Advance Praise for *The G...*

"Both timely and timeless, *The Gre... ...s File* is an environmental thriller extraordinaire. Perry's sterling debut reminded me of James W. Hall's Thorn novels, similar in both theme and style. The notion of a sleepy small town rocked by a series of murders may not be new, but in Perry's polished and steady hand, it feels fresh and original. *The Green Beach File* is perfect for, well, the beach or a cold winter's night, establishing Perry as New England's literary environmental crusader, a northern version of the great Carl Hiaasen."

—Jon Land, *USA Today* Bestselling
Author of the *Murder, She Wrote* Series

"As a true crime expert, I can tell you with certainty, Perry's debut novel feels 'real.' Her knack for storytelling and character development is uncanny—making *The Green Beach File* a must read for anyone in the mood for a top-notch environmental thriller"

—Jon Leiberman, Author and Former National
Correspondent on *America's Most Wanted*

"Karen Perry's strong debut *The Green Beach File* has it all—a shocking murder, a twisty plot, strong characters, and a storyline that stays with you."

—Barbara Ross, Author of *A Maine Clambake* Mystery Series and the *Jane Darrowfield* Mystery Series

K.A. PERRY

THE
GREEN
BEACH
FILE

Whose beach is it anyway?

PERMUTED
PRESS

A PERMUTED PRESS BOOK

ISBN: 978-1-68261-907-0
ISBN (eBook): 978-1-68261-908-7

Cover art by Cody Corcoran

PERMUTED
PRESS

Permuted Press, LLC
New York • Nashville
permutedpress.com

Published in the United States of America

PART I

CHAPTERS 1-17

CHAPTER 1

J enn closed her eyes and pictured herself standing in the forest and looking up at the trees, at all the green of the leaves. The pure and simple beauty of all the leaves moving together, swaying a little in the wind. The image brought her steady calmness. It grounded her and slowed her pounding heart. She took a deep breath and opened her eyes, but the dead face was still there, right there, in front of her.

This dead face looked just like her dead fiancé's face. The cheek muscles were fixed and rigid. Eyes closed, lips curved down and set, and gray skin. No blood circulating, nothing rushing through the arteries. No movement or warmth. Life was gone, just like it had been from her fiancé's face.

Jenn blinked and tried to move past all the emotions rocketing out of her heart. All the shock, anger, and pain that came from Alex's death. She blinked and looked again at the face before her now. She tried to curb her emotions and use her brain.

Yes, it was a dead face in front of her. But really, that was all that the face shared with her fiancé. Alex had been emaciated by the cancer. He had wasted, shriveled, and faded away in a matter of months. This face, this dead face, wasn't like that. It wasn't emaciated. It was full, round, and old. Much older. And fat, really fat now that she noticed. Not really at all like her dead fiancé. The dead face from her past, her fiancé's face, and the face before her now actually had very little in common. Just that they were both dead. Cold, fixed, and dead.

CHAPTER 2

◆

Sideways. It had spiraled sideways. No one could have predicted that the evening would stir up such a tempest of emotion for Jenn and reopen the wounds of losing her fiancé five years ago. Claire, Jenn's sister-in-law, had actually hoped the evening was going to be about Jenn's future. Not her past.

Jenn was heading to meet her sister-in-law, Claire, for an author's book signing. Some big-wig, climate change guru was signing books at P.T. Jane's, an independent bookstore, in Mayfield. As she drove to P.T. Jane's, all the awkward efforts Claire had made on her behalf passed through her mind: blind dates, dinner parties, art show openings, and now setting up a casual meeting at an author's book signing. Today, Claire was going to introduce Jenn to an ear, nose and throat doctor who had recently moved to Connecticut. As with all of Claire's love interests for Jenn, the guy was "just perfect."

Jenn couldn't understand why she didn't say no to her sister-in-law. Here she was, getting dragged once again to something she should have said no to. Claire was on some kind of mission, however, to find Jenn a spouse. And Jenn would not speak up to Claire and tell her not to. Jenn's brother, Peter, a doctor, had married Claire, an art teacher, eight years ago. Ever since Peter and Claire's day of bliss, Claire had been after Jenn to tie the knot, too. It sure hadn't gone well the last time.

Jenn turned into the rear parking lot of P.T. Jane's, lucky to find a parking spot. She was almost into the book store as her iPhone rang. It had been a ridiculously long workday and she thought about declining the call. They, meaning the other lawyers she worked with, just never left her alone. Supposedly, it was a sign of success to be indispensable to the firm. But when Jenn stopped to think about it, her iPhone in particular, and her work in general, mostly felt like a pair of handcuffs. Or maybe one of those leg cuffs that they put on criminals on probation. She paused outside the back door and dug for the "handcuffs" in her purse.

"Jennifer Bowdoin," she answered. Stuart, the partner she mostly worked with, launched right into the details of a client's particular wishes and needs, and the alternative strategies he thought might help the client. Jenn tried hard to pay attention, just in case he was looking for real input.

Other latecomers to the book signing were passing by, and so as not to disturb them, Jenn started ambling away from the small back porch at the rear of the bookstore. She headed back toward her car for privacy. Her car was parked near a dumpster at the edge of the lot. The lot was not paved, but rather covered by small stones with tiny, pale green weeds starting their seasonal creep through the gaps in the stones.

As Jenn moved closer to what she thought was a dumpster, she realized it wasn't for trash, but was actually an ice machine with a wooden fence built three-quarters of the way around it. The cosmetic screening fence was meant to hide the ice machine and was a little shorter than she was at five feet, eight inches. Actually, it was an ice freezer to store already made bags of ice—it did not make ice like ice machines in hotels. The freezer was just a short rectangular-shaped structure that held bags of ice and had two doors on the front of it. Why was it in a bookstore parking lot?

"Yes, I checked the legislative history, and no, there was no comment on your point," Jenn explained to Stuart as she meandered along. Her legal specialty, "environmental law" sounded glamorous, but most days she felt like she just had a routine desk job, some kind of glorified paper pusher.

Stuart was still talking. He launched into a creative solution for the client that involved seeking an amendment of some law. Stuart spoke on and on and on, but Jenn had stopped listening.

As she wandered closer toward the ice freezer, she saw some deep green moss growing amidst the pebbles. The moss was a beautiful, rich green and in such an odd spot for moss. Maybe condensation from the machine provided an extra source of water. She then saw that someone had propped some brown dress shoes on the far left side of the ice freezer. How odd. The shoes were between the freezer itself, and the five-foot high screening fence wrapped around the sides and back of the it. The freezer faced west, and the screening wall stood on its north, east, and west sides.

Focusing on the shoes, and not just the moss, Jenn saw that they had tan slacks attached to them at a weird angle. She stepped closer. Stuart continued talking, but now she wasn't following him at all. She moved toward the left side of the ice freezer. There was a person partially shoved between the machine and the fence surrounding it, and his shoes and pants cuffs were visible.

She leaned in closer and tried to peer behind the left side of the ice freezer, toward the person's face. As her eyes adjusted to the darkening evening sky, she could see his pants, leather belt, white dress shirt, and blood. Yes, it was definitely dried blood on the shoulder of his shirt. The blood was so dark. She could also see his face. His lifeless, still face. Her brain couldn't catch up with the reality before her eyes.

CHAPTER 3

Upon picturing the peaceful tree canopy and pushing down the whirlwind of emotions about her dead fiancé, Jenn focused on the fact that the man before her was really so much fatter and older than Alex. Not quite elderly, but gray-haired with a belly straining the buttons of his dress shirt. Propped so far diagonally on his left side, that his stomach was stopping him from collapsing at the waist and falling behind the ice freezer. His eyes were closed, but his face muscles were frozen in a way that looked like he was in pain.

"Hello?" she called out to the man.

"Yes, Jennifer, I'm still here. Can you hear me?" Stuart asked. She had forgotten all about the call.

"Stuart, I have to go. I'll call you back." She pressed "end" and said, "Hey, are you alright?" to the face behind the ice freezer. The dark brown blood on the shoulder of his shirt looked as though it had come from his head. He was not alright. He had not fallen behind the ice freezer.

"Jennifer Bowdoin, what are you doing?" boomed Claire from ten feet away. Jenn turned her head toward Claire's loud voice, and could almost see smoke wafting up from Claire's ears.

"Claire." It was all Jenn could get out. She looked back at the man's body. The man's dead body, she now realized.

Claire was just far enough away so that she must not have been able to see the shoes or lower legs. She grabbed Jenn's arm and started pulling her toward the bookstore.

"If you didn't want to come, you could have just said so. I saw you almost get to the door and then turn and walk away. Why bother showing up at all if you aren't coming inside?" Claire clearly sensed Jenn's reluctance to come tonight.

After hobbling along a few feet with Claire, Jenn recovered enough to pull her arm away from Claire and dialed 911.

CHAPTER 4

W hile they waited for the police, Jenn and Claire moved to the back porch of P.T. Jane's. The porch was gray and raised two steps above the height of the parking lot, framed by four large orange ceramic pots filled with purple, yellow, and pale blue pansies. It seemed strange to stand close to a dead body, so without discussing it, they had wandered out of the parking lot and up toward the safety of the porch and its cheery flowers.

For Jenn, the blooms were like the tree canopy she had forced into her mind at the moment she saw the dead face. Claire was talking about the book signing and hinting that the doctor, "possibly the one," was still in there waiting to meet Jenn. Jenn didn't look up at Claire, or respond, but just stared down at a pansy, as her eyes were drawn to the contrast of the dark purple and strong yellow colors, both on just one petal. The edge where the strong colors met was not straight, but ragged and variant, with purple veins running through the yellow half of the petal. Together, all the petals created a strikingly beautiful flower. Jenn's focus on the pansy kept her calm, centered her, and kept at bay the emotions that had flared up from seeing the dead face, and the pressure she felt from Claire to go be sociable inside.

Thankfully, the police response time was quick. Within a few minutes, a policeman in his full uniform, who looked like the lead from a *Hallmark* or *Lifetime* movie, pulled up rapidly in his cruiser. He blocked the exit from the parking lot, and walked briskly over to Claire and Jenn. When the first words he spoke were to inquire whether they were okay, Jenn liked him immediately. His second question was whether they had placed the call. Jenn said yes, and pointed to the ice freezer.

Jenn was struck by how reassured she was by the stunning policeman's arrival. The Mayfield police force was rife with problems. She had read that some officers were charged with engaging in prostitution, some with accepting overtime pay when no work was performed, and others with privately using police vehicles to run personal errands. There were also claims of incompetence in the leadership's management skills, since response times to several recent burglaries were unacceptably slow. At one burglary last month in the north end of Mayfield, on a house that was alarmed, thieves were able to rob the house and leave quickly, even before the police arrived. So, the quick arrival by the resplendent officer was wonderful and reassuring to Jenn. Plus, with the policeman's fast response time, Jenn didn't even have to respond to Claire's suggestion that she still go in to the book signing.

The parking lot was lit by two lights, which had turned on in the fading light of dusk. She could see the officer disappear out of view behind the ice machine's fence. After a moment, he reappeared.

"Yes, he's dead," he pronounced and then paused a moment. He said, "I'm going to grab the police tape from my car. You need to stay here so that we can take your statement."

Before Jenn could say anything, a second police car arrived, sirens blaring, and two other officers jumped out. The officers all spoke together and then broke up to perform various tasks. One of the newly arrived officers approached the ladies and simultaneously pulled out a small notebook from one of his many pockets.

"Ladies, I have the pleasure of escorting you to the station. It will be better to take your statement there, in a warmer and better-lit spot." Claire, who, despite motherhood, was still incredibly self-centered, immediately spoke up.

"Officer, I didn't find the body. My sister-in-law did, and she, as a lawyer, will be able to give you a far better statement than I ever could. I have not even been over there to look at the body. I have no desire to see it, and I need to get home to my daughter."

Jenn turned toward Claire with an expression of awe. What a load of crap. Claire had looked at the body, albeit quickly. She had taken a peek behind the ice freezer while Jenn was on the phone with the 911 operator.

"My sister-in-law was supposed to meet me here at seven. When she was late, I started watching out the back door for her, and came out to greet her when she arrived. By the time I saw her, she had already discovered the body. I really can't go to the station tonight. I live on Liberty Street and am a teacher here in town. I have nothing to add, but I'll give you my contact information in case you need me in the future."

"Alright ma'am. Write down your name and address here, and let me see your driver's license." Claire rooted through her handbag for her wallet and did as she was asked. "Miss, why don't you show me your license, too? And then you can follow me to the station in your car. It certainly looks like foul play, so I'll need to get a formal statement."

Jenn started digging in her purse as well. She handed her license to the officer as her phone rang. She saw Stuart's name appear on the screen and pressed the answer button.

"Stuart, I hung up on you because I found a dead body. I'll call you back." Then she hung up on him again before he could respond. Oops. Maybe that was not so smart. When she felt brave enough to look up and meet the police officer's eyes, he looked impatient.

"It was my boss, I was on the phone with him when I first found the body." Jenn felt compelled to explain why she bothered to answer her iPhone.

"So, Jennifer," the officer said, reading her name from her license, "let's head over to the station. I'll follow you. You know where the station is? Where are you parked?"

Jenn nodded her head and pointed toward her car, then started walking in that direction.

The crafty, lying, Claire caught up to Jenn and said, "Phew… that was close. I'm sorry you have to spend the evening at the station, but it would have been a huge waste of my time. I'll let Pete know what happened. Discovering a dead body as a way to avoid meeting a date is a new one in my book."

CHAPTER 5

◆

The evening continued its sideways path. As if the dead body and Claire's lying weren't enough, Jenn's visit to the police station was not as Jenn had pictured it on her drive there. She thought of herself as the helpful Good Samaritan who had called in a dead body. The police, however, did not share this point of view.

Upon arrival, she was led to a room with no pictures on the walls, no rug on the floor, and not even any fake plants in the corners for her to examine. The room held only a folding table and three metal chairs. Jenn sat down in a metal folding chair and waited. After a few minutes, two tense officers entered the room and sat on the opposite side of the metal table. Even worse than the lack of nature in the room, neither of the police were the alluring officer who had been the first to arrive at the crime scene.

As they glared at her from across the table, Jenn tensed up and took stock of the situation. She was in an interrogation room. These had been the subject of many classroom discussions at law school, but she had never actually been in one. And certainly not on the wrong side of the table. She was not over on the side of law and order, with emphasis on the *law*, which, as a lawyer, was her usual place. Nope. She was on the bad side. She was a police suspect in a murder case. That explained the officers glaring at her as they entered the room, and the tension they brought into the room with them.

They began questioning her, and because of her realization that she was a suspect, she carefully and thoroughly answered each question. After what seemed like forever, with some breaks by the officers to leave the room, and some questions repeated, the two police officers seemed to relax a little. Maybe they had left the room to call Stuart to verify her story, she wondered. Eventually, they had her write up and review her statement. She did as instructed, signed it, and was finally free to leave.

She left the station, feeling a like an outsider and a nuisance to the officers. She wasn't treated like she was helpful, and she was told nothing. All she learned, from eavesdropping on the officers' conversation as they left the interrogation room, was that the victim was named Dr. Tilman.

CHAPTER 6

J enn's mother, sister-in-law, and even her brother told her not to buy a house in the woods of Connecticut, after Alex's death and while she was still single. They thought a condo would better suit her "all work, no play" lifestyle. She didn't listen and each night as she faced the house and all its required maintenance, she remembered what they said.

Jenn drove north away from the Mayfield shoreline, toward her needy house. The terrain rose in elevation, and lights from the houses became scarcer. The night was cool and clear, and the darkness of the woods along the road enveloped her car.

Really though, her family just didn't understand. She actually hadn't bought the property for the house at all. It was a small white colonial home with black shutters, just a little big for one single woman. But it wasn't the house that brought her back and distinguished itself from all the other houses its size. It was the two American chestnut trees at the edge of the side yard.

Jenn first visited the house with her realtor on a rainy fall day. As she was walking back up the driveway to her car, unusually large brown leaves were falling and sticking to the driveway. She had never seen leaves like this before. She picked one up, noticing that the young tree from which it had fallen was full of these leaves. Fearful that her realtor might think her odd, Jenn secretly pocketed the wet leaf and carried it home. After drying up on her kitchen counter for a few days, she finally got around to looking up what kind of tree is was. Like most environmental attorneys, Jenn had an insatiable interest in nature. Without it, the analysis of minutiae required to read environmental regulations and laws would have probably turned her into a walking zombie years ago.

The leaf belonged to an American chestnut tree. Back in the 1800s, this type of tree reached a height of 100 feet and grew massive wide-spreading branches around the trunk. Compared to other tree species, it was incredibly useful. It was the tree which was used to build America, but now was extinct, or supposedly extinct. Its wood was used in home construction, for railroad ties and for split-rail fences. Its chestnuts were cultivated for food. Its bark had tannic acid that was used to make leather products. And not only was the American chestnut aesthetically beautiful, but also provided needed shade (back before air-conditioning).

Around the turn of the century, however, everything changed. A forester discovered diseased chestnut trees on the grounds of the New York Zoological Garden. A fungus was attacking the trees and killing them. The fungus was an early-era invasive species, unintentionally introduced into America from Asian chestnut trees. And the fungus was clever—it spread regardless of the weather.

On windy days, it had a dry disc shaped spore that easily dispersed, and on rainy days, the fungus had a smaller, stickier type of spore that easily dispersed. When the spores settled on the tree's bark, the fungus could grow and would produce orange-colored cankers or spots on the outside of the tree. The fungus would enter through any cracks in the bark and choked the tree to death by cutting off its water and nutrient supply from the ground. A slow choke. First the leaves above the point of infection would die, then the limbs themselves would die. Slowly cankers spread through the tree, encircling each branch or stem, and the branches above each point of infection. Within two to ten years, a tree would die.

The blight spread like a wildfire, in the early 1900s, and infected all American chestnuts in its path. The government attempted a number of methods to try to stop the blight. But, tree surgery, chemical sprays, injection of fungicides, and cutting to try and quarantine infected trees just didn't work.

Jenn sat wondering how two extinct trees could be living in a side yard in Mayfield, Connecticut. She found herself engrossed by this strange slow death that had befallen the American chestnut. After further research, and even phone calls to a mysterious government agency called the Connecticut Agricultural Experiment Station, it turned out that this was not some remarkable feat of nature where survival of a species had overcome a destructive, invasive force and grown in a side yard, but rather a tragic story of an ever-shortened lifespan. Chestnut trees would produce sprouts below the diseased portion, and these trees would grow for a few years. Unfortunately, the resulting new saplings would eventually become infected by the blight though and die as well. So the two chestnut trees in the side yard were doomed to a short life from the day they sprouted.

Odd as it seemed, even to her, upon learning this despairing tale, Jenn wanted the house, and the two chestnut trees. Was she attracted to them because of their will to survive or because they persisted despite their tragedy? Did she want to save them because she couldn't save Alex from the cancer? She didn't know. She just wanted the trees, and the house that came with them.

Her family kept pestering her about getting a dog to keep her safe, but she didn't feel like she needed one. Not that she would ever tell anyone, but Jenn thought of these two trees as her pets.

In the past, Claire, when feeling frustrated with her attempts to marry her off, had called Jenn a hopeless romantic in the same vein as *Romeo and Juliet*. It was kind of mean since Jenn's love life had ended in a tragedy like *Romeo and Juliet*, but the hopeless romantic part was also kind of true. When Jenn decided to have names for her pet trees that were destined to die young, she called one Romeo and one Juliet.

Returning home from the police station, she pulled into her driveway, parked her car, gave her usual glance to check on Romeo and Juliet, and headed into her house.

CHAPTER 7

Jenn awoke in the night with the dead man's pained face right in front of her, and her heart pounding. The grim line formed by his lips, and his lifeless gray skin, were awful. She had awoken remembering the moment she realized he was dead. She tried to fall back to sleep, but sleep would not come. She could hear wind, loud thunder, and finally heavy rain outside her window. Weren't they clear skies she had seen on her drive home? Maybe it was the newly arrived storm outside that had awoken her, but it might have just been her pounding heart.

The police had referenced the victim as Dr. Tilman. She turned to her iPad to see what she could learn. One news website already had an article, as a dead body in the back of P.T. Jane's bookstore in fancy Mayfield was headline news. Dr. Tilman, the man with the brown shoes, stuck sideways behind an ice cooler, was really a renowned herpetologist from Columbia University. Ironically, Jenn had even met him once before, years ago, when he had offered an expert opinion on amphibians on a case she was working on. Dead, she did not recognize him. But once she learned who it was, she could reconcile the grimness of his dead face with the way he looked alive.

Dr. Tilman had a faculty webpage on Columbia's site, and she perused it quickly to see if there was any hint of why he was in Mayfield. There were references to his published books and literature on frogs, snakes, turtles, and salamanders, but nothing that seemed significant.

Murder. The news article called the death murder. The location of his body and the angle it was wedged in at, made it clear it was not an accident. That's why they were so serious with her in the interrogation room. But why would someone murder a man who spent his life studying little creatures, studying frogs, snakes, turtles and salamanders?

CHAPTER 8

◆

With a mind foggy from yesterday's events, Jenn opened her eyes to a sunny, spring Saturday. She'd had so much trouble sleeping the night before. Checking the clock, it was already 9:30 a.m., which was shocking to her. She had not slept in so late in years. She was due at her brother's house at 10:00 a.m. for her niece Sophia's fifth birthday party. Peter and Claire lived south of Route 1—the high-end district of Mayfield, near the water, in a gorgeous, newly renovated home.

Jenn quickly showered, dressed, and headed to her brother's house. She passed Romeo and Juliet on the way out of her driveway. Juliet looked a little droopy and frazzled this morning from the thunderstorm last night, but maybe Jenn was just projecting onto the tree. She felt droopy herself after her restless night. Of course, that was the beauty of having trees for pets. She could assign them whatever thoughts, feelings, or emotions suited her. Plus, there was no shedding fur to vacuum, no dirty litter boxes to clean, no trips to the vet, and no running out of pet food.

At her brother's house, Jenn climbed out of her car and walked into the backyard framed by a row of arborvitae on two sides, and a split-rail fence along the rear. A low wooden deck was furnished with an outdoor table, chairs, and a freestanding umbrella. A centerpiece of white hydrangea, pink lilies, and frosted green eucalyptus festooned the table. A, not surprisingly, pink castle cake stood at the head of the table, and a bouquet of pink and white balloons were tied to the head chair.

In the center of the yard, an old maple tree grew, and provided shade over a swing set covered in children and decorated with more pink balloons. A small castle bouncy house was inflated to the right of the swing set. The party was already in full swing at 10:10 a.m. Twenty kindergarteners were playing tag, blowing bubbles, and climbing on the swing set, and there were no adults to be seen.

Sophia spotted Jenn and ran over for a big hug.

"Happy Birthday, Sophia! I can't believe you're five already!"

"Hi, Aunt Jenn!"

"I bought you something special…for later," Jenn said.

Oh, crap, she thought. *I forgot it*. Finding Dr. Tilman dead was wreaking more havoc on her mind than she thought. Sophia's present was still at home tucked out of sight in the mudroom, awaiting the big birthday party.

"Okay!" Sophia ran back toward the jumpy house to rejoin her friends.

"Hi, Jenn. Survived finding a dead man I see?" It was her brother, Peter.

"Yes, but barely. My sleep was all messed up last night, and I managed to leave Sophia's gift at home."

"You can give it to her another day," said Peter. He was still amazingly mellow on the weekends, despite his high-intensity medical practice.

"Maybe I'll run home at some point," replied Jenn. "I feel awful and would rather she didn't know I forgot it."

"Don't bother. She won't even notice," said Peter reassuringly.

A couple approached at that moment with a young boy named Sam between them. Sam was one of Sophia's good friends and neighbors, so Jenn had met his parents, Toby and Kim, at prior parties.

"So, Jenn, do you think Doctor Tilman's death had anything to do with Riverfront Landing?" asked Kim. She was never one to mince words and always knew the latest gossip in town.

"I don't know." Was all Jenn could come up with for a response. Her firm, Shipward & Waters, was well known in town for representing the owner of Mayfield's Riverfront Landing the past five years. The property owner, uncreatively named Mayfield Coastal Development, was trying to construct a community of 127 residential units on approximately twenty-two acres of shorefront land. Although the property to be developed was actually forty-two acres, only twenty-two acres were buildable, with the other twenty acres being coastal wetlands.

Much of Mayfield was one-acre zoning. In other words, one single-family home was allowed per one acre of land. Even in areas south of Route 1, near the water, current zoning regulations only allowed two residential homes on one acre. So cramming 127 residences into twenty-two acres, many of which would have water views and their own private neighborhood beach was, for the developer, the equivalent to the sound of a cash register ringing.

Five years ago, Mayfield Coastal Development had proposed constructing 260 units. But strong opposition by a group of citizens had, as these things frequently do, whittled the number of units down to less than half of the original proposal. The citizen's group had lots of steam because the forty-two-acre property was the largest undeveloped tract of shoreline between New York and Boston. It was the sole remaining coastline in all of lower New England that was still essentially untouched and pristine beachfront. A couple of small hanger buildings and some grass runways were on it from an old country airport, but predominantly the acreage was still green and undeveloped.

Land conservationists fought the development, as they had hoped to preserve the property as open space. It was, after all, immediately adjacent to the 130-acre Hammonasset State Park, which was hugely popular and the crown jewel of the Connecticut State Park system. More people visited the Hammonasset State Park each summer than any other park in the state, and more than many national parks. It functioned more like a popular national park, like Yellowstone, than a state park, with its sandy beaches, coastal wetlands, interesting wildlife, hands-on nature center, and lively campground.

The permitting for the project had been through a number of stumbling blocks, but was still moving ahead. And despite the reduction in units planned, it was a hugely profitable venture. A community of beautiful homes with their own private neighborhood beach was proposed, and the homes would be elegant and expensive. Jenn did not personally work on the project. Since she had grown up and now resided in town, and since the property's development was so controversial, it was for the best (at least in her mind) that she remained off this particular project.

"Did you know him personally? Can you believe he was behind P.T. Jane's?" asked Kim.

Jenn's brother must not have told their friends that she had found the body.

"The rumor is that his stomach kept him from stinking up P.T. Jane's parking lot for weeks. His stomach didn't fit behind the ice freezer, and his shoes were discovered," piped in Toby.

Jenn looked at Toby with a questioning expression. Before she could open her mouth Kim explained, "We went to O'Malley's for coffee this morning. It's all everyone was talking about. He was apparently hit on the back of the head. We even walked over to P.T. Jane's after our coffee, and checked out the crime scene. There really was yellow tape all around the parking lot."

"A murder in Mayfield. Can you believe it?" said Toby. "There hasn't been one since that husband took out his ex-wife, what was that five years ago? At least that was in the fall, not like this murder at the start of the summer tourism season."

Jenn started, "I—", but her brother jumped in.

"Jennifer found the body and called it in," he said. "Claire and I had arranged for her to meet one of our friends last night at P.T. Jane's, and she managed to find Doctor Tilman's body on the way in."

Toby and Kim turned to look at Jenn, astonishment crossing their faces.

At that moment Claire walked up with her mouth already moving. "So you heard the news. We have celebrity Jenn in our midst. Finder of a dead body in our own little quaint Mayfield."

Jenn started again, "It—"

But Claire hadn't stopped and used her teacher voice to loudly exclaim, "Yes. Another dead body. Isn't this the second murder this decade in Mayfield? What is the world coming to? Couldn't folks have the decency to commit their murders elsewhere?"

"New Haven is always a good spot for murders," Peter dryly chimed in.

"We cannot have this impact our summer tourism business," Claire said. "This is just like the shark in *Jaws*. We can't have folks afraid to go to the local bookstore for risk of getting slain in the night."

"Well…" said Peter. "Folks might flee if it turns out to be a serial killer. One murder is not worth losing sleep over. If someone is dead at O'Malley's tonight, then we have a problem." O'Malley's was, after all, one of the two coffee shops located in the center of Mayfield, where residents whiled away the hours.

"That's unlikely—" Jenn began, thinking that maybe she should explain her role as a possible suspect while in the interrogation room, and explain how upsetting it was to see someone dead.

"Cake!" yelled Claire, interrupting Jenn. "Time for cake!" A gaggle of five-year-olds rushed to the deck table and swarmed around it. Jenn smiled at the adorable kids rushing for cake, glad for their liveliness and joy in contrast to the death she saw the day before.

CHAPTER 9

E ver since seeing the dead body, Jenn had had an overwhelming sense of disquiet. She hoped some fresh air and maybe even a walk or jog would clear her uneasiness. At moments, Dr. Tilman's face crept into her mind and she was reminded of not just Alex's death, but her own father's passing, and the renewed shock of realizing death's permanency. She'd slept fitfully for a second night and fresh air seemed like a healthy plan.

At yesterday's party, Jenn had committed to take Sophia out for Sunday brunch, so she could give her niece her belated present. After brunch she would take Sophia and her dog Roscoe on a nice long walk. They left Roscoe in the car until they had ordered and brought their food to a table in front of Larry's Bagels. The table was tucked into a small alcove at the edge of the parking lot. It wasn't attractive, and the tall metal chairs were not comfortable, but Jenn had chosen the spot to spy on the activities across the street.

Beyond the restaurant's thirty-foot parking lot lay Route 1. On the other side of the two-lane road was the metaphoric cash register: twenty-two acres of buildable coastal land that Mayfield Coastal Development hoped to turn into 127 residences. During Jenn's childhood it had been an airport—a country airport, with a dirt road and grass runways. She wasn't sure when the airport closed. There was still a windsock on a tall pole and the wind rolled in from the east, filling the sock halfway. There was also a well-maintained chain-link fence across the front of the property and a closed wooden gate across the dirt entrance road. "No Trespassing" signs were evenly spaced along its length.

Sophia asked if they could get Roscoe from the car. Jenn obliged and looped Roscoe's leash around the table base. While they ate, Jenn and Sophia conversed about Sophia's favorite colors, toys, and animals. As they were finishing their food, Jenn asked, "How did you like your party yesterday?"

"I liked it. The bouncy house was great, and Sam and I played *Hunger Games*," replied Sophia.

At some point after the cake was served and the presents opened, Jenn had seen Sam and Sophia crawling in the grass holding plastic white hangers like bows. They were stalking the other kids, sneaking up on them, and launching imaginary arrows.

Jenn was more than a little worried about what this meant for American culture as a whole and her niece specifically. Even if it were just pretend, weren't five-year-olds too young to stalk and pretend to kill other five-year-olds in a game, for food? Jenn wondered what was so bad about the non-violent games of her childhood like Musical Chairs and Farmer in the Dell.

Before Jenn had a chance to talk to her niece about not pretending to kill other kids, a metallic-green Prius pulled into the dirt driveway across the street. The Prius had a Connecticut state license, which was only on state-owned vehicles. Why was it out on a Sunday? What was it doing at Riverfront Landing? The Prius pulled up to the wooden gate and a lean, bearded man climbed out of the van and walked over to the gate, unlocked it, and swung it to the side. He hopped back into the Prius and drove out of sight.

Across the two-lane road, much of the Riverfront Landing property was visible, consisting of dull, green grassland. There were some buildings, though—old airline hangers—and a grove of taller deciduous trees to the south. The Prius had disappeared behind one of the buildings. Jenn was frustrated that she couldn't see what a state worker was doing on privately owned property on a Sunday morning. Anonymously following the Prius onto the property was simply not a possibility, unless, maybe she could use Roscoe. She looked down at the dog and saw that he was sleeping soundly under the table.

"Shall we take our walk?" Jenn asked Sophia.

"Okay." One half of Sophia's bagel was almost gone, and the other half had been licked clean of its cream cheese.

Jenn looked back at the gate and could still see the "No Trespassing" signs, even with the gate partially swung open. She looked back at Roscoe sleeping and thought better of using a lost dog ploy. As curious as she was, trespassing was against the law.

"Let's go to Meigs Point," said Jenn. "Come on."

She cleaned up their meal scraps and threw them out. She grabbed Roscoe's leash and piled Sophia and her dog into her car.

Meigs Point was part of Hammonasset State Park, which abutted the Riverfront Landing property. The Point was at the eastern edge of the park, and although overcrowded in the summer, open parking spots were still to be found midday Sunday in early May. The Point consisted of salt marsh, covered with tall saltwater cord grass, with some islands of higher ground surrounding the marshy areas. The colors of the sand, grasses, and Long Island Sound were unbelievably beautiful, any time of year. Once summer came, the marshes would be adorned with the yellow and purple colors of common marsh wildflowers— primarily seaside aster, seaside gerardia, and sea lavender.

Today Jenn was glad for the beauty of the spot, to clear the picture of Dr. Tilman's dead body from her head. They slowly walked down the path along the Point, enjoying the surrounding nature and the peace that comes with a Sunday stroll in the great outdoors.

Walking its grounds, Jenn could see why opponents of the project wanted the Riverfront Landing property preserved for public use and annexed to Hammonasset Park. The coastal marshes of the Riverfront Landing property were along the edge of the Hammonasset River, and just as attractive as the marshes of Hammonasset Park. At its mouth, the river took a sharp turn to the east, which created the Meigs Point area and provided shelter for so many acres of salt marsh to thrive.

Jenn believed in the value of public access to land, and to the beach in particular, and part of her secretly hoped Riverfront Landing would be preserved. Whether the public, the town, or the state would raise or commit the funds to preserve Riverfront Landing was a question that did not yet have an answer.

CHAPTER 10

M onday morning brought another sunny spring day, which Jenn unfortunately had to spend in her office. The work was not engaging her. Deciding to do the easy stuff first, Jenn at least made a little headway down her to-do list. She kept checking the news websites for more on Dr. Tilman's death. Why wasn't there an update? What was he doing behind P.T. Jane's? Was he there for the same book signing? Did she just miss the murderer? The blood was dark though, so maybe he was there a while. Why weren't there any details about his death publicly available yet?

On Mondays, there was a weekly lunch meeting for the attorneys who practiced environmental and land use law, to share information about their new cases. Generally, about twenty lawyers sat around a conference table. Attorneys from the firm's offices in Boston, Stamford, and New York also called in to be part of the meeting as well. The partners took turns describing new business and any matters or cases that were changing or had significant developments. The partners also determined which associates would actually do the brunt of the work on each of the new cases.

When Jenn became bored at these weekly meetings, which was…well, weekly, she defaulted to her Snow White and The Seven Dwarfs analysis—determining which partner fit which dwarf. Around the table sat a Grumpy, Happy, Sleepy, Bashful, Sneezy, Dopey, and Doc. She only needed to figure out who was who on any given day. There was one partner who frequently mixed up his words a lot and wore heavy glasses, so he was Doc. Another partner had bad allergies, with an almost constant runny nose and a propensity to sneeze, so yes, he was Sneezy. On certain days, it seemed like there was one partner for each dwarf. But if there was not a lot of new business, and things were slow, or weren't going well, there were only Grumpies at the table.

Today she was thinking that everyone seemed like Happy, until David sternly brought up Dr. Tilman's death. David was the head of the Land Use and Environmental Practice section of the firm. He ran the luncheons and had an amazingly powerful voice, which resonated with more decibels than the average voice. His drawback was his diminished stature and the traditional Napoleonic personality that went with it. He didn't seem to like Jenn. She wasn't sure why, but she tried to steer clear of him as much as possible.

"For those of you who haven't heard, Doctor Tilman was found murdered in downtown Mayfield over the weekend. He had been retained as an expert herpetologist on a number of cases over the years, including our current work on Riverfront Landing. Luckily," David smirked, "his written report on his site findings had been completed."

"Jenn found the body. I was on the phone with her Friday night when she found him," said Stuart.

Ugh. Everyone turned to look at her. Jenn hated being the center of attention. She tried to think of something profound, or maybe intelligent to say. She gave a dramatic pause.

"It was weird. And sad," she responded. Ugh. Neither profound nor intelligent. Just mundane. Oh, well.

"Where was he? What happened?" A fellow attorney asked. "I thought you were going on a date."

Questions were being fired at her. Nothing like being cross-examined by a room full of lawyers. And worse, everyone was still looking at her. She started in on Friday night's events.

"It was a dark and stormy night."

Some chuckles filled the room. Cheap joke, but at least now folks were smiling and she had a friendlier audience.

"No, seriously. I was on my way into P.T. Jane's, a bookstore in Mayfield," Jenn said. "I was on the phone with Stuart when I saw something strange over at the edge of the bookstore parking lot. It turned out to be a pair of shoes stuck behind a commercial ice machine, and there was a dead body wearing the shoes. I didn't even recognize Doctor Tilman, even though I'd met him at least once."

"Why was there a commercial ice machine in the parking lot of a bookstore?" The question came over the speakerphone from one of the other offices.

Jenn had forgotten that there were people listening in. Usually they piped in with their cases toward the end of the meeting, and had been pretty silent to date. Leave it to a lawyer to point out the elements of her story that made no sense.

"Well, it wasn't actually a machine that makes ice. It was a one of those commercial freezers that hold bags of ice, which are already made. As for why it is in a bookstore parking lot, I have absolutely no idea."

"What's the latest in terms of the investigation?" asked Stuart.

"I don't know. There is not much information on any of the news sites yet," Jenn answered. "Only that he was killed by blunt force trauma to the back of his head. I cannot imagine why he would be at P.T. Jane's, except maybe to go to the book signing as well. He's a professor at Columbia."

"Well, as long as you didn't have anything to do with it Jenn, I think we better move on," said Stuart. "Let's keep going with our meeting as we don't have much time left. Any matters we need to discuss from the Boston office?"

Jenn sat through the rest of the meeting, glad that her time in the interrogation room didn't have to be discussed. She tried to pay attention, but her eyes were pulled toward the window, and the cumulous clouds that were patiently traversing the sky. Dr. Tilman's death made no sense, she thought, as she watched the clouds move. She hoped that someone was trying to figure out what happened to him, and why.

CHAPTER 11

T he drive home was a pleasant escape from her office. Loud music and the pure freedom that came with the empowerment of driving allowed Jenn to put the workday behind her. As she pulled into her driveway, she noticed Romeo and Juliet were still standing. Another day older and wiser, and another day that they had stalwartly fended off the blight. Today, she would call them stoic and proud of their accomplishment. She had no idea of their age, but imagined they were around seven or eight years old.

Her yard was bursting with the life that comes in late May. It, unfortunately, needed lots of work. It always did, since she spent most of her time at a desk and not in her yard. Although there was not much daylight, she went inside and changed from her work clothes into her gardening garb and grabbed a beer, a water, and even a lemonade. She wasn't sure when it started, it gave her family endless amusement, her constantly carrying and drinking more than just one substance simultaneously.

She went back out into the fading daylight and enjoyed the last of the sun's rays reaching her skin. Where to start? The pile of mulch needed distributing, the flowerbeds needed weeding, and some pesky leaves that had taken winter harborage against her stonewall still needed raking. She was glad for the few flowers already in bloom. Pink rhododendron and white azalea bushes adorned the front of her home. Red tulips were interspersed in the mulch bed at the front edge of the shrubs.

In the side yard near the garage, at the base of the chestnuts, deep purple iris blossomed in the flowerbed. She thought maybe she should start weeding there. A stonewall and stone ledges framed the bed and one particularly flat stone made a perfect table upon which to rest the three drinks. She pulled weeds, relocated worms, and saved a ladybug from being squished in her quick hands. It felt good to accomplish something as simple as weeding because the satisfaction from the work was immediately evident.

As she settled in to weeding, Mark, one of her neighbors, crept closer. He was a tall, lanky, attractive man around fifty years old, a scientist with a large pharmaceutical company, who walked out each day to get the mail. She had seen him out of the corner of her eye, but kept her head down. She wasn't a recluse or non-neighborly. It was just that she found herself making up lies, about cookies in the oven, or pots on the stove, to avoid conversations with him. The conversations were interesting, but they were never-ending. A while ago she reached the conclusion that Mark must not like conversing with his bossy wife. This explanation seemed more likely than that he was allergic to the inside of his house.

Jenn realized that Mark lingered at the mailbox to try to catch her eye. Normally, when he caught it, he would greet her and then creep closer and start talking. Tonight he hadn't waited for the eye catch. Since she was looking down weeding, Jenn noticed his shoes first. She had just pulled another ladybug from her handful of weeds, and had relocated her to a new home on the iris leaves. He might make a good pet, she thought. An opportunity to expand her family. Maybe Romeo and Juliet would like a pet of their own. Brown dress shoes with laces stepped into view. They reminded her of Dr. Tilman's brown shoes. She really had no choice but to look up.

"Hi, Mark. How are you this evening?" Jenn asked, while tilting her head up, so her eyes could meet his.

"Good. Things are really warming up these days. How are you?" It had been a horrible winter. More snow than Connecticut had seen in decades, covering the ground in winter whiteness for months, and piling up to over two feet. The long, slow snowmelt had taken weeks through March and even into April. The first day of spring had brought one last snowstorm. Spring rolled in cold and stayed cold, as they had remarked to each other on a number of prior evening conversations.

"I'm good. Desperate to at least get this bed cleaned up before sunset." Hint, hint, hint, she thought.

Mark didn't get it. Instead, he stepped closer and sat down on the stonewall, dangling his legs into her flowerbed. He had never done that before. Her head jerked up to look at him in surprise.

"Anything new?" she asked.

"I'll just keep you company while you work tonight. It's a nice warm evening, and pleasant to be outside. It's peaceful out here. Did you hear about the murder in town? Debbie is all worked up about it. She says it's related to Riverfront Landing. You know how she feels about that."

Mark nodded toward the dark-green-and-white yard sign that adorned their lawn. It had been up for almost a year so Jenn had stopped noticing it. It read "Preserve Riverfront Landing. Stop Mayfield Coastal Development" and was placed at the center of a small garden surrounding their mailbox. The garden contained some yellow lilies, a small, pink rosebush, and some late daffodils still in bloom.

"Yes. I know she hates the project," Jenn answered. "Why does she think the murder is connected?"

"She says he was an expert for the developer. I guess Doctor Tilman did a study of the animals on the property and found some that are a protected species or something. Some sort of turtle or salamander. I don't know. She thinks the developer didn't like his findings and knocked him off."

"What?" said Jenn. She stopped weeding and gave her full attention to Mark. Strange news, she thought. She had heard at lunch that Dr. Tilman's report had been good for the developer.

Now she became aware that Mark looked haggard tonight. His hair was disheveled, dark circles edged his eyes, and there was a sharpness to the angles of his face that wasn't normally there. Typically, Mark was pleasantly dressed in either his work clothes or his gardening clothes. This evening though, he had on a little bit of both. Dress shoes, sweatpants, and a button-down shirt. Things were getting interesting. She took a long swallow of her beer, looked at him, and waited for him to continue.

"Well, I guess a group of the ladies opposed to the project had lunch today down at the Beach Hotel, and some real cat claws came out," Mark said. "Debbie mentioned that the other ladies were rude to her, that they ganged up on her. She's awfully upset tonight, angry about everything, really. I had to hightail it out of there and find some quiet." He looked at her sheepishly. Maybe he didn't want to be the target of his wife's misdirected anger. Jenn realized his rush to exit his house must explain his mismatched attire.

Debbie was an angry woman. Over the years, she complained to Jenn about everything from the aphids eating her rosebushes to the other neighbors to pretty much every decision ever made by any of the local boards or politicians in their small town. Although she couldn't do much about the neighbors or small-town politics, Jenn had once tried to stand up for the aphids. They were just doing their part in the food chain, she had kindly explained. Debbie had scowled and, as though someone had pulled a light switch, the anger shifted from the aphids to Jenn. A litany of reasons why aphids were the scum of the earth fell from Debbie's lips, which left Jenn feeling like the scum, even though Debbie kept referring to the aphids. Since that day, Jenn had just listened to her complaints, and stuck up for no one. She neither encouraged nor discouraged the complaints. The only thing she really could do was to remember something in the oven that she had to go back to her kitchen to take out.

"What do her friends have to gang up on her about?" Jenn asked Mark.

"Well, apparently, Shelby Williams asked Debbie if she had visited the property last week. Shelby said she had seen Debbie's car one morning at daybreak when Shelby had made an early morning bagel run," Mark answered. "Debbie explained that she had not been on the property."

Debbie drove a silver Lexus station wagon. It really didn't stand out in Mayfield, where luxury cars were more prevalent than most places. Mark explained to Jenn that apparently, Shelby didn't believe Debbie, and wouldn't leave Debbie alone. Shelby actually voiced the idea that maybe Debbie had compromised loyalties. Debbie was a realtor and worked for Northeast Realty, the largest realty company in Mayfield. Shelby voiced the opinion that more houses in town would lead to more sales for Debbie and so maybe Debbie wasn't really opposed to the development.

"That's a stretch. Who even knows if Northern Realty would get the listing?" replied Jenn.

"It's weird," Mark agreed.

The folks Debbie lunched with were the core of Save Riverfront Landing. They had a regular luncheon to strategize efforts to mobilize citizens to rally against the development project when needed. Their photo had made the local paper the first time the project was before the local commissions. These folks were the fuel that stoked the fires against the project and inspired folks to come out and state their opinions. The evening meetings would drag on for hours with different town residents expressing their concerns about the project. They would cite possible problems from increased pollution of Long Island Sound to increased school children, and therefore higher taxes from more residences, noise from the construction, and traffic issues at access points to the development.

Jenn always felt for the goodhearted unpaid volunteers who served on these commissions and had to sit for hours listening. Not only was it public service in its purest form, it made you a target in the community. No one would like all the decisions of a commission all the time. The folks had to decide on the issue before them regardless of their friends' or neighbors' heartfelt opinions expressed to the contrary. At the grocery store, the coffee shop, or in church, these people were a bull's-eye for the folks in the community who loved to criticize.

Jenn knew a little about the four "Grand Marshals" of the citizens' group, who paraded against the project. Shelby Williams, a seventh-grade science teacher at the middle school, was able to rile up the local parents about how this land would be better off undeveloped, preserved for future generations. Shelby was an attractive, fit blond, who appeared to be in her mid-thirties in the photo.

Dot Hutchinson was a longtime resident, whose family once owned planes that used the old airport. She lived on the water on Mayfield's Middle Beach Road, which was once lined with quaint, old summer cottages that had been replaced with mansions. She was in her late fifties or early sixties, very well kept and clothed, and seemed to be in the local paper almost weekly for her involvement in various community events, fundraisers, and committees. Dot was well connected among the well-heeled of Mayfield, and could get them out to meetings if needed.

The third member of the group was Robbie Hayden, a young father of three athletic boys, who advocated strongly for open space for recreation and more sports fields for the youth of the town.

And Debbie, Jenn's neighbor, was the fourth member of the group.

Mark continued with his tale, "Nat, the leader of the opposition, was having lunch at the same restaurant, but surprisingly not with his four lackeys. He was eating with an older gentleman, who is the state archeologist."

Nat Harkins was a money manager. Although the sign he hung was affiliated with one of the national investment companies, he had a small office right on Route 1, which was the main street of Mayfield. Personable, handsome, and witty, he had a following of folks that loved him. Jenn didn't know why he opposed the project so strongly or why he had taken on the role of leader of the citizen's group. She had read a number of his statements in the local paper, which he had made over the years opposing the project. He only ever attributed amorphous reasons why the development just wasn't right for the town and why the property should stay in its natural state.

Mark continued his tale. "Debbie had expected Nat to join them for lunch, but he only came by the table to say hello, and then he and Dot brought up some great news. You would probably know best, but a state-listed endangered species could maybe help slow down the project, right?"

Before Jenn could answer, Debbie appeared, marching in full stride toward the Preserve Riverfront Landing sign on her lawn. She was a rotund woman who didn't move much; so full stride was something of note. Mark and Jenn stopped talking and watched Debbie move, well, kind of move. She grabbed at the sign, pulling up, as though to pull it out, and loudly exclaimed, "That's it; I'm done!" But she lost her footing and slipped backward and down onto her legs and back. The sign had disintegrated in her hands from its year outdoors. Debbie now looked like a ladybug stuck on its back, arms flailing, and frustration mounting. Even worse, Jenn realized, Debbie had squashed the small rosebush in the garden, probably ruining its buds, and killing its aphids.

Mark jumped up and started over to help. Jenn made a lurch to get up, but thought better of it and let Mark do his puppy dog run to her side. He helped Debbie up, pulled the remains of the sign out of the ground, picked up the other pieces, tucked it all under his arm, and ushered her into their home.

Jenn was left perplexed, wondering exactly what Dr. Tilman's report had found. Were there endangered species at Riverfront Landing or not? And why wouldn't Nat eat with those who marched to his drum and helped him in his cause to stop the Riverfront Landing? None of the facts were adding up.

CHAPTER 12

T uesday brought rain. Lots and lots of rain. A long, slow commute to her office was inevitable. Before she could get out the door, a call came in from her sister-in-law, Claire.

"Jenn, another body has been found!" exclaimed Claire.

"What? What do you mean?" asked Jenn.

"Well, apparently, just like Peter joked Saturday, a woman was found murdered behind O'Malley's."

"No way! You're messing with me!" said Jenn.

"I am joking about the location, but, get this, even worse, there was a body found behind Starbucks."

Starbucks was the other coffee shop in Mayfield. They were competitors in some sense, O'Malley's and Starbucks. Both were on the same main street, in close proximity to the bookstore, P.T. Jane's. Mayfield was a town that still had a quaint town center, with stores lining both sides and an island down the middle, decorated with pots of flowers for the summer tourists. It was common practice that the year-round citizenry of Mayfield went to O'Malley's and that the summer residents, particularly the New Yorkers, went to the generic Starbucks. To Jenn, the Starbucks coffee was much better. But for most Mayfield residents, even more important than the taste of the coffee was the prospect of who you might run into while getting it. So many Mayfield residents never bothered with Starbucks. After all, Starbucks were everywhere. O'Malley's was one of a kind.

"I don't believe you," said Jenn.

"I'll meet you at O'Malley's and we can talk. I have something else to share as well," Claire explained. "I can be there by quarter of nine."

"I was about to leave for work," Jenn said.

"This is worth going in late for," demanded Claire.

"Don't you have work today?" Jenn asked.

"I'm taking a personal day—a mental health break from all those budding Picassos," Claire said. She taught elementary art. "You have no idea what it's like to spend the day with children who don't know an abstract from a landscape."

"Yes, I know. You are a poor, tortured soul. Harder than going down into a coal mine," Jenn retorted.

"So I'll take it you're meeting me. See you in a bit. Buy me a grand decaf latte with one-percent milk and a shot of caramel, if you beat me there." Claire hung up.

Jenn didn't remember committing to meet Claire and going in to work late. And she certainly didn't commit to buying Claire her latte. She thought about calling back, but she was curious about what was going on. She checked the local newspaper website and found nothing about another dead body. Nothing at work this morning was pressing, and she could always work into the evening to make up for lost time.

On the way to her car, Jenn took the few extra steps and checked out Romeo and Juliet. Romeo still had three visible canker marks, which meant the flow of nutrients from the roots to the leaves was starting to get cut off in those spots.

The cankers were orangish and circled around the base of some of the limbs, visible if one looked closely and knew what to look for. Juliet now had six cankers that Jenn could see. Two more than last time she looked. She thought about getting out the stepladder and checking some of the higher branches. This was not good news. The leaves up above the limbs, with the cankers, were not as fully green or large as the leaves on the rest of Juliet. Nutrients and the tree's water supply was already reduced. *Every day older is a day closer to their deaths*, thought Jenn pessimistically.

But on the flip side, for us humans, Jenn philosophized; every day we grow older is one more day to learn something new, which we may then use to handle each of the days ahead. She wished her trees could learn from the blight and find a way to stop it. One day Jenn would have to learn how to handle Claire, who seemed to walk all over her lately.

CHAPTER 13

✦

Jenn arrived at O'Malley's first. She ordered Claire's latte—a ridiculous masterpiece of marketing—along with a plain old small coffee and a water for herself. She recognized a few faces in O'Malley's from growing up in town and smiled at an elderly couple that caught her eye. Since the early morning rain had stopped, she headed back outside with their drinks to one of the four outdoor tables, choosing to sit at the one with the loveliest potted blue hydrangea on it. The potted hydrangea on the other tables were already browning or wilting at the edges of the flowers, and not quite as perfect.

As the minutes ticked by, Jenn pulled out her "handcuffs" and checked the latest work texts and emails. Her stress level mounted as she saw how busy the day ahead looked, and how little she was accomplishing sitting with a coffee she didn't even want.

Claire came around the outside corner of the shop with a policeman at her heels. He was not just any policeman though; he was the one from central casting, who had arrived first at P.T. Jane's. He followed Claire to the table and remained standing while Claire grabbed a seat and reached for her latte. Claire took the lid off her latte and buried her head, examining its contents with a stirrer. Jenn looked up at the officer and smiled. He was looking right back at her and smiling. Boy, he had the nicest eyes, she thought, like the color of really rich potting soil. He looked about her age, too—and he was even tall, which she liked. Well, he looked tall, but then again, she was sitting. She was still looking into his eyes contemplating all this, when she heard Claire.

"Matt, don't you want to sit?"

"If you ladies don't mind, I'd rather we head somewhere a little less public?" He glanced at the front of O'Malley's, which was an entirely glass storefront. Jenn tore her eyes from him and saw that half of the folks in O'Malley's were looking back out the glass window at them.

"Okay." said Jenn, and stood up. Whoa, he was tall. Even with her heels on, he was taller than her by a couple of inches.

"Do we have to?" said Claire. A small voice rose up from down inside her. Claire stayed seated, still staring at her latte, stirring the foam that cost so much.

"Claire, come on. Half of O'Malley's is watching us. Let's walk," Jenn answered. She turned her eyes back to the officer and introduced herself. Sticking out her hand, she said, "I'm Jenn. I saw you the other night at P.T. Jane's."

"Matt," he said, shaking her hand and meeting her eyes. "I wouldn't forget you, or the night I saw my first murdered body."

"Okay, let's move," piped in Claire, as she stood, and slurped down some of her latte with a grimace. Claire led them back around the outside corner of O'Malley's building down a narrow alley to a rear parking lot, only two parking lots away from P.T. Jane's. Claire stopped at the edge of the lot and started talking.

"So a body was found behind Starbucks almost two hours ago. It's Dot Hutchinson. Do you remember who she is, Jenn?" Claire inquired. "I saw Matt there and he remembered me from the other night. After he eliminated me as a suspect," Claire said, sneering at him, "we started chatting a little and I told him about your knowledge and expertise as an environmental and land use attorney. I guess he thought I might be a murderess, since I was present when both bodies were found."

"Dot Hutchinson?" said Jenn. "What happened? My neighbor was just talking about her yesterday."

"She was found dead, and had been hit with a blunt force object to the back of her head. At this point it looks like she was killed in the same manner as Doctor Tilman," Matt explained.

"Anyway, Jenn, I told Matt you could explain to him what in the world a herpetologist is, what they study, why we care about them, and probably sixteen thousand things he doesn't really want to know about on the topic of nature, animals, or even the Earth in general."

"Thanks, Claire," said Jenn sarcastically. "Way to make me look appealing," she mumbled under her breath and gave Claire a hard glare, hoping she would realize how attractive Matt was, that here was dating material, right before their eyes. Claire looked back at Jenn, and as their eyes met, she seemed to get it, and made a small "oh" sound.

"Sure, I could," Jenn smiled up at Matt. "But are you a detective? Is there a sergeant or detective assigned to the case? I don't think I've ever seen you around town before the other night and you weren't in the interrogation room when I was questioned. There was a Detective Moffitt, right? He took my statement."

"I moved out to Mayfield almost a year ago from Darien," Matt said. Darien was another wealthy Connecticut shoreline town; larger and closer to New York, but similar in many ways to Mayfield. "And no, I am not a sergeant or detective, and I am not assigned to the murder investigation. I'm just trying to understand some of the history here. It seems like some kind of war is being fought here over land. Only the fight doesn't involve sticks and rocks like it would have thousands of years ago, or even bows and arrows, and guns, like it would have hundreds of years ago. Seems like the fight, up until this point, has only been with words, and environmentalism, to prevent a landowner from building homes on his property."

Wow, thought Jenn, dramatically phrased, but in many ways, true.

"That's exactly what's been going on for many years around here, and in lots of other places," Jenn said. "My firm represents the developer, so I'll tell you the facts and let you decide."

Jenn explained the history of the Riverfront Landing, how it started on a larger scale five years ago, but was now down to only 127 residences. Fewer homes meant less profit. Then she explained that herpetology was the study of amphibians (such as frogs, toads, and salamanders) and reptiles (such as snakes, lizards, turtles, and crocodiles).

"But," Matt interrupted, "why would a developer hire a herpetologist?"

"Well, there was this law in the '70s that a bunch of states enacted to make regular citizens the protectors of the environment. Any person could file lawsuits and be in lawsuits, not because the person would be injured by a development, but because the person could show that the environment or some part of nature would get unreasonably hurt by a development plan."

"Ahh," said Matt, "like the Lorax from Dr. Seuss—someone who speaks for the trees." He smiled broadly.

"Yes, exactly," said Jenn, smiling back at his quickness. "A regular person could go to court and speak for the trees. Not just for the trees, but for all of nature, and all the animals. So a regular person could sue a developer and argue the developer's plan would hurt the environment or a particular animal or plant. The Lorax guy though, would need an expert in court to say the animal would get hurt. The expert could be a general wildlife biologist, or a bird expert, a plant expert, whatever suited the facts."

"Okay, I get that, but why would the developer hire the expert? You're talking about a regular person hiring an expert to stop a development."

"In court, there are always two experts, one for each side. The judge or a jury picks which one to rely on. The developer would hire one to counter or stop whatever claims the Lorax guy might be making." Jenn paused and took a breath. Matt was looking right into her eyes and actually seemed to be listening. Not just listening. Intensely listening.

Jenn kept going, hoping his eyes wouldn't glaze over with boredom. "You know, it's about money. Developers are in it for the money. And lawsuits slow projects down, or stop them. If you get your own expert, say an anti-Lorax, and pay them to say an animal or species is not getting unreasonably hurt, you might get your project built."

"Would it be unreasonable for me to ask you out to dinner?" Matt asked. He was still looking right into her eyes, but now his eyes had a twinkle in the corners.

She laughed at his line. Was he serious? She dropped her eyes to the ground. She didn't know what to say. Had he been listening? Did he get the point? Now he seemed to just be flirting with her. A moment passed while she thought all this, and when she looked back up at him, he asked, "Well, so was Doctor Tilman hired by Mayfield Coastal Development?"

Jenn went all lawyerly and hedged answer. "I can tell you generally about the laws and the process, but you'll need to ask someone from Mayfield Coastal Development. It's been in the papers, so it's public knowledge that the head of my law depart-ment, David Webster, represents them. I can't answer any ques-tions though that could disclose anything confidential or privi-leged." Jenn paused.

"It's also public though that Charlie Martins is the head of Riverfront Landing. Hasn't anyone from the Madison police force, maybe it would be Detective Moffitt, talked to Charlie Martins?" Jenn altered her tone slightly and inquired, "Why are you asking about this anyway? Why are you getting involved if it's a detective who would be leading the murder investigation?"

Matt shifted his stance. His previously slightly stiff body language had transcended to bristly. "I just want to understand things. I care about this community and its citizens and I hate to see bad things happen."

"Come on, Jenn," Claire chimed in. "He doesn't trust his fellow officers. You've seen all the articles suspecting corruption in the Mayfield police force."

The public troubles of the Mayfield police force flick-ered through Jenn's mind. "You don't trust Detective Moffitt?" she asked.

"I just want to do what's right," Matt replied. "Dot Hutchinson was a sweet old lady. Stubborn, opinionated, and crusty, but sweet. She used to call the force last August when someone parked where they shouldn't on her street, Middle Beach Road." He smiled at the memory. "As the newest guy on the squad, I'd get sent over to her house. Seemed to me she really hated the summer crowd, like all the crusty old year-rounders who hate that New York wave that rolls in around July fourth. But she didn't mind sharing her beachfront with other folks from Connecticut. She only ever called in troublesome parkers trying to get to the beach when they had out-of-state plates."

Matt hadn't remotely answered Jenn's question about trusting his fellow officers. She decided he must not. The police radio on his belt made some noise and he excused himself from their conversation, took a couple of steps away, holding it to his ear to listen. Jenn looked at her cell phone and realized she really had to get to work. Matt mouthed, "I have to go," and started for his police cruiser.

Jenn said goodbye, realizing that she now regretted that in her shock at his asking her to dinner, she hadn't even gotten out a real answer. She would have liked to go to dinner with him.

Claire continued to nurse the bitter end of her latte, head down looking at the foam, stirrer spinning round and round the cup like a slow twister. Jenn suddenly realized Claire's Achilles' heel.

"You said that Dot Hutchinson's body was found at Starbucks and that you were there this morning. I have only one question, Claire. I thought you were a true Mayfield girl. What were you doing…at Starbucks?"

Claire smiled and reddened a bit. "Oh, it's simple really—O'Malley's lattes stink. The foam is like meringue mixed with jelly and it sticks to the inside of my mouth. Starbucks makes the better latte," Claire said with a sheepish grin, as she walked away.

CHAPTER 14

◆

Jenn spent the day completing her work and logging her billable time. Most of the day, she had worked hard on a document for court. It may have been called a "brief", but was really more appropriately called a "lengthy." Like too many lawyer's documents, this brief seemed to boringly drone on and on, all the way to the page limit set by the court. As the evening hours slipped away, Jenn made a quick trip to the break room to refill her water bottle. She was hunched over a water dispenser, and her bottle was almost full when she heard, "Two dead bodies in Mayfield. I bet the locals are abuzz." Jenn looked up to see David leaning against the left side of the doorframe into the break room. He had hunched shoulders, squinty eyes and a large belly. As he stared at her, she realized she was the "local" having grown up there, so maybe she better add something.

She gave a placid smile, and said "I think folks are upset. Mayfield has so few violent crimes, let alone murders." Jenn kept it vague. No need to burden him with the local gossip from her neighbor's husband or the strange suspicions of Officer Matt.

Jenn was a little afraid of David and avoided him as much as she could. She acted like she respected him and wanted more work from him, but she really didn't. He was a man controlled by his own ego. When the economy had been booming, David had wallowed in clients developing all sorts of projects all over the state. Grocery stores, big box stores like a Lowe's or Target, affordable housing developments, country estates, mansionizations along the Connecticut shoreline. David had done the work for all of them. He was the land use guru of the state. Each week he wrote an opinion piece on a land use issue that was published in the weekly statewide newspaper for attorneys. Although, he didn't really write it. One of the associate attorneys did, and David took all the credit. The associate's name didn't even make the end of the article.

"Are you hearing anything else in Mayfield about our client's project?" David asked pointedly. He moved across the room as he spoke, took a seat at one of the four tables in the break room, and patted the back of the chair to his left in a motion that directed her to sit down. *Oh Lord*, thought Jenn, trapped in the break room for a conversation.

The break room was actually pretty large, and well equipped with tables, a kitchen, even a flat-screen TV and a couple of stiff couches. Jenn hated it because it was located in the center space of the twenty-seventh floor and contained no natural daylight or plants. She always felt badly for the employees of Shipward & Waters who weren't attorneys. The lawyers had all the office windows in a circumference formation on the top four floors of their small skyscraper, and the rest of the employees, assistants, paralegals, administrators, and mailroom folks were in internal spaces. Jenn thought it stunk for employees to take their break in a windowless room and made it a point to go there as little as necessary.

Since Jenn had frozen for a second, dreading the thought of being trapped in the break room, David patted the back of the adjacent chair again. "Hey, come on Jenn, sit down for a second, and tell me about what the Mayfield folks are saying."

Jenn grabbed the chair and pulled it away enough to preserve some personal space, answering, "I'm not really hearing much. I'm not sure if folks are connecting the two murders to the Riverfront Landing project. Although Dot Hutchinson was a vocal opponent, she had her hands in practically everything in Mayfield. Her photo is constantly in the paper for the gardening club, or this committee or that fundraiser," she paused, adding, "and as for Doctor Tilman, I'm not sure it's general knowledge he was a consultant for our client, Mayfield Coastal Development. There has been nothing further in any of the papers on his murder. A few years ago, when the last murder occurred in Mayfield, I seem to recall a new story every day, even though there wasn't much to report."

"I'm not asking what you're reading, Jenn," David interjected impatiently. "I've read everything available myself. I'm wondering what you're hearing from your connections. Your neighbors. Friends. Family."

He paused dramatically. *Ugh*, thought Jenn. He wasn't letting go of the issue. She held her ground, though, and took a sip of her water to have time to think. Her gut told her not to start in on who had said what.

"I really have been so busy working, I haven't had a chance to read the community's tea leaves," she said. "I'm hoping to get to the Memorial Day Parade this weekend with some family members, so I'll let you know what I learn." Oh no, she had faltered in her resolve. Now she might have to supply more information next week.

She wasn't sure why she had caved, probably the same reason she had caved and met Claire for coffee earlier in the day, some kind of personality flaw. But David did know she was homegrown in Mayfield, and basically couldn't go anywhere in town without running into someone she knew. Memorial Day weekend was coming up and Jenn's family always went to the local parade. It lasted maybe ten minutes, but it had been a family tradition since she and her brother were young. The parade marked the start of the summer season in Mayfield and was always a festive event. Besides the Mayfield High School band, fire department, police department, local Lions and Masons, and many of the youth organizations marched, which made it so entertaining to watch. Cub Scouts and Daisies, Little Leaguers, lacrosse teams, a dance group, and even a small local martial arts club walked the length of the parade.

"Well, I'm not at all sure their deaths are connected. It could be random acts of violence," David stated plainly.

"They were both killed by blunt force trauma to the back of their heads," responded Jenn.

Wait, maybe it was good that she had committed to report back after the parade, because David then said, "It hasn't made the news yet, but Doctor Tilman had a small summer cottage in Mayfield. He would stay at it when he was consulting for us on a Connecticut case." Jenn didn't know this fact previously and Officer Matt hadn't mentioned it.

"Where is it located? What part of town?" asked Jenn.

"Over near the Surf Club," replied David. The Surf Club was a public park on the water in Mayfield, which consisted of a beach, a clubhouse type building, a playground, picnic areas, basketball courts, and a turfed field. For the community, it was an amazing asset that pulled the community together. The Mayfield High School football team played their games at the field, along with some of the other Mayfield sports teams.

Jenn had always wondered why it was named the "Surf Club." Connecticut beaches didn't have surf in the sense that there were no real waves. The state's southern shoreline lay along Long Island Sound, so there was little opportunity for waves to develop, as they do along much of the Atlantic Seaboard. Unless it was an extremely windy day, there was no "surf," just a calm, placid surface, with some small ripples rolling peacefully in to shore. In addition, the public park wasn't really a "club," since everyone in town could go without an invitation, but somehow the name "Surf Club" was a permanent addition to the Mayfield vernacular, and no one but Jenn seemed to notice the name's idiosyncrasies.

"Does—or I guess did—Doctor Tilman and his family come out from the city for the whole summer every year then?" Jenn didn't really know if he had a family, but she thought she would see what David knew.

"As much as he could. You know Jenn, I've been using Doctor Tilman as my expert for years, whenever I've needed him. When a citizen group has gotten a bee in its bonnet about any state-listed amphibians or reptiles, he has typically been a great expert for my developer clients. He's such a renowned expert and he's so thorough in his knowledge, site visits, and reports that he always wows local zoning and wetlands commissions into believing a proposed development won't hurt nature."

"Did he have family?" Jenn asked, trying to learn more.

"He left behind his wife, Ingrid, and two grown children. His children are both academics themselves. I believe one is at Berkeley and the other is in Baltimore, at Johns Hopkins."

"Has he had the Mayfield house for long?" Jenn tried again.

"I really don't know. I think I've heard him talk about it for at least the last five years, but I really can't say," replied David. He dropped his eyes, turned sideways as though to rise, but stopped to look down at his dress shoes. He reached over his large belly to try to brush something off the inner side of his right shoe. He was off by a millimeter or two, and kind of swatted the air on his first attempt. His belly really had grown especially large lately. Did he need help putting those shoes on in the morning? Jenn wondered. David lifted his right ankle up over his left knee, and then swatted again at what looked to Jenn like a small aspen leaf. This time the leaf wafted toward the ground. As David watched it fall, Jenn realized she had time for one last query.

"So you mentioned at the Round Table that Doctor Tilman had completed his report for Riverfront Landing?" She decided she'd better confirm what she had heard, given the discrepancy in what her neighbor Mark had told her. "And he found nothing. That no habitats of reptiles or amphibians would be unreasonably impaired or destroyed as part of the development?"

"Yes. We have a final report from him to that effect. He had conducted all of his site walks to review the species and their habitats at Riverfront Landing, and he finished it about two days before his body was found. Well, I guess two days before you found his body. It is terrible he's gone, but given the current timeline on the project, I'm glad we received his final report before he was murdered." David stood up as he spoke, and took two steps away from the table.

"Current timeline?" Jenn asked David's back as she stood up from the table.

David looked back over his left shoulder to face Jenn. "Yes. It's no secret," he replied. "Mayfield Coastal Development is under some financial pressure from its New York investors to get Riverfront Landing shovel-ready before the end of the year. The resistance by Save Riverfront Landing has been effective in the sense that we are now over three and a half years into the permitting approval phase, and we still have no local land use approvals in sight."

"I recall the news when the coastal permit was obtained from the Department of Environmental Protection and Energy," Jenn said. A project this close to the Sound needed both approval by the state to make sure it would not unreasonably hurt coastal resources, as well as approvals by the local commissions.

"Yes. We've been cleared by the state, which, as you know, is typically the greatest hurdle," David said, "and the application for the latest version of the development of 127 residences is before all three local commissions."

Jenn knew this to mean applications were pending with Mayfield's Zoning Board of Appeals, the Zoning Commission and the Inland Wetlands Commission.

David continued, "The citizens just filed an intervention petition in the Wetlands Commission matter, claiming the proposed development will unreasonably hurt the natural resources of the property. They claim that there's a vernal pool on the property in the grove of trees remaining on the site, and that a rare population of salamanders live on the property."

Jenn blinked in surprise. "A vernal pool so close to the Sound? I thought vernal pools were more for upland, wooded areas." Jenn stepped toward David to make sure she heard him correctly.

"Yep, a vernal pool. They're usually in real wooded areas," said David, "but I guess there's enough trees in the grove, and the right type of soil, so that a seasonal pond is there for the salamanders, turtles, and frogs to breed in."

"I'm so surprised there is a vernal pool so close to the Sound," replied Jenn. "I thought you were using Doctor Tilman to look at turtles or snakes, not at species which are dependent on a vernal pool."

"It surprised me, too, Jenn," David said. "Look, after we got the state coastal approval, I thought this project was a go. I did not expect the citizen's group to come up with vernal pool issues. It's thrown a wrench in the whole thing, and getting Doctor Tilman out there this spring, and getting his report completed has become critical for keeping the project in line. Plus, why didn't the state environmental guys see or raise the issue of the vernal pool when they issued the coastal permit?" Jen felt her brow furrow, because the facts weren't making sense. "You know, Jenn, I'm asking for your help here," David pleaded. "I'm not sure how you feel personally about the property getting developed, but I'm asking for your help professionally. I know you are careful to keep your mouth shut down there, but please let me know what you hear. I have got to get this one through."

Jenn was stunned. David had never spoken to her in such a personal manner before. His words seemed to come from his heart. He needed help.

"I'll let you know what I hear," she assured him.

"Thanks, Jenn," David said, and he turned back around and left the break room.

Jenn didn't move. She thought about their exchange for a moment and what it was like to be David. In good economic times, he had bathed in money. He had a large sailboat, a mansion in the best suburb, and a house on Block Island. He had a ski house at Stratton, and a place in Florida, too. Lately, with the slower economy, his business generation had fallen off, and with such a large and public property case, he really did need this to go well. Jenn looked down at the leaf on the floor of the break room, and then bent over to pick it up. She couldn't resist. No, not a small aspen at all, she realized. A locust leaf. She went to throw it in the trash, but decided to keep it instead, and carried it back to her office.

Entering her office, she stuck the leaf on her bookcase, and immediately realized the day had passed into night while she was stuck in the windowless break room. It was the same shocking sensation as going into a movie theater in daylight and coming out into darkness. It scared her that the sky could go from light to dark so quickly. The arrival of darkness led her to the dark thought that now two folks lay dead in Mayfield, not just one, and only the murderer knew why.

CHAPTER 15

"Who are we vessing?" screamed an agitated Sophia. "Who are we vessing?"

"Honey, calm down," said Claire.

Jenn had just walked in the side door of her brother's house. Despite knocking, no one had opened the door, so she just let herself in. They were expecting her. It was the morning of Memorial Day, and time for the Bowdoin family to go to the parade.

Sophia and Claire were in the kitchen. Claire was kneeling on the kitchen floor, tying Sophia's sneaker. Sophia was dressed in her yellow T-ball shirt and hat. She was clearly upset about something more than soggy breakfast cereal.

"Mommy, who are we vessing?" whined Sophia. "I want to know."

"Oh, hi, Jenn. Glad you made it," Peter said. "Sounds like you've been taking your turn as the family workaholic this week." Their father had been a workaholic, desperate to be financially successful, and "get ahead." Although Jenn and Peter tried hard not to follow in his shoes, they did occasionally exhibit too strong a work ethic, if there was such a thing.

"Mommy, Mommy, who are we vessing?" repeated Sophia loudly, reaching up, putting her hands on her mom's face, and trying to turn Claire's head toward her.

"Say hello to Aunt Jenn," Claire told her daughter. "She's come to watch you."

"In my game? Mommy, who are we vessing? Is it the green team?"

"Oooh," said Claire, finally understanding her five-year-old's speech. "You are not versing anyone today. Today is not actually a game. It is a parade. You get to walk in the parade with your team."

"No game? A parade? Will the green team be there?" asked Sophia.

"Yes. The green team will be there," answered Claire. "Now, please say hi to your aunt."

"Hi, Aunt Jenn."

"Hey, Sophia," replied Jenn, giving her niece a hug.

"We're off," said Claire, standing up and rubbing her hands together. "We have to get there by eight-thirty."

"Mommy, wait, wait, tell me again, what happens at a parade?" questioned Sophia again.

"Bye, Peter, see you there," yelled Claire toward the stairwell, as she pulled Sophia by the hand toward the back door.

"Bye, Daddy," yelled Sophia.

Jenn sat down at the kitchen island and surveyed the room. Clutter was everywhere. Breakfast dishes and glasses were still strewn on the island, papers cluttered one entire counter, and recently washed pots and pans, probably from the prior night's dinner, lay air-drying next to the sink. One counter captured Jenn's interest though. It contained uncapped canning jars of various sizes and shapes. But there wasn't anything edible in the jars. Instead, they contained recent treasures her brother had found. Treasures to him that is, but trash to most.

About twenty-five years ago it had started as a joke. Peter had been out on a day hike, and brought home some moss and lichen samples. He said he wanted to learn more about them and their role in our ecosystem. Their father had been upset. He didn't want it in the house and thought Peter was just trying to "torture" him as they both had when they were younger and had brought home whatever creatures or natural wonders they could. Sticks, rocks, leaves, shells, snakes, frogs, salamanders, baby birds, and turtles had all been brought to the back door, usually with them begging, "Please can I keep it?" Their father did not want "that stuff" in the house. Their mother didn't care and allowed them to keep their collections and pets in their bedrooms.

Jenn started reeling in the years as she waited for Peter to come downstairs. They were going to walk to the parade together as they had since Jenn could walk. She recalled her father telling Peter's missing snake story. Peter's pet snake, Ben, had escaped and they were all helping to look for it in Peter's bedroom. Their mom lifted a corner of the area carpet and she and her dad saw there was nothing there. The carpet lay askew though, and their dad scolded their mom, "You didn't put that back right. It's not pulled straight." Their mom replied, "Well if you don't like it, you fix it."

Their father marched back over to the carpet, lifted the corner, and screamed. The snake was looking right at him. He had never screamed in his life, and probably wouldn't ever again. Sometimes their parents referred to it as "The Scream." Jenn had turned when he screamed, and his face had looked like the Munch painting. For such a strong, serious man, it was an image she had never forgotten.

"Do you like my latest collections?" asked Peter as he walked into the kitchen. "I pulled them out of Cockaponset State Forest last weekend."

After "The Scream" their father had requested that they stop bringing home so many animals, at least absolutely no more snakes, and preferably nothing else that was alive. Peter was already eleven years old and had just learned about lichen. Since lichen are not just plants, Peter found a way to fool his father. Lichen don't have roots that absorb nutrients and water the way plants do. Instead they are a composite organism based upon a symbiotic relationship between bacteria and fungus. The bacteria or algae produce food for the fungus through photosynthesis, and benefit from being protected by the fungus inside its filaments or threads of cells.

Once Peter learned that lichen can grow almost anywhere— on bark, leaves, other lichens, mosses, rock, even gravestones— and that there were about 20,000 known species of lichen, he set out to start collecting them all. Peter's fascination was fueled in part because that same summer, they had seen the movie *Ghostbusters*, in which Egon Spengler proclaimed that he collected spores, molds, and fungus. Although lichen wasn't exactly the same thing, the idea of collecting something so odd stuck with Peter, and sparked a desire to learn a great deal about this phenomenon of nature.

He and Jenn had mostly chuckled, though, because it was fun to fool their father, who didn't realize the lichen was alive.

Jenn pulled herself back to the present.

"Sure, they look great. Anything rare or exceptional?" she asked.

"Come on Jenn, you know each one has its own unique beauty," replied Peter. "I did pull two samples I wasn't sure of, but you know lichen, almost its own ecosystem. It can grow so differently, it can be difficult to determine species."

"I like the orange one especially," said Jenn. It was bright orange, with a scalloped edge and fingerlike projections fanning out from a deeper orange center.

"Yes, that one is especially cool," Peter agreed. "Sophia called it the Heat Miser."

Jenn wrinkled her brow in confusion. The Heat Miser?

"You know, Jenn, come on, you could not have forgotten *The Year Without a Santa Claus*." It was one of those Christmas movies that was on one of the networks every year, and one of the characters could make fire and had bright orange hair, which stuck straight up into the air.

Jenn looked at it again and laughed, finally recalling the Heat Miser and seeing what Sophia saw. It looked exactly like a miniature version of the Heat Miser from the movie, with flaming hair. There were even some evenly spaced indentations, which kind of looked like eyes. *Sometimes you really had to look at things closely*, thought Jenn, *to see what's right in front of you.*

She thought about the murders, and Dr. Tilman's face. Then Dot Hutchinson getting killed and her body dumped in with the coffee trash. She was missing something. There was something right before her eyes that she couldn't see.

CHAPTER 16

❖

On Memorial Day, the weather was perfect and the crowds were out. The walk from Peter's house to their standard viewing spot was a short quarter mile walk. On the way, Jenn and her brother greeted folks they knew, including their mom, Linda. She was seated in a chair in the front yard of one of her friend's houses, surrounded by about ten elderly men and women. The group had gathered for a morning of parade watching and an afternoon of card playing and eating.

Peter and Jenn stopped and visited with their mom and said hi to her friends. Last year, the first Memorial Day without her husband, Linda had decided to watch the parade with friends, rather than from their typical family spot. At first Jenn had felt hurt by this, but this year she took it in stride. She wasn't sure she understood it, but she accepted it.

The Bowdoin family had always watched the parade from a small commercial property, which had been a gas station in Peter's and Jenn's childhood, and was right near the beginning of the parade route. The building had since been razed, and the plot sat empty and covered in grass and dandelions. This spot, so early on the route typically didn't have many spectators, but it was their tradition to gather there.

The gasoline tanks from the old gas station had leaked underground and the property was contaminated. You couldn't tell from looking at the grass-covered lot, and most folks in town probably didn't know. Jenn, however, knew an application had been filed to have the property cleaned up with some of the leaking underground storage tank funds available from the state. The application process for state funds to clean up a contaminated gas station took years. Jenn knew it might be a while before the property was cleaned up and developed again. When they were kids, the former gas station had sold Coke in glass bottles, from what was then an ancient vending machine. On Memorial Day, they were each allowed to get one, a special treat, and it became part of their tradition.

The parade started, and they watched the first selectman, or mayor as most of the country called it, walk by. This year Fritz Robinson was in a light red jacket, white dress shirt, and blue pants. "How many years in a row has he worn that red, white and blue outfit?" Jenn asked.

"I can't recall him ever wearing anything else," Peter replied. Robinson had ruled Mayfield for over fifteen years. He was followed by the other members of the Board of Selectmen, or Town Council, who each smiled and waved, as the folks on the sidelines clapped their appreciation.

The chief of police, Chief Scalini, followed by his officers, was next in the parade. Jenn saw Detective Moffitt, who had taken her statement at the police station, walk by and caught his eye and waved at him. She thought for a second of Officer Matt, and his potting soil eyes, but did not see him. Maybe she missed him in the crowd of officers walking by.

As they stood watching the parade, Peter asked Jenn, "Do you think I'm a good dad?" He didn't even turn to look at her.

He kept his eyes forward and watched the Lions Club march by in their matching blue blazers.

Jenn assured him that he was great and not to worry about it. Peter still didn't turn to look at her, but seemed to be listening. Their own father had never stopped to play with them. He wanted to provide, but he didn't really know how to play. All work made for a sort of joyless life, and as children it felt as though their father didn't really know how to stop working. He had never been fun. He was too serious, too busy, and too opinionated. There was a right way to live one's life, and a wrong way. Peter and Jenn had tried to live up to his expectation of what was the "right way," but maybe they had each given up some of themselves in the process.

Peter leaned the other way too much. He overcompensated. All Peter did with Sophia was play. He never scolded, minded, or even directed her. Sometimes Jenn wanted to say something, but she never did. She could see Claire took on all the discipline, and Peter only took on the fun. While she was still contemplating whether today was a good day to actually have this discussion, Sophia marched by with her team.

There were lots of Little Leaguers clumped together by shirt color. The oldest baseball players seemed to come in the front, some of them holding the Little League banner. At the very end of the section were the T-ball players. Parents of the T-ballers marched with their sons and daughters, and some pulled wagons filled with five-year-olds, or even carried their players.

Sophia was walking, holding her mother's hand, and holding hands with a boy, who wore a green T-ball shirt. The little boy had blond hair curling out under the edges of his hat and a huge grin on his face. Sophia had dropped Claire's hand to wave frantically at Peter and Jenn, but held onto the boy's hand tightly. Peter snapped some photographs, and after Sophia and Claire passed, he commented, "So now we know why she likes the green team."

At the very end of the parade, there was a ten-foot-wide banner carried by two high school boys that said "Save Riverfront Landing," and referenced a website in smaller font. Behind it marched Nat Harkins, the lead opponent of the Riverfront development. Jenn also recognized Shelby Williams, the seventh-grade science teacher, and Robbie Hayden, the father of three, who was pictured in the local paper as well. There were a few other folks marching behind the banner who she didn't recognize. She could not recall a Save Riverfront Landing banner in prior years. Jenn turned to ask Peter about it, when Officer Matt tapped her on the left shoulder.

Turning around to face him, she smiled at the sight of those deep brown eyes. He smiled back. She tried not to say anything stupid. When nervous, she rambled at moments. She recalled that the best moments with Alex had no words. The best moments so far in her life seemed to involve looks she had shared, or maybe small actions or gestures, but with time she found that words sometimes rang hollow. Some folks were all talk, no action. She stared into Matt's eyes and thought about how they were so brown and rich, almost endless.

"Hi, Attorney Jenn. How are you today?" Matt said, interrupting her wandering mind.

"I'm good," she replied. "How are you, Officer Matt?"

"Good," he answered. "Glad to not have any new dead bodies on this beautiful day. It's been a little too crazy around here lately. Happy for a nice normal Memorial Day Parade." He leaned in closer to her, and finished with, "I see you look beautiful in the morning too."

Jenn smiled at him, in shock at his compliment, and looked into his eyes. She was begging her brain to please come up with something funny to reply, when she heard high-pitched shouting from the parade route.

"Yes, we will march," shrieked Shelby. "We have every right to march in this parade. I pay my taxes and I want to march with my group." Jenn turned back toward the road, and could see Shelby about fifty feet to her right. Shelby had stopped marching and was yelling at a middle-aged man.

"You're not on the official list," boomed back the man. He was not yelling. He was just very authoritarian in his tone. "You cannot just jump on the route. Now please stop marching."

"We will march," yelled back Shelby. "I don't see you stopping any other groups from marching." Shelby then turned away from him and started walking in the parade route.

"We will march. We will march. We will march," chanted some of the other people who had stopped and stood with Shelby. As she started her walk, they started to walk again, too.

"So much for a nice normal parade. I better go check that out," said Officer Matt, and he headed down toward where the commotion had been.

Jenn watched Matt walk toward the man who had spoken to Shelby. She watched the conversation for a moment, until the crowds milling about at the parade's end blocked her view.

Jenn wanted to walk toward where she had last spotted Matt. She looked to her right to see Peter looking down, checking his phone. He glanced up and said, "Claire wants us to walk toward her. Sophia's breaking down. She'll probably need to be carried home."

They started walking along the edge of the parade route, to the right, toward its end. Jenn scanned ahead, trying to see what had happened to Officer Matt and whether the Save Riverfront Landing group had been allowed to continue in the parade. She couldn't see the back end of the parade, as it was already too far ahead. The parade had passed in an instant this year. As a child, folks seemed to march slowly up the street and in her childhood mind the parade had lasted hours.

Most parade watchers headed toward the Mayfield town green for the short Memorial Day ceremony that followed the parade. To Jenn, town greens like Mayfield's represented the idea that even hundreds of years ago, the settlers supported the concept of public parks. Even historically, some property was held as open space in trust for all people. The greens were for all to use and enjoy. The law, under which the Save Riverfront Landing group had filed a petition to join into the wetlands approval process, was based upon the same basic premise. Some natural resources, or some parts of nature, needed to be kept for all the people to use, preserved so that future generations could see and experience their undisturbed beauty.

The Mayfield town green was the size of about two standard city blocks. Around it stood a protestant church and a community meeting building. The grass covering was broken up with some older interspersed oaks and maples. The leaf canopies created by the old trees provided some much-needed shade.

There were large swaths of grass, cut up by some sidewalks. Many Connecticut towns had almost overfilled their town greens with war memorials, so that there was little grass left. Mayfield had not done this, but rather had smartly set all the memorials in the southeast corner with a flagpole located at the center of the engraved stones, which honored those who fought and died in wars, from the Revolutionary War up to Vietnam.

Peter and Jenn walked onto the green, surveying the crowd. Near the war memorials was a temporary stage with a couple of rows of chairs, and a podium with a microphone at its left side. Folks were milling around the stage with some chairs already taken, and others still open. Peter spotted Claire and Sophia, pointed toward them, and led Jenn through the gathering crowd. Jenn noted that Sophia was playing what appeared to be "rock, paper, scissors" with the boy in the green T-ball shirt. Jenn was glad Sophia was not stalking other children for food today. Claire was talking to Robbie Hayden, who Jenn now realized must be the father of Sophia's friend.

As they got closer, Claire turned to look at Peter, and said, "Excuse me, Robbie, but let me introduce my husband, Peter, and his sister, Jenn. Robbie's son Freddy is quite a favorite of Sophia's."

They greeted Robbie, and Peter and Robbie engaged in the usual small talk about the weather, and commented on their children's blooming friendship. Peter suggested maybe they'd end up as prom dates, much to everyone's amusement.

After the chuckles died down, Claire opened her big mouth. "You probably know Robbie, but it is Jenn's firm, Shipward & Waters that represents Mayfield Coastal Development."

Robbie turned to Jenn, and suddenly anger appeared in his eyes. Jenn just smiled and said nothing.

"I'm against the development," he said angrily. "We need more fields in town to support our growing athletes. The state and the town need to preserve the property."

Although Robbie's words were benign, the intensity of his voice and the rage in his delivery was not normal. She was about to say something when a clergyman took the microphone up on stage, and stated, "I've been asked to give the invocation on this beautiful Memorial Day."

Jenn chose not to respond to Robbie, but instead bowed her head to hear the minister's words.

Sophia and Freddy were disruptive during the ceremony. At one point when they became particularly loud, Claire finally took Sophia by the hand, had Sophie say goodbye to Freddy, and mouthed that she was headed toward O'Malley's.

Peter and Jenn stayed for all the speeches, including a rather lengthy one by Fritz Robinson. He made a generic reference to the recent tragedies in town. He pontificated that during times of war and strife, Mayfield residents had worked together to fill in the cracks and seams in the community, and that he hoped as a community, Mayfield folks would continue to help and tend to others in these modern times.

Jenn thought it was nicely done. The community had to be shaken up by two dead bodies found brutally murdered, right on the same main street the parade marchers had just walked down. Everyone needed a little reassurance now and then that things would be okay. Citing a history of collectiveness and community made it seem as though the current murders were just another bump in the town's long and successful history.

When the ceremony was over, Jenn looked around and realized that Robbie and his son Freddy had also departed at some point. She must have been more engrossed in the ceremony than she realized. Thank goodness, she thought, and said so to Peter.

"Yes, that guy had it in for you," he replied.

"Just because I work at Shipward & Waters doesn't mean I'm part of the evil empire," replied Jenn.

"I know," said Peter. "You're not evil. You just work at The Death Star."

CHAPTER 17

J enn could have hung out at her brother's house the remainder of the day, but she chose not to. And although there was plenty of housework to be done that needed more attention than her yard, she could not bear to spend such a gorgeous day inside. She still didn't have everything mulched, and here it was Memorial Day itself, so Jenn went right to work distributing mulch by wheelbarrow and raking it out around the bushes at the front of her house.

Jenn's neighbors were having a party. There were probably ten extra cars on the street and music coming from Mark and Debbie's yard. It was loud enough that she could hear every word of what sounded like The Beach Boys' Greatest Hits, which although happy, summer music, was painful to her ears today.

She decided to get a beer and a water from the kitchen and miss "Surfin' U.S.A." While inside, she did a few dishes, and returned outside to a more tolerable "Barbara Ann." As she came around to the front of her house, balancing her water and beer while pushing the wheelbarrow, she saw Freddy, the little boy from the green T-ball team. He was standing at her front door about to ring her doorbell.

"Hey," said Jenn. "Hi!"

"Hi! Is Sophia here? I saw you in the yard when we drove up and I didn't know if Sophia lived here. Does she live here?" He was still in his T-ball shirt and hat and looked very eager.

"No sweetie, she doesn't live with me. She lives with her mom and dad," Jenn explained. "I'm her aunt, her dad's sister. Are you here for the party next door?"

"Yes," said Freddy.

"Does your mom or dad know you came over here?" Jenn asked.

"No," replied Freddy. He looked sad. "They're all busy drinking Pina Coladas and Hurricanes. The adults have all the fun drinks with umbrellas and fruit and the only kids' drink is apple juice boxes. The party sucks. Plus, I'm the only kid. My older brothers are at one of their friends' houses with a pool, but I didn't get to go because I can't swim yet. There are no kid toys at the party and the dog isn't even fun to play with. And the music stinks."

"Well," said Jenn, walking toward Freddy, and then sitting down on the top of the brick stoop at the front of her house, "I can't say much about the party in general, but I agree with you about the music. It definitely stinks!"

Freddy smiled and sat down next to her. The stoop was brick and three steps high. Moss grew on the mortar between the bricks, as the front of Jenn's house faced north. She touched the moss, noticing how soft it felt under her fingertips. Freddy reached out his hand and started to touch the moss, too.

He said, "Is this stuff moss? I think it is, but it's funny how it just grows here." He pointed to the little strips between the bricks.

"Yes, it is. Moss grows in damp, shady places. It doesn't have any flowers or seeds," explained Jenn, "but it has spores, like mushrooms. The wind helps blow the spores around, so moss can grow in all sorts of places, as long as it has a water supply. Have you ever looked at the lines on the back of a leaf?" she asked, reaching over and pulling a leaf off one of her rhododendrons.

Jenn showed the back of the leaf to Freddy.

"See these lines?" she asked him. "They act like straws and carry the water and nutrients to all the parts of this bush." Jenn gestured toward the rhododendron. "The water and nutrients are carried all the way from the roots to the flowers. The moss doesn't have a straw system like that. Even we have a straw system like that, and she pointed to the veins showing on her wrist. The moss doesn't have that, it doesn't have a vascular system, so it has to live somewhere with a big enough water source to support it."

Freddy took the leaf and ran his finger along the lines on its underside.

"How does the moss survive here?" he asked.

"This side of my house, the north side, doesn't get any direct sunlight. Moss is believed to grow better on the north side of trees and rocks because the north side of things gets less sun than the south side of things. When the bricks in the stoop get really wet, the bricks soak up the water and without direct sunlight to dry up the water, there's a source of water for the moss until the next rain."

Jenn took a sip of her beer, and remembered looking at moss the other day, but she couldn't recall where. It was growing in the cracks, just like this. Where was that? she wondered. She took another sip of her beer and felt Freddy's eyes following her. Then she thought of poor Freddy stuck with plain old apple juice.

"Do you have any toys?" he asked.

"You know, I do have a toy truck Sophia rides on sometimes, and I think I have something fun for you to drink. Come on."

Jenn led Freddy around to the western side of her house, toward her driveway. She grabbed the toy gator for him to play with and then went back inside to find him a fun drink. She quickly made a pitcher of lemonade from mix, cut some orange slices, and found some maraschino cherries and blueberries to stick in it. She returned outside with the concoction in a dazzling plastic dragon cup she had for Sophia, decorated with the cut fruit.

"Here you go, sweetie," she said as she walked back out her door. Robbie, Freddy's dad, was standing next to his son, looking annoyed. Oh no, she thought. This is the guy that thinks I'm Darth Vader. Jenn audibly felt herself exhale in a sigh, and then took a deep breath in, ironically just like Darth Vader, anticipating a possible confrontation.

"Thank you for minding Freddy," Robbie said pleasantly enough, but with no trace of a smile.

"No trouble," replied Jenn. "I made him some lemonade." She handed Freddy the cup and his eyes lit up.

"Say thank you," Robbie directed Freddy before Freddy's hand had even reached the cup.

Over parenting seems to be the new in-thing, thought Jenn. Let's jump in and tell kids what to do before we even see how they respond. Her sister-in-law did that, too.

"Thank you," said Freddy. "Daaaaddd, I was going to. You don't have to tell me."

Hmmm, thought Jenn.

"Freddy, after you finish that drink, you need to come back to the party. You can't bother Sophia's aunt all afternoon."

"It's fine," said Jenn. "He is no bother. The Taylors don't have any toys and I have some for when Sophia visits me. I have some bubbles, Freddy, if you want to do that next." Freddy was eating the fruit from the top of his cup with his hands.

"I really don't feel comfortable leaving him with you," said Robbie, whose eyes had been replaced with lasers that were boring into her. Anger suddenly seethed from him. *What a quick change*, thought Jenn. He seemed fine a second ago—somewhat annoyed at the world, but not enraged.

"You know it pains me to see Mayfield Coastal Development walk all over our community, for the almighty dollar," he said. "The children in our community need more playing fields. They need green spaces and fresh air. We don't need more houses with more children for our children to compete against."

Jenn said nothing. She wasn't even sure she followed him all the way. But she could tell he was just getting going.

"When will folks be rich enough?" he continued in a louder tone. "How much money does your developer client have? I bet he already has at least a few homes in the fanciest spots. At what point does someone who loves conspicuous consumption have enough? Does he have to destroy the whole world, build on all the open beachfront, and use up all our natural resources before he's satisfied?"

Jenn wasn't even sure who Robbie was talking about. Did he mean Charlie Martins, the spokesman for the project? Did Robbie know something about the investors of Mayfield Coastal Development?

Despite Jenn's close proximity, he yelled, "I don't know how you sleep at night! You're on the wrong side! You work against nature! Your firm represents the destroyers of the environment! When will man's greed for stuff stop? It's our children who'll be deprived of the natural world and the kind of childhoods we had!"

Freddy, who had been happily focused on his drink, noticed his father's escalating voice. "Dad, Sophia's aunt is a nice lady. She's not out to ruin the earth. Look at her beautiful yard. Daddy, look."

Robbie looked at Freddy. He tried to reign in his anger, remembering where he was.

"Oh good, Freddy, you're done. Time to go back to the party."

"But what about the bubbles, Dad?"

"We have bubbles at home. Come on, time to go back to the party." Robbie took the dragon glass from Freddy's hand and gave it to Jenn. "Thank you again for the drink. It was kind of you to look after my son."

Robbie led Freddy away by the hand. Jenn stood there for a second and then walked back over to her front stoop and sat down. That was one of the strangest things she'd ever seen. It was like he had a switch in his head that made him go from normal to deranged, and then back again. Moody, she thought. Mental health issues, she guessed. He had such intense anger seething out of him. She was glad she didn't live with him. Poor thing, she thought of Freddy, to have a father with such uncontained and intense anger.

"Kokomo" played next door. Jenn wouldn't mind going to any of those places. Aruba, Bahamas, Jamaica, all seemed better than being the recipient of unleashed rage. She looked down at the moss between the bricks of her stoop, and started to quietly sing along. She rubbed her finger along the moss again, and suddenly remembered where she had seen it.

At P.T. Jane's. There was moss along the front of the ice cooler. That's what she had seen when she was on the phone with Stuart. That's what she had walked over to look at. Why would there be moss there? The ice cooler faced west, not north. It had the full afternoon sun on its face.

The ice cooler must be in use, then condensation would provide a water source. Why would a rusted ice cooler be in use in a bookstore parking lot? None of the stores on either side of the bookstore sold food or drinks. There was a wine shop, but that was four or five properties away. Jenn decided she needed to take another look at that ice cooler. Immediately.

PART II

CHAPTERS 18-27

CHAPTER 18

S o much for immediately going to the ice cooler. Jenn might have appeared to be in control of her life, but it just wasn't really the case. She was always putting her own agenda on the back burner, and helping others with their agenda instead. Sunday afternoon was spent helping her mother with her yard work. Then, most of the work week, Jenn toiled away in her office getting things done for the attorneys she worked with.

It wasn't until Friday morning when Claire called that Jenn refocused on her desire to check out the ice cooler. Claire started the phone call with, "I'm going to the viewing." Claire wanted Jenn to go with her. Jenn did not want to go. She didn't know Dot Hutchinson. She had been in school with Dot's daughter Peg, but she didn't like her. Although she had empathy for Peg losing her mother in what appeared to be a heinous crime, it seemed disingenuous to go. If Dot had died of natural causes, she wouldn't be going. Claire was friendly with Dot, so Claire had a legitimate basis for going. Claire just didn't want to go alone.

"I really don't think I can swing it. I have two briefs due this week and a mediation memo. It really would be best if you just went without me. Can't Peter go with you?"

Jenn asked.

"Peter doesn't want to go. He says half the town will be there, and the viewing line will be a mile long," Claire answered. "He said he'd rather match socks than go."

Peter hated laundry and avoided it like the plague. From the outside looking in, their marriage seemed to balance two careers and one child pretty well, but part of that was that Peter did most of the kitchen work when he was home. He might not be so great with the laundry, but if the sink had dishes in it, and he walked by it, they would be promptly washed, dried, and put away.

"I need you, Jenn," Claire paused. Still, it really seemed fake and inappropriate to go.

"They'll know you are just coming to keep me company. They won't think badly of it," said Claire. "I doubt they know you found the first body, or even remember you work at Shipward & Waters. They're going to be consumed by grief and sorting out their new finances."

Dot had been a widow, a very wealthy widow. Her daughters were her only heirs and were both married with children. Leave it to Claire to point out the more practical facts of a situation.

Jenn had read a few more details about Dot Hutchinson's death in the local online news website. Oddly enough, her body was found in the dumpster itself behind Starbucks. The dumpster also had a screening fence, but apparently, whoever was disposing of the body decided on the dumpster and didn't just stash it inside the fence. The article didn't provide much information about the condition of the deceased's body or the person who had found it.

Jenn guessed it had been a Starbucks employee taking out trash. The article mentioned only that she had received blunt force trauma to the back of the head at a prior location, and had been moved to the dumpster. The majority of the article was a summary of the lifetime of community service Dot had provided to the Mayfield community. It was impressive in both its length and variety. Dot had served as a volunteer member of several town commissions, as a fundraising leader for the library, as a director of the historical society, and as a lifelong member of the Mayfield Garden Society.

Jenn wondered why the younger generation didn't understand the concept of giving back. It seemed like so many folks her age just took from the community. They used the roads and schools and civic services, and thought paying taxes was a sufficient return. Taxes were only half the picture—small communities needed an active citizenry to thrive and prosper. Dot's generation, and Dot particularly, seemed to understand that. Hit on the head and dumped with the coffee grounds seemed like such a horrible ending for a life that was primarily spent giving in service to others. Her murder bothered Jenn more than Dr. Tilman's. Maybe this was why. Although opinionated about preserving Riverfront, Dot generally was about helping others.

And although Dr. Tilman's murder was shocking, the idea that someone brutally killed an elderly woman, who only meant to further good, was downright appalling. And of all the places to end up, a dumpster just seemed trashy. Why would a murderer drop a body in a dumpster? There were miles and miles of deserted forests in Connecticut that a body could be placed in and never found again. Jenn wondered about the choice of Starbucks. Was it just a location that was convenient? After the brutal act and getting rid of the body, did the murderer just need a quick latte pick-me-up?

There were no details on Dot herself or about the time of day. The only quote in the article wasn't even from Detective Moffitt, whom Jenn understood was investigating Dr. Tilman's murder. It was the state police spokesman, Paul Rance, who mentioned that the state police were now involved in the investigation as well since more than one murder had occurred in Mayfield. Apparently, serial killer investigations merited involving more than just the local police.

"I'll meet you at Dunville's after," said Jenn. She wanted no part of funeral or viewing crashing, which is what it really was. Jenn decided to wait Claire out, so she sung "Jingle Bells" in her head. Jenn sometimes used this tactic with opposing lawyers in phone negotiations. Never underestimate the power of silence, she thought. Claire was clearly waiting for Jenn to backslide on her position. Jenn got to the end of the song, and took in a big sigh to start it again in her head.

"Fine," said Claire finally. "I'll meet you at Dunville's." Claire hung up without even saying goodbye.

Jenn put the phone down, a little exasperated by her sister-in-law, and went back to her law work. She was so focused on it, she lost total track of time. She looked up to realize she'd be late if she didn't move fast. Grabbing her cell phone and car keys, she headed home. Claire was going to be mad, so she pressed the right pedal a little harder to make up some time. Jenn was almost to Dunville's when she heard a police siren behind her. Cursing, Jenn looked in the rearview mirror, and saw a police car with its lights flashing. She saw her speedometer as she hit the brake. Fifteen miles per hour over what was the likely speed limit. Nervously, she pulled her car over to the road's shoulder, and started fishing in her purse for her license. As she leaned toward the glove box, she noticed that she'd been pulled over right next to the Summerhill Cemetery, where her father was buried.

Great, Jenn thought, *Dad will be proud of me now.*

She noticed the many tulips along the front of the property and the daisies interspersed among the grass and stones. Her father used to say that any day you weren't six feet under was a good day. I guess by his standard, expensive speeding ticket and all, it was still a good day, Jenn realized. She couldn't see his gravestone, as it wasn't visible from the road. But she knew it was there.

Jenn opened her glove box and pulled out her registration. As she turned back toward the window, she could see the policeman approaching her vehicle. She opened the window and turned to greet the officer. It was him. The potting soil eyes were looking right back at her.

"Well, if it isn't Attorney Jenn," he said, smiling. "Guess you're in a hurry tonight. Late for a hot Friday night date?"

"Hi Matt. I'm supposed to meet Claire at Dunville's. I'm late. There was a lot of traffic getting out of Hartford tonight."

"There's always traffic getting out of Hartford," he said. "Maybe you shouldn't have stayed and finished that one last thing."

Jenn shrugged and turned a little pinker. How did he know? she wondered.

"Now, I really know it's your own fault you were late. You just gave it away." He grinned and laughed a little.

Jenn laughed and smiled, partially because it was funny he guessed it, and partially in the hopes of getting out of an expensive ticket. Too far over the speed limit in Connecticut meant an extra fine, and it seemed to Jenn that she had been going pretty fast.

"Don't think that smile will get you out of a ticket," said Matt. He started to turn back toward his police car. "I'll be right back."

Jenn grabbed her phone and texted Claire that she was coming, but would be later than expected. Officer Matt showed up back at Jenn's door with a pink tulip. He smiled and handed it to her. She reached up to take it and smiled back at him. "Thank you," she said.

"Your smile worked after all. You're free to go," he said. "No ticket for you tonight."

CHAPTER 19

D unville's was kind of a dive bar. It had been around for decades and mostly served the drunken summer beach crowd. Jenn and Claire were a decade too old to be in it, but neither of them felt like making the move to a more sedate bar for the middle-agers. Jenn had come here in her youth, and was a creature of habit.

Claire liked coming because she had a huge crush on the very attractive bartender. Although Claire was married, she couldn't resist the little extra attention Rob, the bartender, lavished on her, whenever she walked in the door. Jenn thought he probably used that technique with all the clientele, but Claire didn't seem to care. On the plus side, there was always excellent people-watching, as drunken teens and twenty-year-olds were highly entertaining.

Surprisingly, the food was good. Claire had apparently been there long enough to order, as a giant plate of nachos sat in front of her. After greeting each other, Claire launched into her report about the viewing. Half the town had been there—the mayor, the chief of police, all the Save Riverfront Landing folks, including of course Jenn's neighbors, Debbie and Mark. The sisters Peg and Allison, and their husbands and children were in the receiving line. The mayor even said a few words about what a loss to the community losing Dot was, and how dedicated she was to preservation.

Claire explained that the funeral home had a photo compilation running across a couple of flat-screen televisions, as well as some old-fashioned picture boards. The casket was closed of course, and a photo of Dot from her youth sat on a table at the end of the casket. Claire said the photo was barely recognizable, as Dot must have had quite a bit of handiwork done on her over the years to preserve her youthful appearance. When Claire reached the end of her summary, Jenn asked, "How were the flowers?"

"The flowers?"

"Yes, any unusual arrangements? Anything unique?"

"For God's sake, Jenn, I wasn't there to look at the flowers," said an exasperated Claire. "I'm not sure you get it sometimes, Jenn. There is a murderer living in our midst and it doesn't seem like anyone cares, except maybe Officer Matt."

"Come on, Claire. I care. You know I care a lot. I even care about the flowers. When you're done with the nachos, we're going on a road trip. We're going to check something out."

Claire called over the handsome Rob, and flirted away for a bit until she had their tab reduced to just the nachos and one beer. Although Jenn appreciated the discount, she was a little uncomfortable with the behavior, given that Claire was married to her brother. After they had settled up, Claire turned to Jenn and said, "Now, what is this road trip about?"

"Oh come on," replied Jenn. "We'll go in my car."

Jenn led Claire to her car. She drove them out onto the main road toward the center of Mayfield, then pulled around to the backside of P.T. Jane's and into the rear parking lot.

"We're robbing a bookstore?" squeaked Claire, who had been playing with the radio most of the short drive.

"No," said Jenn.

She jumped out of the car and headed over to the ice cooler. The lovely Friday evening had turned cloudy, blocking the stars, and it was warm and humid. Jenn was a little spooked by the darkness of the night, but she kept moving toward the cooler.

The parking lot was dimly lit with safety lighting. It seemed dark in comparison to the bright lights of Dunville's. She walked between the south edge screening fence and the cooler. Half scared she would see a body, she slowed her movements and mentally braced herself. She leaned in between the cooler and the screening fence and checked behind the cooler. Instead of a body, she saw that there was a cord coming from the lower back of the machine, which plugged into an outdoor outlet with a plastic cover mounted about a foot above ground on a metal pole. *The electricity wires must have run under the parking lot,* thought Jenn. She reached and touched the back of the cooler, where the motor was likely located. It was warm.

Jenn scurried back out of the narrow space and reached down to touch the front side of the cooler, about six inches to a foot off the ground. It was moist. Beads of water were accumulating, and as she rubbed her hand across the front side, the beads commingled into drips, which ran down onto the moss along the front edge of the cooler. Jenn looked down at the moss. The condensation formed a source of water for its growth. She reached back up to waist height and pulled on the right door. It didn't budge. Maybe it was rusted shut. She pulled even harder on the left door. It opened. Although there was some safety lighting in P.T. Jane's rear lot, it was dark inside the cooler.

Claire must have gotten out of the car and come over to investigate because she said, "Here, the flashlight on my phone." She passed over her iPhone.

Jenn shined the iPhone flashlight into the cooler and could see that it was empty. Unlike if it were at a convenience store, there were no bags of ice in it. She scanned the cooler with the light from side to side. There was an empty painter's bucket in the far right corner, behind the door that wouldn't open. She tried the other door again, but it wouldn't budge.

Claire walked closer and tried it herself to no avail. Jenn leaned into the freezer to look at the bucket that was filled with trash or leaves. As she leaned in, she realized it wasn't freezing in the cooler. It was cool, but not cold. She reached in further to see what was in the bucket.

"If you're looking for ice, Jenn, I have some at home in my refrigerator. It even has a button you can push, and believe it or not, ice cubes come out, right into your cup."

Jenn didn't reply. She pulled her arms and torso out of the ice cooler, and lifted her left leg over the three-foot high front edge and climbed halfway into the freezer. She felt a chill traverse her back and shuddered. Jenn saw a metal bucket handle, so she handed Claire back the iPhone. With two free hands, she reached over and pulled on the handle. The bucket was very heavy and barely budged. It was apparently filled with rainwater. Jenn lifted her right leg into the freezer, too, so she was standing in it. Using the handle, she dragged the bucket toward her. When she had it in front of the open door, she lifted it up to the edge of the freezer and swung it out and over the bottom edge of the freezer. Jenn climbed back out of the freezer and knelt to examine the bucket.

"Weird, it's not frozen," said Claire.

"Let me see the phone again," said Jenn. She turned away from the bucket and carefully shined the light from the iPhone over the inside of the cooler again. She noticed a thermostat at the top rear left, which read 55 degrees. At the bottom of the thermostat was a small lever that apparently allowed one to set the cooler from 30 to 60 degrees. "It's not a freezer," Jenn noted. "Well, it looks like it could be a freezer, but it's set to be a refrigerator at 55 degrees."

Jenn shone the light at the right door that wouldn't open. She slowly examined the sides of the door, stopping along its right edge to see that the hinges were rusted and gnarled, and its left edge to examine what looked like a break in the seal behind the metal door.

"It looks like someone tried to pry their way into this right door and messed up the hinges," said Jenn. "The seal is broken around the door and it's been warm enough these last few weeks for some condensation to form and water to drip down the outside of the cooler. It's probably been almost constantly running to keep itself cool. The water source has allowed that moss to grow along its front edge. You know, it's that light green moss down there which first drew me over here when I was on the phone with Stuart. This type is cushion moss. It can tolerate the afternoon sun that this western side of the ice cooler gets. When I was on the phone with Stuart, I thought it was rock cap moss, because it seemed like it was growing on the rocks, too, and not just the spaces between the rocks."

"Jenn, you're killing my beer buzz, enough about the moss already. What's the deal with this painter's bucket?" asked Claire. "I wonder if the police even looked in the cooler or noticed it. It looks like an old bucket that's collected some rainwater."

Jenn leaned over and turned the light so it shone into the painter's bucket. The water inside was over a foot in depth and filled with old brown leaves. Jenn turned away from the bucket and started shining the light from the iPhone around the ground. She walked toward the back of P.T. Jane's where a red maple grew at the edge of the parking lot. She leaned over and picked up a foot long stick, and came back to the bucket. She reached into the bucket and began fishing to see if there was anything in it. As she moved some of the leaves on the surface of the water, she tilted the bucket and poured off some of the water. In the water she could see a gelatinous like substance attached to a small stick. It was a jumbled cluster of about a dozen small circular clear spheres, each with a dark center.

"Eggs," said Jenn. "Some kind of eggs."

"I'll take mine in an omelet with some ciabatta bread and a side of bacon," retorted Claire. "Come on, let's go home. Tomorrow Sophia has gymnastics in the morning and two afternoon birthday parties. I'll be all small-talked out and ready for a G&T by two o'clock."

"No, Claire look, these are some kind of salamander eggs. I don't think they're frog eggs. They look a little different. Maybe the cooler was on to keep them from hatching.

I don't think they hatch until the water temperature warms up some."

"Jenn, come on. I think that's just some algae or trash in an old painter's bucket," Claire said. "The police would have taken it if it were important."

"They only saw an old painter's bucket filled with rainwater," Jenn insisted. "They didn't see salamander eggs carefully preserved at the right temperature. Plus, you mean our Mayfield police that are so caught up in getting laid that they've been caught hiring prostitutes? Or did you mean the Mayfield police that like to collect overtime when they aren't even working? I'm taking these home."

Jenn tilted the bucket and drained a little more water off the top of it. Then she lifted the bucket's handle and started carrying it to her car.

"Hold on Jenn. If it's important, shouldn't we let the police know about it?" asked Claire. "It could be evidence related to Doctor Tilman's murder."

"It's definitely evidence related to his murder," Jenn said. "He was an expert in salamanders and there are salamander eggs right where his body was found. But I don't trust the police; even Officer Matt has me suspicious. You know, he pulled me over tonight on the way down to Dunville's."

"He did?" asked Claire.

"Yes. He pulled me over for speeding, but then he let me go without a ticket," said Jenn. "Oh, and he gave me a tulip."

"He gave you a tulip?" repeated Claire, suddenly very interested and smiling.

"They were growing on the side of the road right next to where he pulled me over," Jenn answered.

"Did you make plans to go on date with him?" Claire said. "Did you?" she said waiting for Jenn's response. Jenn ignored her. "So you're just going to take his flowers, but not actually talk to him?" said Claire in a somewhat annoyed turn.

Jenn opened the passenger car door and busied herself with lifting the heavy bucket onto the floor of the car.

"Let's go, Claire. You can straddle the bucket while I drive you back to your car."

"What's gotten into you, Jenn? We can take the bucket, but don't you have to tell Officer Matt or Detective Moffitt?"

"I know you're right, I just don't feel like calling it in now and trying to explain the relevance of these little cloudy spheres in an old bucket of water. I'm afraid it will take hours and I will only end up back on the suspect list. I'd rather see what these things hatch into, or look up what type they are, before we give them up."

Claire was walking toward the car when a police car pulled into the small lane adjunct to the back parking lot of P.T. Jane's. Claire kept walking and sat down in the car and closed the door. Jenn got in her car and started the engine. She opened her window, backed out of her parking spot, and started to turn onto the lane. She waved at the police officer and he waved back. It was not Officer Matt.

The officer, however, must not have been watching or was not concerned with them, as he did not pull her over or stop her. Jenn returned Claire to her car at Dunville's and then headed home with her painter's bucket of salamander eggs. She wondered what in the world she was getting herself into, and if the salamander bucket could really be connected to Dr. Tilman's murder.

CHAPTER 20

Running. Jenn was running. She looked at the ground in front of her. It was a paved, narrow two-lane road on which she ran and trees lined both its sides. The canopy from the trees met over her head, and the shadow of the trees lined the ground·in front of her. Blotches of shade covered the ground, creating a mottled landscape on the pavement from the sunlight and shadows.

Mosquitoes swarmed by Jenn's ear. She lifted her eyes from the road, in order to turn her head to see if there was a mosquito to her left. She swatted at what she thought was one and missed. Instead of swatting again, she picked up her pace to outrun the mosquito. She turned her eyes back to the road. Then suddenly from the left, a large object swooped down toward the right. As it approached, she started to shrink away and duck, and her heartbeat quickened with the thought that she couldn't get out of the way in time. But then Jenn realized the object was actually just a bird, and was nowhere near her. The bird was high in the sky, way up in the tree canopy, and it was just its shadow in front of her feet. She didn't need to duck. She was not going to get hit by it.

Jenn woke and lay in her bed sweating. I guess from the run, she thought. Wait, she realized, she hadn't really been running. It was just a dream about a run. It was just a shadow from a bird. She was fine, safe in her bed.

Jenn thought about the bird for a moment. She didn't know what species it had been. She had only seen its shadow and even a bona fide birdwatcher would be hard pressed to come up with a species based on a shadow. If it were a clear, open road with no tree canopy, the bird's path would have been visible the whole time. It was not. Jenn could only see the shadow in the sunlight. In the shade, the bird's shadow was masked by the spots of shade from the tree's leaves and branches.

The bird, the dream, seemed poignant to her. What was at times masked by a shadow for much of its path, but at other moments, glimpses of it were out in the light of day?

CHAPTER 21

◆

T he work week flew, and Jenn focused solely on that until Saturday morning brought a beautiful beach day. She took her coffee outside and inspected her garden and the outside of her home. Romeo and Juliet seemed chipper. Their leaves rippled and swayed in a slight breeze. She inspected the canker marks and decided that nothing had changed in the last few days. Both trees had reached almost thirty-five feet in height. Jenn hadn't thought they would grow as tall and wide as they had. She had thought about calling back the mysterious Connecticut agricultural research place she had contacted once before. Were they really supposed to get this big before they were overcome by the blight? They would definitely make the summer, she thought. Maybe not next winter, especially Juliet who had more cankers, but at least they could enjoy one last summer together.

Jenn looked around her garden and her home and thought of the endless tasks that awaited her. She noted the deep blue color of the sky without a cloud in it and decided today was not the day to chip away at her to-do list. She went inside, changed into a swimsuit and cover up, packed her book, beach chair, and towel, and headed out the backdoor for the beach. As she walked by the painter's bucket tucked in the corner of her garage, she peeked her head in to see the gelatinous eggs still attached to a stick.

She climbed into her car and drove to the Hammonasset Park so that she could soak up some sun at Meigs Point. A few hours reading at the beach in solitude would recharge her body and mind. After a busy week, she didn't mind a little time alone.

Jenn set up her chair with her toes in the water and picked up her novel. The beach was not yet crowded. Dark, olive green seaweed blew gently to the right of her chair, not quite rolling, but rocking back and forth in the offshore breeze.

She tried to focus on her book, but she found her mind wandering. What were those strange eggs sitting in a paint bucket in her garage? They must be salamander eggs, and they must be from an endangered or threatened species. Why had she brought them home? All she was doing was getting herself in trouble. If they had something to do with Dr. Tilman's murder, they were evidence. For God's sake, she knew that. And if they weren't connected to the murder, why would they be in an ice cooler? She was an attorney, even if she wasn't a criminal one. She knew it was wrong to tamper with evidence. At the rate she was going, she would need her own criminal defense attorney.

Restless, Jenn stood up, closed up her chair, and dragged her stuff above the high tide line from the night before that was evident from the debris of seaweed, shells, and sand patterns. In Connecticut, it was the average, or mean high water line that was the demarcation as to where public lands started. On the beach though, you couldn't visually see any demarcation at the average location of the high tide line. You could only see if you looked closely, where the high tide had swelled to the night before.

Jenn thought about the concept of certain land belonging to the public. The concept of public trust lands dated back to Roman times. America's coastal states held the submerged lands and waters waterward of the mean tide line in trust for the public. Citizens were allowed to use these lands and waters, whether beach, rocky, or open water for traditional uses such as walking, sunbathing, fishing, or shellfishing. Court cases in Connecticut dating back to the early colonial times, upheld the concept that private ownership ends at the mean high water line.

She stood and watched a group of five sandpipers run back and forth on the shore. First they ran on the waterward side of the high tide line she could see from the night before, and then they ran on the shore side of the high tide line. Jenn thought about how animals, birds, frogs, salamanders, and turtles had no concept of property lines. At one moment a species was in one location on private property, and the next moment they were on public land free to be enjoyed by everyone.

Jenn also thought about how the public in many land use disputes had a say in what happened to private property, partially because of social pressure to be pro-environmental or green. Who is not for helping out the animals, plants, and the environment in general? Even just admitting that you don't recycle, or use plastic bags, or, God forbid, use plastic straws would get you socially shunned in a town like Mayfield.

Traditionally, public trust lands were used for survival necessities like grazing sheep and shellfishing, but nowadays humans needed public trust lands, parklands, and untouched, open to the public, green beaches for respite. Researchers seemed to be trying to fully understand the connection between spending time in nature and one's happiness. Jenn wasn't alone in taking refuge in the woods from the stresses of all her responsibilities and human interactions. More and more news articles seemed to tout the need for nature in people's lives, whether it was nature walks or the term she heard lately, which called it "forest bathing."

Jenn looked down at her flip-flops and realized she wasn't wearing the right shoes for a nature walk. She could not, however, sit still any longer, and picked up all of her beach belongings and headed toward her car. She stashed her belongings in her car and started to the far side of the parking lot, moving away from the beach area. Traveling north across the spit of land that formed Meigs Point, she walked toward the Hammonasset River.

Beyond a grassy patch and a public pavilion, there were tall coastal wetland reeds, or phragmites. As she neared the phrag-mites, she could see a path between them, so she started down it. She slowed her pace due to the uneven ground and her flip-flops. The reeds grew from clumps of mud interlaced with water, and it was difficult to find a dry spot to place her flip-flops. She slowed her pace and tried stepping at the base of the phragmites, where her feet were least likely to sink.

On her jump across a large expanse between the clumps of mud and roots, Jenn's phone slipped from the pocket of her cover up and fell into the water. It floated for a split second and she grabbed it. Her iPhone was in a waterproof case and when she quickly checked, it looked like it was working. She ripped off the case and dried it with the skirt of her cover up. What was she doing, she wondered, and why? She paused, realizing she could go no further without sinking into the warm, mushy mud.

Jenn looked up from drying off her iPhone and could see the expanse of the Hammonasset River and across it to the Riverfront Landing property. In all her years in Mayfield, she had never seen this view of the river, where it took its curve to the east, which created Meigs Point. To her surprise, she could see that in the far distance there were three vehicles parked on the west side of the old airport hangers. One was clearly a silver Lexus wagon, one looked like it might be a Prius, and the third looked like a white pickup truck. Although she could not see the plates on the Prius, it was the same metallic-green color as the one she had seen last week. Jenn could not believe her eyes. It was the weekend and again there was a state vehicle on the property.

She decided it was time to find out why a state vehicle would be present, particularly on a Saturday. Her options were to call David and ask him, or to drive over there, trespass, and ask for herself. A third option popped into her brain, and she impulsively went with it. She looked up the non-emergency number for the Mayfield police.

"Good morning. Is Officer Matt, um...what was his last name?" she thought. How could she not know his last name?

"Matt Banks," responded a female voice on the other end.

"Yes, I believe that was his name, a newer officer, brown hair?" offered Jenn.

"Yes, he's at his desk. I'll transfer you over."

"Matt Banks here."

"Matt, it's Jenn. Jenn Bowdoin. I met you last week. You pulled me over last night, but didn't give me a ticket.

"Hi, Attorney Jenn. How are you today? How can I help?"

"Well, there are a few things I need to talk to you about. Is there a chance you could meet me at Larry's bagel shop this morning, in like fifteen minutes, or later if that won't work?"

"What was that? I can't hear you. It's bad reception."

Jenn repeated herself, shouting back at him a request to meet. She looked at the phone and there was only one bar of service. It didn't seem to be from the iPhone falling in the water, just a bad cell service area.

"I'm just finishing up," Matt answered. You're lucky you caught me. I'm actually off today and looking forward to some time at the beach. Sure, I'll meet you there in fifteen minutes, at eleven o'clock."

"Okay. See you there." Jenn yelled at her phone. She signed off and suddenly realized where she was. Still at the end of the reed path overlooking the river, a good ten to fifteen minutes from her car, plus a good five to ten minute drive to Larry's. What the heck, she thought. She jogged out of the path through the phragmites, with her flip-flops occasionally slipping and sliding out from under her. She practically ran across the grassy pavilion area, and full-fledged sprinted across the parking lot.

Climbing into her car, Jenn started the engine, backed out of her spot, and headed onto the road that traversed Hammonasset State Park. A Saturday at Hammonasset was generally very busy, and traffic on the road out was slow. Although a bike/walking trail ran parallel to the road, for some mysterious reason the bikers, runners, and walkers, all seemed to prefer using the road itself. Jenn would have to sort that mystery out another time though. Today was for confessing about the salamander eggs, and trying to actually talk to the cute and mysterious Officer Matt. She felt her heart pounding in her chest as she pushed to get to Larry's on time.

CHAPTER 22

J enn pulled into the parking lot of Larry's Bagels at 11:02 a.m., glad to not be any later. Jenn jumped out of the car, and then thought to look down at her flip-flops. They were speckled in mud, and so were her ankles. She popped the trunk, pulled out her towel, and wiped down her legs and feet. They were still a little grubby because the mud had dried enough that it wouldn't wipe off all the way without water.

Larry's Bagels was crowded. She headed right to the table where Officer Matt was seated. He looked different without his uniform. Cuter. Casual in his T-shirt, and scruffy, as he hadn't shaved. There were two sandwiches and two Snapple iced teas in front of him.

"I thought you might be hungry. Your choice. Turkey…or turkey. One with mustard, one without."

"Thank you. You pick first. I'm good either way," Jenn responded. She started to sit down, but stopped, and said, "Would you mind if we sat outside?"

He grabbed the sandwiches with one hand and the drinks in the other and stood up.

"Sure."

Jenn led the way outside and sat at the same table she had shared with her niece Sophia a week ago. She looked across the street and saw that all three cars she had seen from the opposite side of the property were still there. Matt sat down in the chair opposite Jenn, put the sandwiches and drinks down in the middle of the table, and looked into her eyes and smiled. They really were the exact color of potting soil. Plants would grow like crazy in there.

"It was so kind of you to order two sandwiches. Thank you," she said.

Matt kept looking at her. Ugh. She probably had sunscreen globed on her face or mascara smudged below her eyes. Oh no, Jenn hoped she didn't have boogers on her face. Nothing like dried mucus on one's nose to impress a man. She really should have checked the mirror before she jumped out of the car. She was too worried about mud on her legs that he probably wouldn't even notice, and should have worried about whether her face was clean.

Matt was still looking at her. Oh no, even worse, what if it were egg from breakfast? The proverbial egg on her face. *Figures it would be more than an expression for me,* she thought. She smiled right back at him, though, and hoped for the best.

Jenn reached for the sandwich, and looked down to make sure she wasn't grabbing Matt's hand by accident. Although maybe that would have been a good move. He slid the sandwich toward her, opened his sandwich and took a bite.

After Matt had swallowed his first bite, he asked, "So what is it that you called about?"

"Well, it's actually two items. The first is across the street." Jenn gestured with her right hand in the direction of the

Riverfront Landing property. She could see that three cars were still parked there.

Matt turned his head to take a look.

"One of the three cars is a state vehicle. I can't imagine why a state-owned vehicle would be at the property on a Saturday," she said. "I was hoping you could find out. It's a metallic-green Prius. Also, I believe the Lexus wagon belongs to my neighbor, but again, I was hoping you could find out. My neighbor, Debbie Clifford, is one of the vocal opponents of the development."

As Jenn spoke, the green Prius started moving toward them. The gate on the access road was swung open, and the Prius continued to the intersection of the access road and Route 1.

Matt said, "Excuse me," and jumped up from the table. He started for his car, got in, and was about to drive away.

The Prius turned left out of the access lane to the Riverfront Landing property. Matt turned right out of Larry's Bagels' parking lot, following behind it.

Jenn started to shrink in embarrassment. She couldn't tell whether she had just been cruelly ditched or whether Matt was running after the Prius. *Well*, thought Jenn, *definitely the shortest date I have ever had.* She looked around the restaurant, and realized no one seemed to have noticed his quick departure. So, she took a bite of her sandwich and mulled things over. On the plus side, if Matt didn't come back, she had scored two sandwiches and two iced teas.

As Jenn chewed, she looked back toward the Riverfront property to see two more cars headed up the access road toward her. She knew she would not be able to read a license plate from so far away, so she hopped down from her chair and headed across the parking lot, moving southwest toward the intersection of the access road and Route 1. She reached the intersection right as the silver Lexus reached it from the access road. She didn't have to read the plate. She could see it was her neighbor, Debbie.

Debbie was looking for a break in the traffic and had not noticed her. Jenn turned her back and headed to the nearest parked car and pretended to bend down and tie her shoe. She thought she made it out of sight before Debbie saw her, but she wasn't certain. Now, why would Debbie be at Riverfront Landing? And why did Jenn not want Debbie to see her? Was she watching too many spy movies? Subterfuge and slyness were not her normal patterns of functioning. Even if she wasn't the most outspoken and direct with folks about what she actually thought sometimes, she generally didn't sneak around spying on them.

Jenn straightened up and saw that a tall man stepping out of a white pickup truck was walking toward the gate to the property. He had driven through, but was heading back to close the gate. He looked like the same tall, bearded man whom she had seen driving the Prius last week.

Now he was climbing into the pickup, and as he looked up, he stared at her. He kept staring, as though he was wondering what she was doing. Since she was still next to a car, Jenn looked down and reached for the closest car door handle, to open the door. It opened, and she started to move to get in. She braved a glance up to see that the truck had pulled forward and was about to turn west onto Route 1.

She hadn't quite made it to sitting, so she started to back out of the parked car. As she stood up, and turned back toward Larry's, Jenn saw Officer Matt pulling his car into the parking lot. She closed the door, and headed back to their table. She reached the table at almost the same time he did, and sat back down. He smiled at her and said, "Do I need to arrest you for breaking into a parked vehicle? You know, I let the speeding thing go, but you're pushing the envelope, Jenn. Do you need to empty your pockets for me?"

Matt's face looked strange. He was smiling at her, like it was a joke, but he seemed tense, as though he thought she might have done something illegal. Jenn reddened and looked down.

"No," she laughed, hoping to lighten his mood and expression. "I know I was speeding last night, but today I only opened the car door to make it look like I was getting in. I had moved closer to Route 1, and was watching the other two cars leave. The man in the pickup truck started staring at me, and I felt like I needed to hide since I was standing there staring at him. I just reached out and tried the car door. I guess I was trying to pretend like it was my car."

"Well, next time, don't actually open someone else's car door. It's not right."

Wow, Matt was deadly serious, Jenn realized. He is a stickler for the rules, but then again, he is a policeman. I guess that's a good thing. She let how serious he was sink in for a minute.

"What's the license number of the truck? Is that why you went closer?" Matt asked in a lighter voice and reached into his pocket and pulled out a pen. He grabbed an extra napkin from the table and pulled it closer, as though to write on it.

"I forgot to get it," Jenn admitted. She had thought of getting the plate when she got up from the table but became flustered seeing her neighbor Debbie.

"That's okay. It looked like a Ford truck. Was it an F-150 or a Ranger?" Matt asked. " I didn't get a close enough look."

Hanging her head, Jenn said, "I don't know. I didn't notice that either. It was the same white bearded man I saw here last week on Sunday. But last week, he was the one driving the Prius. I'm sorry. Guess I'm not cut out to be a policeman."

"Well, you're clearly not a man," said Matt. "I'm sure you would make an excellent policewoman if you put your mind to it, but there's no way you would be mistaken for a man."

Jenn looked up to see Matt smiling at her.

"No worries, Jenn. Hey, you were right about the state employee. A Robert Flannigan was driving the Prius. He works for the state environmental agency. He lives in Colchester."

"Did you see what his job title was?" asked Jenn. "I don't know him, but I do know a lot of folks who work there." From her work as an environmental attorney, Jenn knew many of the state environmental agency employees, as she had interacted with them on various matters over the years.

"No, I could have asked for his work identification," Matt answered. "I examined his license and took his word that he was allowed to drive the vehicle. I did check the vehicle registration and everything is up to date."

"I wonder why the lean, white-haired man was driving the pickup truck today, instead of the Prius?" said Jenn.

"Robert Flannigan is dark haired and pretty young, maybe just mid-twenties or early thirties at most," Matt said.

Jenn took another bite of her sandwich, as did Matt. They sat in silence for a few minutes, eating.

"So," said Matt, "I asked him why he was down this way on a Saturday."

Jenn looked at Matt and felt a spark tingle through her as she met his eyes. She waited.

"He said there were some follow-up issues that needed to be sorted out under the coastal permit issued for the property," Matt said.

"Follow-up issues?" asked Jenn.

"Yes. Follow-up issues."

"Well, typically when the agency issues a coastal permit, they put conditions on it that might need to be met," Jenn said. "But those conditions might require some additional monitoring or study. But they'd usually be met by the applicant or property owner, not by an employee of the agency doing something or having to come out to a property."

"I think I know what you're saying," said Matt.

"Well, suppose I was your mom and I said you had to clean up your room and keep it that way, or you wouldn't have dessert on any given day," Jenn explained. "If, on a given day, you didn't keep it clean, you wouldn't have dessert. But you would have to do the cleaning. Your mom wouldn't go up and help you. It doesn't really add up. The agency never has to do anything under the conditions; Riverfront Landing should have to do something."

"Okay, I get it," Matt said. "Basically, it's my responsibility to keep my room clean and at no point can my mom help me. In other words, despite what he said, there is still no reason for Robert Flannigan and his Prius to be out here on a Saturday morning."

"Exactly," said Jenn.

"Well, what if I asked you to come up to my room and inspect it to determine whether it is clean?" said Matt with a sly grin.

Jenn smiled back, "Well, I could inspect your room if you asked me to, but that's not the way it's typically done. Typically, you just tell me about your room, and I might come up one day and do a surprise inspection, but that would be on a weekday, not a Saturday morning. Besides, if it were a surprise inspection, Robert Flannigan should have just said that and he didn't."

"What if instead of inspecting it in the morning, I wanted you to inspect it on Saturday, or even a Saturday night?" Matt said. Jenn laughed. "I would know you were up to no good."

CHAPTER 23

J enn took one last bite of her sandwich, realized she was full, and put the rest of it on the table. She noticed Matt was already done and was watching her chew. It was time to fess up to the smuggled salamander eggs. She took a sip of the lemonade and cleared her throat.

"Matt, I have another item to talk to you about. I'm not sure what to do about it. You know Claire, my sister-in-law? Well, Tuesday night, we had a few beers and then went back to the location where I discovered Doctor Tilman's body. Except this time, we actually looked in that ice cooler in P.T. Jane's parking lot."

Jenn looked at Matt, who was listening intently. "In the cooler there was a painter's bucket filled with what looked like old rain water and leaves. But in the old bucket it turns out there are some sort of amphibian eggs. Based upon how they look, and some research I did this week, I think they may be from a blue spotted salamander, which is an endangered species. I'm not one hundred percent certain, and they're still not hatched. You really cannot tell one species of amphibian from another until they hatch. The eggs look like little balls of clear Jell-O and although you can see the center, I didn't want to start dissecting them."

"Jenn, do you have these eggs?" Matt asked when Jenn finally paused to take a breath. "It sounds like they're in your possession."

"Well, here is the sticky part, and I don't mean the sticky salamander eggs. You know they're stuck to a branch," Jenn answered. "Salamander eggs are often stuck to a branch, whereas frog eggs just sort of float around free, not really stuck to anything."

"Uh, Jenn. I'm sorry if this seems rude, but try to focus for me on the most pertinent facts," Matt said. "Where are these eggs now? Did you remove them from the cooler?"

"Yes, as I was saying, the sticky part. I took them home with me," Jenn said. "They're in my garage. I know I shouldn't have. I lost my judgment, and wasn't so sure about your police force, and it was so late, and I didn't want to have to explain how I thought of looking in the cooler. Why wouldn't your Detective Moffitt have looked in the cooler? Or maybe he did and just saw a painter's bucket filled with rainwater and dismissed it as irrelevant. Since Doctor Tilman was a herpetologist, the salamander eggs must be related to him or his death."

"The eggs are in your garage?" asked Matt.

"Yes. I couldn't leave them outside, because a predator might have gotten them."

"Why don't we ride up there together and get them? We can go in my car," said Matt.

"Okay. But I could drive there, too and then you won't have to bring me back to my car," replied Jenn.

"Okay, let's go. You lead the way." Matt stood up and collected the trash before she could grab any.

Jenn walked to her car and turned as she climbed in to see Matt getting into his cruiser. She started the drive away from the shore, into the woods, and wondered whether it was safe to have Matt to her house alone. He certainly seemed like a great guy, but he sure was serious when he accused her of breaking into someone's car.

She used Siri to call Claire and Peter's house phone. There was no answer, so she left a message explaining that Officer Matt was coming back to her house to collect the eggs they had found the other night. That way, if she ever disappeared, they would know whom to blame.

As she reached her house, Jenn saw that her neighbor Mark was out in the yard. She waved hello, and again wondered what his wife Debbie was doing at the Riverfront Landing property. It was strange, too, how disheveled Mark was the week Dr. Tilman died. He was generally very well kept in matching clean clothes. Even when he actually gardened, he wore a pressed polo shirt, and not an old T-shirt like most people.

Matt pulled into the driveway and parked next to her car. He climbed out of his car and walked over toward the two trees in her side yard. "These are lovely trees," he said, "Very unusual leaves. So large."

Jenn bit her tongue. How to scare away a possible boyfriend? Tell him you have pet trees. No, seems a little too strange, too lonely. Or worse yet, explain why the trees are important and give him a fifteen-minute lecture on something called a blight or invasive species. Both options seemed bad to Jenn, so she went with, "Yes. They're great."

She led Matt into the garage and pointed to the bucket. "Here it is. I know I should have left it at P.T. Jane's. Again, I really wasn't thinking clearly."

Matt crouched down and peered into the bucket. Jenn crouched down as well, and pointed at the eggs. She was about to speak when she caught a whiff of Matt. *He really smells good*, she thought. *That's a smell I could get used to.* Remembering why she was crouched, she said, "These are the eggs. It would be easy for an officer to just see this as a bucket of dirty rainwater."

Matt didn't move for a moment. He just looked at the eggs, and then he lifted his face and looked at her. Their faces were no more than six inches apart. Jenn smiled at him.

"Are you going to put me in handcuffs and lead me away?" she asked.

Matt smiled back. "Not today. But we do have to do something about this." He stood and reached for his cell phone, and started walking back outside.

Jenn turned and headed into her house. She put down her beach bag, made a quick stop at the bathroom, and started to straighten up the kitchen. Her breakfast dishes were next to the sink, so she loaded them into the dishwasher to get them out of sight. Living alone, well, alone with pet trees, and working all the time, she really didn't have many dirty dishes, so she rarely needed to run the dishwasher. But it seemed quicker today to tuck them out of sight than to wash them by hand. What the heck was that handcuff line that came out of her mouth, she pondered? She had some kind of strange attraction to Matt that prevented her from employing her standard tactics and editing herself before she actually opened her mouth and spoke.

Jenn heard a knock at the door. She had left it partway open, as she figured Matt would come in when he was ready.

"Jenn?" she heard.

"Come on in."

"Turns out I have to take you and the eggs to the station," Matt said. "We'll need another statement from you. Let me take you down in my patrol car."

Jenn was still in her bathing suit and cover up, her legs still smeared with dried mud. She smelled of sunscreen mixed with the dank aromatic stench of coastal mud.

"Now?" she asked.

At Matt's knock, she had stopped loading the dishwasher and started toward the doorway from her mudroom into her kitchen. She met him at the corner of the doorway. They almost collided, but she managed to stop short by a few inches.

"Could I shower quickly?" she asked looking up at him.

"Only if I can too," said Matt with a devilish grin.

Jenn reflexively smiled back. For a split second, she thought he meant he needed one, and almost looked to see if he was dirty, too. But she caught herself and realized he was hitting on her.

"Ha ha, nice try," she said. "Seriously, I just need a couple of minutes to change and get cleaned up. Make yourself at home." She motioned to the kitchen and family room with her arm. "There's beer in the refrigerator, if you'd like one."

"Technically," said Matt, "I'm on duty, having to get this evidence in and recorded, so I better not. Maybe later."

Jenn headed up to her bedroom, got cleaned up, and changed. By the time she came down, Matt had hauled the painter's bucket to the front seat of his police cruiser. He suggested Jenn sit in the front so that she could keep the bucket from spilling over.

She didn't protest, and climbed into the car with him. She had no desire to ride around in the back of a police cruiser.

At the start of the five mile drive down to the station, Matt asked Jenn a couple of questions about her life. Where had she gone to college and law school? How had she ended up practicing environmental law?

Jenn tried to avoid the questions as best she could. Talking about herself was not her strong point. She was able to learn that Matt had grown up in New Jersey, gone to a branch of Rutgers, and decided to become a police officer because his father had been one. His father was shot in the line of duty in Trenton and died in middle age. Matt decided not to be an inner city, or really any kind of "city" police officer. He defiantly explained that he opted for the cushy route, as some cops would call it, patrolling the suburbs for small-town trouble, and keeping traffic under control.

The move out to Mayfield from Westport had happened almost by accident. Matt's partner had become unbearably difficult. Although he requested a partner switch, in a small town, there really was no one else available and it didn't happen. Matt said he found it difficult to spend so much time with an angry, grumpy person, someone who was never happy. Plus, he wondered how his partner would handle an emergency if one arose. He started to look for other towns to transfer to and impulsively applied to the Mayfield position. In hindsight, he should have done more research about the state of affairs of the Mayfield police force. But he was so worn down by his time with his partner each day that all he could think about was a change.

Jenn asked Matt what he could share about the Mayfield police force. Jenn was thinking of all the public problems of the police force which had been recently exposed in the local papers. Some officers had been charged with prostitution, some claimed false overtime pay, and the police chief's competency was being questioned because of long response times. But Matt clammed up and told her that he had to be really careful. He was new to the police force and knew very few folks in town. He had so recently taken the job that he was unmarketable and felt he should just learn to live with the other members of the force for now.

As they pulled into the Mayfield police station parking lot, Jenn couldn't help but notice a gigantic flowering dogwood tree adjacent to the lot. As she walked by, she could smell the tree as well, and slowed her pace for a couple of deep breaths. She didn't want to go inside a police station on such a nice day.

Because of Jenn's dawdling, Matt had pulled ahead of her. He set the painter's bucket down for a second on the cement sidewalk, and turned back to look at her impatiently. "I won't let them arrest you, Jenn, don't worry. But we do actually have to go into the station. They won't take your statement in the parking lot."

"Thank you, I just don't really want to go in there. It's so great out here," replied Jenn.

"I get it," said Matt. "And the dogwood tree is so lovely." Jenn was pleasantly surprised that he noticed the tree and knew what type it was.

Inside the station, Jenn was walked back to the interrogation room, faced again with only a metal folding table and three metal folding chairs. Sergeant Moffitt followed her and Matt into the room with a folder and some papers.

"Attorney Jenn Bowdoin," he said. "So you found something we missed. Grab a seat."

"It was just a hunch, because an ice cooler is so unusual in the parking lot of a bookstore," Jenn said. "I still don't understand why it's there, or why it would contain salamander eggs."

"Why don't you start from the beginning? How and why did you go trespassing looking for salamander eggs?" Sergeant Moffitt asked.

Trespassing, thought Jenn. *Oh no, great. I forgot about that crime. Stealing evidence. But he's right. I shouldn't have been on P.T. Jane's property in the first place. Let alone looking in their ice machine. Might as well hand over my law license now.*

This could get ugly.

"Sergeant Moffitt, I didn't go looking for salamander eggs," Jenn said. "As you may imagine this murder has been on my mind, particularly since I found Doctor Tilman's body. I have been ill at ease for the last two weeks, and have not been able to get Doctor Tilman's dead face out of my mind. My sister-in-law, Claire, and I had gone to Dunville's for some food."

"How much did you have to drink?" intoned Sergeant Moffitt.

"Two beers. We weren't intoxicated. I had been thinking about how unusual it was to have an ice cooler in a bookstore parking lot. It seemed like an odd place to stash a body, and it also seemed like an odd place for Doctor Tilman to end up. At some point since the murder of Mrs. Hutchinson, I started to wonder if your police force had looked inside it," Jenn said.

"Pardon my honesty, but the Mayfield force has not been the subject of the most favorable news articles lately," she added. "I hardly expected to find possible evidence that your officers had missed less than five feet from the body. Plus, I had thought your officers would be more thorough than to just assume something was an old painter's bucket filled with water. The evidence sat around for almost two weeks since the murder. In some ways, you're lucky I found it."

Jenn paused for effect. Maybe she wouldn't be in too much trouble. The sergeant looked taken aback by the prospect that his officers had missed evidence that was less than five feet from a dead body.

Jenn hadn't mentioned the moss. The deep green moss that had drawn her over to the ice cooler in the first place. Did they even realize the cooler was plugged in? How could they not have noticed the electric plug or the cool air inside it? Although, Jenn reflected, the young Mayfield cops were hardly used to seeing dead bodies and their thinking may have been muddled.

"Who owns P.T. Jane's now?" asked Jenn. "Have you looked into why there even is an ice cooler still in that lot? I know at one point there was a restaurant in the adjacent building, which may have needed the cooler, but as I recall that closed years ago."

"Jenn, I know you're a lawyer and you guys like to be in charge, but we'll ask the questions here. Now take a look at this photo."

Sergeant Moffitt placed a photo taken with a flash of the inside of the cooler in front of her. The painter's bucket was clearly visible in the same exact spot Jenn had found it. Even in the photo, it looked like an old abandoned bucket in which rainwater had accumulated. It didn't look like evidence or anything of significance.

"Is that the same bucket you found on Thursday night? And was the bucket in that exact location when you found it?" Moffitt asked.

"Yes, and yes," replied Jenn. "So, you guys opened the cooler and found the bucket, but didn't examine it further."

"Jenn, our actions are not the ones at issue here. You were the one trespassing and hoarding evidence," he said.

Almost two hours passed before Jenn's statement was taken, reviewed, and signed. They weren't going to charge her with anything and seemed somewhat grateful to her. Sergeant Moffitt would not answer her questions about P.T. Jane's or why there was an old ice cooler in its parking lot. She did explain about the moss, that it was what drew her back to the ice cooler. The moss meant the cooler was in use, as the moss had a lifeline of water from the condensation caused by the broken seal on the cooler's right door.

Apparently, their investigation hadn't noticed any of these facts. Officer Matt had been silent the entire time. He just sat next to Sergeant Moffitt and watched Jenn. He didn't give her any looks of disapproval or otherwise. Occasionally she would catch his eye, and he just gave a small smile.

Finally, Sergeant Moffitt said she was free to go. Jenn was so relieved, she felt a tear forming in her left eye. Until he said those words, she hadn't realized how tense she was about getting into trouble for stealing salamander eggs. Her whole career, and years of fostering her career, would have been ruined if they had charged her with trespassing, or stealing, or some kind of crime. Matt followed her out of the room, and said close to her ear, "Come on, I'll drive you home. Let's enjoy some of this beautiful Saturday, before it's over." Jenn wasn't sure what he meant, but just happily climbed into the police cruiser for the ride home.

CHAPTER 24

A s they reached her driveway, Mark was standing smack in the middle of it. His arms were crossed and he slowly backed out of the way toward the passenger side of Matt's cruiser, as Matt pulled the cruiser into the driveway. Through the open window, as soon as the car had stopped, Mark called, "Jenn, are you okay? What's going on? Is your mom okay?"

Mark had been in his yard hiding from his wife the day Jenn got the call about her dad. Jenn flashed back in her mind to that day, vividly recalling the moment she had received the call and her childhood world had collapsed abruptly. Although they had bantered earlier about the weather, Jenn had forgotten Mark was on the other side of the bushes when Peter had called. Their dad had died at night in the hospital. His heart had given out. Mark must have overheard the whole conversation, because when she was done with her cell phone call, he walked over to her, looked her in the eye, and then gave her a big bear hug. She had been taken aback by his humanity and warmth. He was typically so reserved she was surprised to find herself in his embrace.

The next few days after that moment were filled with details and logistics, and just plain grief and sadness about her father's passing. She had forgotten that moment until just now. She had forgotten that part of Mark, as he always seemed so sheepish gardening, or pretending to garden, in his yard.

"Jenn?" Mark repeated. "Your mom?" He reached out and opened the car door. He bent over and reached his hand toward her, offering her assistance in getting out of the car.

Jenn grabbed Mark's hand briefly and dropped it as soon as she was vertical.

"Oh, no, Mark. No worries. My mom is fine. Everything is okay. I had to go back to the police station and give another statement on Doctor Tilman's murder. That's all. I'm sorry you were worried."

"Jenn, I saw you driven away by the officer here and I've been worried since." His whole body and face visibly relaxed. He stood up straight and sighed. "That's good news. I would hate for you to lose both parents so young."

Jenn smiled at him. "That's so kind of you to be worried. You know, I'm not sure I ever thanked you for the support you gave me the day my father died. That was such a crazy time; I had forgotten how you were there for me the moment I first got the call he was gone. Thank you."

Officer Matt had walked around the patrol car while Jenn spoke and stood, giving Mark a once-over. Jenn looked at Mark, as someone might see him for the first time. She had always seen Mark as someone older and in a different life stage. Mark had already been married for probably decades and his only child, a daughter Jenn rarely saw, attended a boarding school a couple of hours away. Mark's hair was already speckled with gray and he had to be in his fifties. It never once occurred to her that Mark was possibly attracted to her.

It occurred to Matt though, because he stepped closer to Jenn and said. "Jenn, it's been a long day. How about we go in and get you something to drink. You could probably use some water and a chance to relax."

Jenn stood still for a moment. She had been looking at Matt as he spoke. She turned to see Mark's face and caught a glimpse of something. She was not sure what the emotion was, but there was some kind of feeling there. For a split second it had not been contained.

"Boy, it's been a long day, and I am thirsty," Jenn said. She turned toward Mark. He had already started backing away. "Mark, thank you for worrying about me, but I'm okay. I'll see you later."

"Yes," said Mark, looking disappointed. "Just glad nothing awful happened." He turned and walked toward his house.

Jenn started through her garage and Matt followed her. He stopped at the doorway. She was a few steps into the house before she realized he hadn't followed her into the mudroom.

Turning back toward Matt, Jenn said, "Oh come on in, Matt. You're not imposing." She reached into the refrigerator and pulled out two beers. She reached into the freezer and pulled out two mugs. She slowly poured each beer, and then handed Matt his.

He found his way into her kitchen and stood hesitantly. He accepted the beer, smiled and said, "Thank you."

Jenn proceeded to pour two large waters. She handed Matt his water, and he accepted it with his other hand. Then she started to fix herself a tomato juice, as well.

Matt was just standing and watching. As she was about to pour the tomato juice into its glass, she said, "Would you like a little tomato juice, too?"

"No, thank you," he said. He didn't ask about her three drinks, or give her a hard time about it. When she was done, she picked up all three and said, "Would you like to sit outside?"

He nodded okay and she led him out the backdoor to a small brick patio. She placed her three drinks on the table and sat down.

What a long day. Jenn was used to long workdays, twelve, even sixteen-hour days at the office lawyering, writing, talking on the phone, and reviewing documents. She was not used to busy weekend days.

Often on the weekends, if she wasn't doing a little work and getting in a few billable hours, she had quieter days at home, organizing, completing chores, and paying bills. She took a sip of her beer and looked around her.

The sun was still shining in the west and there was a shadow from her trees on the patio. The breeze blew Romeo and Juliet and the shadows of their branches and leaves swayed back and forth across the bricks of the patio. She watched the shadows move and thought back to her run this morning.

There had been shadows on her run that masked the bird and then blotches of sunlight that revealed its shape. She had ducked and run for cover when she didn't even need to. The bird wasn't where she thought it was. It was way up in the sky and Jenn's feet were still firmly running on the ground. She remembered the feeling of ducking or dodging when there had been nothing to dodge. *Wait, I didn't run.* For the second time that day, Jenn realized it was all a dream. She hadn't really run this morning.

"Jenn," said Matt, "Are you there? Are you okay?" Matt was talking, she realized. She pulled herself back down to earth and smiled at him. "Yes. I'm okay. I was up for a while last night and it's been a full day. Tell me again what you were saying."

This time, she heard him. Matt was talking about Dot Hutchinson's funeral. He had been able to go, not just to manage traffic issues, but had actually attended the funeral and paid his respects. Matt explained how he was glad to attend. Jenn resisted the urge to crack a joke about how he was the first person she had ever met who was eager to go to a funeral. Folks usually avoided funerals like the plague, and others could barely make it through the service without a little nip of something.

"Every character in town was there," Matt continued. "I thought you would be there. The daughters even asked First Selectman Fritz Robinson to say a few words. He spoke of Dot's countless hours of community service through practically every organization in town. I even thought I saw the sisters cringe when he mentioned how the art of giving to a community was lost on younger generations. Guess they're not so involved in giving back?"

"No, I don't think they do much in terms of community building, despite their wealth," Jenn answered. "I know the younger sister, Peg, is really into showing horses for competition. That's what she posts about on Facebook. For each post she writes about her kids, she writes about a dozen posts for her horse and the ribbons he's won. Not sure what that means, but it's telling of something."

Jenn hardly used Facebook. She had an account and had made friends with lots of folks she had known at different points in her life, but she didn't post anything and hadn't in a few years now.

It was risky as a professional to create a permanent record of one's thoughts, feelings, or actions. Occasionally, she would look at the news stream and see what her "friends" were posting, but it didn't really interest her. The variety of uses of Facebook were shocking, everything from pure narcissism, with a post about a person's every action, no matter how mundane, to pure bragging about their new pool, new kitchen, or better yet, new boat. She didn't get it. Sure, the funny, quirky posts were the best, and probably the only ones worth reading, but there was an awful lot of other chaff to stumble through to reach the wheat.

"It tells you she's prouder of her horse," said Matt with a twinkle in his eye. "The horse is out there achieving and her kids are just growing up. A childhood without achievement seems like a death sentence nowadays, at least it did in Darien, where I moved from."

"You're cynical about parenthood, and you're not even a parent yet?" asked Jenn.

"I'm not cynical about the whole thing, I just think sometimes people have kids for the wrong reason these days. They dress them up and take pictures of them and value their achievements, but what about just valuing a person for who they are inside?"

Jenn thought about what Matt said. Immediately her thoughts turned to her niece and the photos of her in adorable outfit after adorable outfit, which lined the walls of her brother's house.

"You've thought about parenting more than I have," said Jenn. "But I think you raise a good point."

Out of the corner of her eye she saw that Mark was standing on the other side of the fir trees separating their properties. He was holding clippers and waved his hand.

"Hi, Jenn. Just getting these trees the way Debbie likes them."

Jenn waved back.

Matt stood and followed her into the kitchen. "So," he said, "looks like you have a stalker."

"What? I do not," Jenn replied. "He just spends his evenings gardening so he doesn't have to hang out with his miserable wife. She's an unhappy, bossy woman, and I think it takes its toll on him."

"Are you sure about that Jenn? Does he know your every movement? You might be too naïve. You're a beautiful young lady and he may have become obsessed with you."

"Don't be ridiculous, Matt. "He's a nice normal guy, who's just tired of being married. Now, would you like to stay for dinner? The big choices up this far north in Mayfield are pizza or Chinese?"

"Jenn, I am sorry, but I can't stay. I'll take a rain check though."

"Okay," said Jenn. "Rain check it is." She took a long hard look into Matt's eyes and saw him looking right back. She wondered what he was so busy with on Saturday night that he couldn't stay. He didn't seem to have a girlfriend, the way he kind of hit on her. Matt leaned in closer, and she realized he might be going for her lips. No such luck though. A quick peck on the cheek, a thank you for the beer, and out the door he sauntered.

Wow, weird day, thought Jenn. At least she was no longer harboring evidence. Those little salamander eggs had stressed her out. She grabbed another beer and headed back to the deck to think about the day.

CHAPTER 25

T he dragonflies were putting on their almost nightly performance. It was that special time in the evening, when they seemed to swarm her yard and perform their aeronautical wonders. They were hunting their prey, but it had taken a while for Jenn to figure out if there was a purpose to the show. Mating was the first thought that popped into her mind, but the dragonflies never connected or showed any interest in each other. They zigged and zagged at odd angles, moving in an upward diagonal direction. After a careful study, she realized they were hunting insects, sneaking up on them from below, and catching them in their legs.

It was a special treat to watch and appreciate. Some folks could sit on a deck all summer drinking cocktails and talking about their neighbors, and never notice the dragonflies darting backward, forward, and diagonally. Dragonflies had four wings and unlike other insects, they could uniquely move each wing independently. The hind wings on dragonflies sometimes flapped just a bit ahead of the front wings. This staggered flapping allowed the back wings to catch the air generated by the front wings, which generates more lift with less energy than the typical two-winged system used by butterflies and other insects.

Jenn observed with fascination these creatures with their unique double winged system, that had lived on the earth for over 300 million years. As she watched them, she thought about the last two weeks. Two dead people in the small idyllic shoreline town in which she had spent her life, all connected with one controversial piece of land. Land with a future that was up in the air. Homes, open space, playing fields, what would happen to the last two-hundred feet of beachfront of the New England coastline, not set aside as public land? Why should only a few wealthy individuals get to enjoy this shorefront land with another private neighborhood beach? Maybe it should be a green beach, accessible and open to everyone? The existence of blue spotted salamander eggs would certainly slow the development down. But who would kill others over that? It didn't mean the development was impossible. It was just another potential hurdle. Jenn thought about who had a vested interest in the outcome. Who would benefit financially if the project went through?

Certainly, Charlie Martins, and Riverfront Landing's corporate investors, she concluded. After all, Charlie was the spokesperson for the project and was the most vested in the outcome. Rumor in town was that he was personally all-in on the project. He had staked his retirement savings and the equity in his house on its success. But who were his other investors? Jenn really didn't know. She might have to find out.

Jenn thought about her boss for a moment, well one of her many bosses, David Webster, the attorney representing Riverfront Landing. He also had a financial and career investment in the project succeeding. But development projects failed all the time and lawyers were not to blame. Some land use battles were won and some were lost. Even aggressive clients understood that all developments were multi-faceted and had innumerable variables, which led to their success or failure.

Jenn realized she was smack in the middle of mystery. She thought for a moment about all the mysteries she had ever read, going all the way back to those Nancy Drew books that lined her childhood bedroom bookshelf. Why did people murder one another? Money, love, hate, revenge, insanity, and fear. But here the two people dead were from opposite sides of the conflict. Dr. Tilman was the paid consultant for the developer, and would ostensibly be murdered by someone who wanted to stop the development.

Dot Hutchinson was one of the leaders of the citizen's group, and wouldn't she be murdered by someone in favor of the development? Murder; such a crazy action. Who would actually kill someone over what happened to a parcel of land?

I guess, Jenn thought, maybe there were combined motives here. Of all the various characters in town, why would those two be the ones to end up murdered? Wouldn't murdering Charlie Martins, the main proponent of the development, make more sense?

That would be a much better way to slow things down and possibly stop them for good. Or on the other side, wouldn't murdering Nat Harkins make the most sense? He was the most outspoken and zealous of the citizen opposition group. How could the same person want those two individuals dead? Maybe the murderer was just inept? Maybe the murderer was such an idiot, they couldn't even figure out who to murder?

Jenn was out of her league. She had no experience with murder. She wasn't a criminal attorney, and the only cop she knew just blew her off for dinner. So, getting back to mystery novels she had read, she thought about how sometimes motives were combined. The more complex mysteries often had one murder lead to other murders because one person's actions led to another person's reactions. Sometimes the reactions were copy-cat murders, done in the same manner as the original murder.

She thought of the dragonfly's wings, the ripple effect, and how one action might fan the air and provide the fuel to stimulate someone to act, and the momentum from the first action, could set another pair of wings in motion, or someone else to act. It must be a ripple effect at play here. There had to be either two motives, or two murderers. But that just seemed so crazy for such a small town.

Jenn had started to believe, as she aged, that most folks were closer to losing their sanity and going over the edge than she had imagined when she was younger. Sometimes it seemed like all adults had a tendency toward a particular mental health problem that was exacerbated during times of stress and chaos. It was with self-awareness that adults seemed to stay sane and manage their lives. So, if the ripple effect theory was true, there were two murderers running around in Mayfield, who had totally lost it, and were now hitting folks on the back of their heads.

CHAPTER 26

◆

C
rowdfunding: a novel empowerment concept that let folks find funding to create their ideas. Claire had just called Jenn during her short drive to school to share the latest local gossip on the murders, and the gossip was all about crowdfunding.

Shelby Williams had posted on Kickstarter, one of the most popular crowdfunding sites, a proposal to obtain commitments to preserve Riverfront Landing as open space, as part of the Mayfield Land Trust. In just two days, various local Mayfielders had committed over $2 million, so it was the talk of the town. Claire said she felt she had to contribute today or she would get side-eyed at the PTO meeting that night, which she didn't want. Claire maintained that she was side-eyed from time to time for her artistic wardrobe that didn't fit the standard name-brand attire of Mayfield moms.

As if Jenn's desk wasn't already piled high with tasks to complete and papers to push, now the unsolved murders snuck back into the edges of her brain and consumed her thoughts. She pulled up the website to see the total amount funded. It looked like many of Shelby Williams' relatives had contributed. There were Williams after Williams listed, almost eight in all.

Jenn called Claire back, and surprisingly Claire picked up. Usually teaching the budding Picassos kept her from answering her cell phone during the school day.

"Crayons keeping them happy today?" Jenn asked Claire.

"Crayons keep everybody happy. When is the last time you picked one up?" Claire retorted. "You could use a little more happiness in your lonely existence."

"Please, no life analysis this morning, and no more blind dates. Doesn't this latest one show you it's not the path to happiness for me? It led me to a dead body! Anyway, didn't you get the message?"

"Nope, what message?" Claire asked. "Peter and I did hear from our friend Brian and he wanted to know why we stood him up. He apparently left by the front door after the book signing, and never knew that there was a murder in the back of P.T. Jane's. He works all the time, like you. It would be a great relationship. What's better than one workaholic, but two?"

"So, I'm calling because I wanted to see what you know about Shelby Williams," Jenn ignored Claire. "I mean she looks around our age, but she didn't grow up in Mayfield. She teaches science in the middle school, right? Do you know her personally? There are so many Williams on that crowdfunding site listed as donors."

"Jenn, this is so unlike you. What's going on?" asked Claire. "There are clients to milk with your overly priced billable hours, and you're reading through a website's list of donors? And then taking those frog eggs home? You were skirting way more closely to the edge of the law than you usually do. I'm not sure I've ever seen you even roll through a stop sign. What gives?"

"They were salamander eggs, not frog eggs. It is a big difference. In your world that's like confusing a Jackson Pollack with a Renoir," Jenn answered.

"Who cares?" said Claire. "Same thing to me and to most people."

Jenn put her hands on her hips and cleared her throat. At moments, Claire drove her nuts.

"Claire," she said loudly, "I care. Not the same thing to me. But I guess it was seeing the dead body. I can't get past it. This poor old guy gets hit in the back of the head and that's it. Game over. It's really bothering me. And then poor Dot Hutchinson," Jenn went on. "Same thing. One false turn and someone is hammering you on the head. A life ended in a second by someone's crazy and possibly impulsive action. Remember the Beatles song, 'Maxwell's silver hammer, came down upon his head'….? You think someone's obsessed with the song and is taking it out on folks?"

"Yep, that's it, Jenn. Someone's obsessed with a song from the 1960s and acting it out. That's definitely what is going on. You are not Sherlock Holmes. Just let the police worry about this. Your hunky new friend Matt is probably examining the crowdfunding website right now, too. The police will get their heads around this and find the hammerer. Is that a word, 'hammerer?' Well, they'll find the carpenter, or whoever it is running around with a hammer, hitting whoever they feel like," Claire concluded. "Then we can resume worrying about our more typical Mayfield problems, like how our lawn looks compared to our neighbor's, if we have stylish enough patio furniture, whether our pool is big enough, where the summer tourists are parking, whether the town should allow food trucks at lunch time on the green, and my personal favorite, whether the foam in my latte has the right size bubbles."

"You are absolutely no help, Claire. So, you don't know anything about Shelby Williams?"

"I heard she is having an affair with Robbie Hayden."

"What? You're making that up."

"Yep. I really don't know anything about her," Claire said. "I've been told her husband travels an awful lot for work and is never at any of the kids' events, according to a mom I know. The same mom said that Shelby and Robbie are always seen together around town, getting coffee, eating lunch—that kind of thing. The mom was implying that it's unnatural to spend so much time with a male that's not your spouse, but I didn't pay it much mind. I've seen them in Starbucks myself, and they don't look like a couple. They look like they're trying to right the wrongs of the world and preserve some land as open space.

"Hey, I got to go," Claire said abruptly. "My next class is coming in. Brian is going to call you directly to go out. Don't blow him off. And maybe we should go for drinks again this Friday at Dunville's. We have to get you out of your house. Life's complicated and messy and if you don't play, you will never enjoy it."

She hung up before Jenn could even get out a goodbye.

Jenn turned her office chair around and stared out the window. Today the clouds were high and thin. Stratus, she thought, was the proper name for them. Wispy with a light blue sky behind them. It would be great to be outside and not stuck in here.

Jenn thought about her conversation with Claire. Maybe the murderer was someone who used a hammer for work. Like one of the contractor guys who would help build all the houses after the project was approved. That would make sense. If they knew about the salamander eggs, and they knew about Dr. Tilman, they would have wanted to stop the egg information from becoming public. Plus, they would want to slow down the opposition. Dot Hutchinson was probably the glue of that group, since she had her hand in everything. Killing her would certainly keep her from getting her name in the paper. Well, it would get it in the paper one last time, but not every week like before.

Stuart knocked on Jenn's door. She tore herself from the clouds, turned her chair and greeted him as he casually plopped himself down in one of her visitor chairs. Stuart was probably her favorite partner. He never got worked up over work and didn't sweat the small stuff. He just wanted to go over the cases they worked on together and check the status of a few projects Jenn was working on for each of the cases. The conversation motivated her and she dug into her work as soon as he left.

CHAPTER 27

Saturday morning, Jenn felt the beach calling her, until her mom called and asked her to meet at the cemetery. It did not sound like a request. She took a fast shower and went to meet her.

Jenn's mom had bought a plot in the Summerhill Cemetery in north Mayfield. The large family marker about four feet wide by two feet tall read "Bowdoin" and a smaller marker read "Peter Edward Bowdoin." Jenn's mother had grown up in Mayfield, and there were prior generations of her mother's family buried in the cemetery as well.

Jenn didn't mind cemeteries. They were calm, quiet, and peaceful for the deceased. Often those visiting were not yet at peace, but at least a peaceful place helped calm the minds and souls of those who were grieving.

Strange as it sounded, Jenn liked the small and overgrown Summerhill Cemetery. The grass was not trimmed perfectly around the stones. A sloppy weed whacker had rushed his work and left behind blades of grass that gave the stones a more natural, unkempt look. The grass was long, as though the lawn mower had not been pulled out in a couple of weeks. Grape vines, Virginia creeper, and poison ivy all encumbered the bushes at the sides of the grassed area, some of these vines were even growing out onto the grave markers near the edges of the cemetery, or even stretching toward an occasional tree that was interspaced between the gravestones.

The days following her father's death had been tricky. Death is always a little tricky, but her mom unduly complicated it. She wanted her husband buried, but she also wanted him cremated. Jenn had almost lost it when her mom asked if they could just cremate half of him. The funeral director had calmly explained that they could only cremate someone's whole body. Then some or all of the ashes could be spread, or buried in the cemetery. Jenn's mom had wisely taken that approach, rather than have her deceased husband sawed in half.

Peter had a field day over this concept. "So, when I go to the cemetery, which parts of Dad's body am I paying tribute to? His left eye, maybe his right arm, and a little of his pinkie finger?"

Jenn thought it was funny, but her mom had gotten angry at the ill-placed humor. It maybe even inspired her mom because next thing Jenn knew, in the first couple of months after her dad died, her mom started dispersing his ashes all over town.

Jenn's mom had already placed the ashes in the more typical spots: A corner of her backyard growing up; in their childhood church's side garden, since her dad had been somewhat involved in the church; and into the beautiful, blue-green Long Island Sound, from the shore of the Surf Club. They had gone to the Surf Club in their childhood as a family, playing at the beach all day, staying and picnicking for dinner into the evening.

But lately Jenn's mom had taken it a little too far. She wanted some of their father on the local golf course, and had asked the groundskeeper when she ran into him in town one day if she could put a little bit of her deceased husband on each of the eighteen holes. Jenn guessed the groundskeeper did not know what to say to that request because he stalled her mom by saying he would talk to the club manager.

It was just when they were eating outside at one of the restaurants her mom and dad had frequented that Jenn decided it was finally time to speak up. Her mom had reached into her purse, pulled out her dad, or the urn rather that held his few remaining ashes. Her mom was about to fling a handful across the outdoor patio when Jenn got up the nerve to say, "Mom, what are you doing? Have you lost your mind?"

Jenn had raised her voice slightly, and reached to steady her mom's hand, which was already on the urn. For a split second, her mom's arm resisted Jenn's pressure, but then she met her daughter's eye, and her arm relaxed. She looked around the room, as did Jenn. Only a few people glanced back at them. Most of them didn't seem to have noticed. Her mom's eyes filled with tears, and she simply responded, "No, I have not lost my mind. I lost my heart when your dad died, and I just miss him." Jenn's mom pulled her hand out of the urn, replaced the lid, and reached for a tissue from her purse.

Jenn thought about staying quiet, but instead thought maybe she could help her mom. "I'm sorry, Mom. I'm sorry Dad's gone. But spreading him all over town isn't going to bring him back."

"I just have so many memories of him everywhere I go," her mom replied. "I want him to keep being in those places with me. If I put some of him there, then I'm not alone. He'll still be with me, always with me, like he used to be."

Jenn got it. Her fiancé's death had shattered her life. Three weeks after the diagnosis of pancreatic cancer, he was gone. Jenn didn't know if she ever wanted to get so close to someone if it meant her whole world would shatter once they were gone. Since Alex, there were a few guys she had liked, but she quickly lost interest.

Peter, Claire, and Sophia pulled into the cemetery, drawing Jenn back to the present. Peter parked and once released from her car seat straps, Sophia ran toward Jenn and Nana, as she called her grandmother, to give both of them great big hugs.

Claire and Peter walked over at a more leisurely pace and greeted them as well.

"I didn't know Peter was coming, too," said Jenn. "What gives?"

"I'm ready to spread the rest of Dad's ashes on the top of his grave," replied her mom.

"Are you sure?" asked Peter with a twinkle in his eyes. "There might be a port-a-potty in town that you haven't blessed with Dad's presence yet?"

Ignoring Peter's teasing, their mom began, "Gather around and let's hold hands and say a quick prayer." At the end of the prayer, she opened the urn, turned it ceremoniously upside down, and out sprinkled a speck of ash, or maybe two.

"Not much left," said Peter dryly. "Good thing you dragged us out here for that."

"Nana, does that mean we won't be putting ashes on any of the other Little League fields?" asked Sophia.

"Years of therapy," said Peter. "I'm thinking she's going to need years of therapy, Mom, for this. Thanks. And I was hoping to raise an emotionally well-adjusted child." Peter's words were harsh, but he was smiling, and didn't seem truly annoyed or worried—just more inconvenienced by another trip to the cemetery.

"Oh, Peter. Sophia will be fine. She understands," their mom said. "Maybe just prompt her not to talk at school about us spreading Grandpa around town."

Jenn smiled at her, happy to be with both her mom and brother, and enjoying her brother's attempts at humor.

Claire had started back toward the car and, pausing beside a newly dug grave, said, "Hey, Jenn, here's Doctor Tilman's grave."

Jenn walked over toward Claire to a patch of grass that was thinner and a lighter green than the rest of the cemetery. A gravestone stood at the end of the patch.

"William Jonathon Tilman," read Claire out loud. "Terrible to be killed behind a bookstore. Murdered. Why was he hiding frog eggs in the bookstore's old cooler anyway? Strange stuff."

"They are salamander eggs," Jenn corrected her.

"Oh, they are siblings," said Linda. "I grew up with the Tilmans. Patty and Billy Tilman. Patty, she used to run a restaurant instead of a bookstore. I've been meaning to tell you, Jenn," Linda said. "That's why there's that old ice machine behind the bookstore now. P.T. Jane is just Patty's married name, Patty Tilman Jane. Anyway, the restaurant failed, like so many do, and she started up the bookstore, instead. I went to a book group for years at her store and occasionally she would even join in the group's discussion. She's a lovely woman. Now that I think about it, Doctor Tilman came to the bookstore when we were meeting one day, and Patty introduced us. He had some definitive guide on frogs on display in the bookstore. Doctor Tilman was her older brother."

"Well, being her brother, he would have knowledge of the ice cooler and feel comfortable stashing the salamander eggs in it," said Jenn. "That makes some sense, but why wouldn't he just put them in his own refrigerator?"

"You know, Jenn, now that I think of it, Patricia Jane had a son about your age," her mom said. I wonder if he's married yet. He might make a good husband for you. Have you ever met him? Was he in your year at school, Peter? Daniel? Or maybe Robbie, was his name? Do you remember him, Peter?"

"Oh, sounds promising, maybe I can find out where he is now?" chimed in Claire.

"Mom, Claire," said Jenn. "Knock it off."

Before Jenn could say anything else, her mom continued, "You know, Jenn, it really is time for you to find a spouse. You really don't want to get buried alone. You need someone you can lie next to in the cemetery."

Jenn was annoyed now. Enough with the matchmaking. She gave them each a quick hug goodbye, and then just said, "Seriously, Mom, Claire, please stop the matchmaking. It's not helping."

Jenn drove away upset. Not wanting to lie alone in a cemetery was definitely not a reason to start dating again. Jenn felt too emotional to think about it all. Instead, Jenn thought about the murders. Maybe she could contact P.T. Jane, and find out if she knew anything about why salamander eggs were in a book store ice cooler.

CHAPTER 28

❖

U nfortunately, the rest of Saturday was filled with chores. Suddenly, it was Saturday night and Jenn had no plans. Kind of depressing. She hadn't bothered to ask her brother and Claire what they were up to tonight. She liked to give them space, or maybe she liked some space for herself, she wasn't sure which. Jenn sat on the back patio with her usual potpourri of drinks, and a novel.

Tonight's drink choices were water, chardonnay, and lemonade. Some folks might not like the chardonnay and lemonade at the same sitting, but Jenn liked the acidity it brought to her mouth as she switched back and forth. She examined Romeo and Juliet from afar, and they looked happy. One really couldn't tell that they were a tragedy in the making. The wind rustled their leaves and they swayed back and forth together in what seemed like a happy fashion. That's how it was today, Romeo and Juliet, and all the leaves on each tree, swaying together.

Other days the wind rustled individual leaves, and each leaf shook or danced to its own rhythm, with no uniformity or cohesion. Jenn didn't know what caused it to differ so much or if anyone else ever even noticed it. She guessed it had to do with the velocity of the wind or the variability of the wind's direction. Watching Romeo and Juliet sway together made Jenn think of them as a couple, a pair. She wondered if they would last the same length of time, or would one be left grief stricken as her mom was without her dad. She thought about what her mom had said that morning, and the day Jenn called her out on the ash distribution. She watched the trees sway, and then saw something move at Romeo's trunk.

"Hello, Jenn," called Mark. "How are you this lovely evening?"

"Hi, Mark." She recognized his voice, and he seemed to creepily have appeared from behind Romeo's trunk. He stood in front of her expectantly, so she said, "Would you care for a glass of wine?"

Jenn thought about what Detective Matt had said. There was no way her neighbor Mark was a stalker. He might lurch around and suddenly appear out from behind trunks of trees, but that had to be normal behavior, right? She was suddenly worried there was more to Mark than she realized.

Mark ambled over to the patio and said, "That would be great. Hate to go inside yet. Such a lovely, lovely evening."

Jenn got up and fetched a glass of wine. She grabbed some crackers and dip while she was in the kitchen, and returned to the patio. Mark had sat down in the chair next to hers and looked completely comfortable. He really did not look like a stalker, even if he occasionally acted like one.

"Thank you," said Mark, as Jenn handed him the wine. She waited for Mark to start a conversation, but he didn't. He seemed content to just sit and enjoy the quiet.

"So, Mark, did you tell me last week that the state archeologist was at the Mayfield Beach Hotel, having lunch with Nat Harkins, the leader of the opposition group? I feel like you said something about that, but so much has happened in the last week or two, I can't recall what you were saying."

"Oh, you mean the day Debbie broke the rose bush? Boy, was she upset about that. She takes so much pride in every particularity of the yard being perfect. Yes. Debbie said she had been to lunch at the Mayfield Beach Hotel and that Nat Harkins sat with the state archeologist instead of her group. It was the same day Dot Hutchinson accused Debbie of mysteriously visiting the property and inferred Debbie had mixed alliances."

"You said that Dot accused Debbie of wanting to make money as a realtor when the development occurred. And the basis for the inference was that Dot had seen a car like Debbie's at Riverfront Landing, right?" Jenn thought for a moment about seeing Debbie herself leaving Riverfront Landing last week, and whether she should tell Mark.

"Yes, I think that was the story," said Mark. "Debbie hasn't really said anything else about it. What is a state archeologist, anyway?" asked Mark.

Jenn started to answer, "I know there is one, but that's about all I know. I recall working on a case once where the state archeologist's opinion was given about whether or not a property should be developed, which had cairns on it."

"Cairns?"

"Cairns are stone rock piles that are believed to have been made by the Native American Indians eons ago, and might mark graves or other spiritual sites," Jenn explained.

"Neighbors opposing a development project didn't want the rock piles disturbed and the property owner had to design his plan around the existing cairns. It seemed kind of silly to me, since we really don't even know what we are preserving by preserving a cairn. What if it was just how the Native Americans marked their outhouses? Or just piles of rocks from when European settlers cleared the rocks out of a field? We really don't know what we're preserving. We're just affirming the philosophy that because something is old it should be preserved. Taken to an extreme, in our current culture, that's called hoarding. If you save all your newspapers because they're old and might have some value, you now have hoarding issues and could be the subject of ridicule on national television."

"Well, I don't know about that, Jenn," Mark responded. "What if the cairns are gravesites? Is there any inherent beauty or workmanship in them?"

Jenn pulled out her iPhone, typed in "Cairns in Connecticut," and pulled up a picture of one. It was just a pile of rocks in the shape of a small mound. There was no workmanship involved in how the rocks were cut, layered or chosen. Jenn handed the phone to Mark and he examined the photo.

"A group of children could have done it," said Jenn. "They could have been building a pretend fort."

Mark handed the phone back to Jenn. She glanced at it again, but the picture had been switched. Mark must have scrolled through the photos, which came up with her search. The phone now depicted a cairn with a tall, lanky bearded man standing next to it. Jenn recognized that man. He was the guy she had seen from Larry's Bagels when she had gone there with Officer Matt. So, who was this man standing next to a cairn?

On a hunch, Jenn did a quick search and typed in 'Connecticut state archeologist.' A different photo of the bearded man appeared. This time the photo depicted him in a suit jacket and button-down shirt. So the bearded man was the state archeologist! The state archeologist had been down at Riverfront Landing, and on a Saturday? Why?

"What is it, Jenn?" asked Mark. She looked up to see him staring at her.

"Oh, the state archeologist is this man, and I saw him leaving Riverfront Landing last weekend." Jenn handed her phone back to Mark. "It was the day the police officer was here, and you were worried about me. Earlier in the day, I was at Larry's Bagels and saw this state archeologist pulling out of the entrance to Riverfront Landing."

"Maybe he was checking out the property for some reason?" asked Mark.

Jenn thought for a moment, but then decided there was no point in holding back information from Mark about Debbie.

"It's just weird that it was a weekend. State employees really don't work on the weekends, for typical routine matters," she said. "Plus, it is so late in the game for anyone to claim there is something of historical significance at Riverfront Landing. One of the questions asked as part of the coastal permitting process, is whether there is anything historically or culturally significant about a property. Mayfield Coastal Development, or Charlie Martins, would have already thought about this issue."

"Well, Charlie Martins would not have been particularly motivated to admit to any kind of historical or cultural significance, correct?" Mark asked.

"Yep, Mark, you are correct. It would have delayed, stopped, or altered development," said Jenn, looking right at Mark and laughing a little at her naiveté. Of course a developer would not be motivated to be honest about a question like that on a permit application.

"I wasn't born yesterday, Jenn." said Mark. "In my work, I sometimes see lies by omission. There are lots of peer review requirements and incentives for veracity. But lies by omission still occur and can substantially alter research results. Certain man-made systems or structures encourage lies by omission, by default, or by mistake, really, especially when they involve self-reporting."

"Mark," yelled Debbie from her own backyard. "Where are you? Mark!" A little louder this time.

"Looks like I need to go home. Thank you for the wine and company," Mark said. "So here's my lie by omission tonight. I'm not mentioning this drink on your patio because I would have to hear about it for the whole evening and maybe even into the next evening or two or three." He smiled as he said this line. "I really enjoy your company, Jenn. You know, at work I'm the lead toxicologist, head of twenty scientists, but at home, I can't even take out the trash correctly, or properly trim the cherry tree. It is hard to spend time with Debbie because I'm constantly criticized."

Mark stood as he spoke, then turned and started back toward his own yard. Jenn was shocked at both his honesty and perception. She had long thought he was miserable at home but here was an actual admission.

"Mark," said Jenn at his back, "You need to know. Debbie was down at Riverfront Landing last Saturday. She met with the state archeologist and with someone from the environmental agency named Flannigan. She doesn't know I saw her from Larry's Bagels across the street. I didn't know it was the state archeologist until just now. She's involved somehow, Mark. I don't know how. And hey, we'll have more wine another time."

Wow, thought Jenn. Lies by omission. Maybe she did have a stalker and maybe Mark was a lot more complicated that he appeared.

PART III

CHAPTERS 29-44

CHAPTER 29

J enn was running in the woods across the motley ground, with a beautiful collage of patches of sunlight and shadow created by the tree canopy up over her head. She wasn't running in her usual place or usual route. It was somewhere different. And she was running fast, full speed, her heart pounded, and she was scared. It wasn't a leisurely jog. Someone was behind her. She could hear them. A man or a woman, whoever it was, they were right behind her. She could tell because she could hear not just their footsteps, but also their breathing.

Jenn was afraid to turn and look to see who it was, and suddenly the motley ground ended and she found herself running where it was familiar, into her own yard. She didn't have her house key and the house might be locked. There was no time to try the door. Whoever she could hear walking and breathing was right behind her.

Leaping for the bottom branches of Romeo, Jenn climbed and climbed as high as she could. Some of the branches had cankers and she tried to avoid those branches and reach for the ones she knew were strong. But she couldn't avoid them all. She needed to step on some just to get higher. She didn't think her pursuer had figured out that she hadn't headed for the house.

Jenn could no longer hear anyone breathing. She was a good fifteen feet off the ground, but if she reached up a little higher, she might have been able to peek out toward the house where there was a break in the leaf coverage. She climbed toward the next branch and transferred her weight onto her right leg. She heard a loud crack where the branch connected to the trunk. Catching herself with her arms, Jenn stood back on the lower, stable branch. She didn't fall, but wondered if her pursuer heard, and would find her in the tree.

Another crack. But wait, Jenn realized this crack sounded different. Not a tree limb or branch breaking.

Jenn opened her eyes and realized she was in her bed, and the breaking sound was coming from downstairs. She sat up startled. The running, it was a dream. Climbing Romeo was just a dream. She heard another sound from downstairs—a long, slow grumbling sound. The sliding glass door, Jenn realized. Was someone in her house? Her phone was downstairs. She stayed still and listened. Nothing. She patiently waited it out for another few minutes. Nothing. The sliding door sound must have been someone leaving, she decided.

She thought for a minute. If someone was still here, better that they know I'm coming, and have time to leave, she rationalized. But chances were that they were already gone. Trying to stay calm, Jenn climbed out of bed and called out, "Hello? Is someone downstairs? I've already called the police. They're on their way. You better leave quickly." Her voice started out shaky, but she tried to give it more volume and authority, as though what she said about the police was true.

Hands shaking, Jenn turned on lights in her bedroom, the bathroom, the upstairs hallway. She didn't hear a sound and wished she didn't have to go downstairs for her cell phone. Had the crack of the tree branch in her dream been real? Did that crack occur in real life? Or was that just her imagination? She wasn't certain where her dreaming stopped and the sounds from downstairs began.

Jenn made it down the stairs and flicked on all three light switches at the bottom of the staircase. She headed toward the back of the house to the kitchen and sliding glass door leading to the patio. The iPad was on the kitchen floor. Cracked. The screen was cracked. Maybe the sound she heard was it falling to the floor, but why would she have heard the sound twice? Some of her work papers were disheveled and sticking out from her briefcase. When she finished her legal work yesterday, she had packed up her bag and closed it, so it was at the ready for Monday morning. Now the flap of the briefcase was open, but the papers' edges weren't lined up properly. They were stuffed back in and some of the corners were folded over, where they caught the edges of the briefcase.

Jenn's heart still pounded. She looked at the sliding glass door. It was not locked. She was not good about locking her doors at night. It was semi-rural Connecticut and it seemed so unlikely that anyone would break in. Jenn walked over to the sliding door and locked it. She checked the rest of the first floor. No one there.

She sat down at the kitchen table, trembling. She tried to calm the wild heart pounding in her chest. What the heck? Who would break into her house? Well, technically, they hadn't broken in, since she was so bad at remembering to lock the doors. But who would have the audacity to walk into her house in the middle of the night, and why?

Besides, she really had nothing of value to steal. What did she really have? Let's see, if someone wanted some wine and lemonade, seltzer, soda, juice, or beer, it was definitely the house to break into. If someone was really thirsty, overly parched, then her house was the way to go. But she didn't really have any valuables.

Jenn's eyes scanned her kitchen; everything seemed to be in order except the iPad and briefcase. She got up and picked the broken iPad off the floor. The screen was cracked. She had been meaning for the longest time to buy one of those durable cases for it so it wouldn't get broken. Guess she could remove that item from her to-do list. No need to buy a case now. She hit the button. It was on the same news website she frequented, probably too many times a day, to pick up the latest inflammatory news. She surfed and read a variety of news sources in a given day. She liked to compare and contrast articles sometimes, to see how the different news sources could present the same story.

Jenn looked at the history and didn't see anything out of sorts. It was harder to see the sites because the screen was so cracked. Oh no, she realized, after she had pawed it thoroughly, there may have been a fingerprint on it. Jenn put the iPad down on the kitchen table and decided to let it be until morning. She checked the clock and realized it was only 1:00 a.m. As she glanced back at the iPad, she noticed it had two different cracked patterns on it. Maybe it had fallen twice? She had heard two loud sounds in her dream. Maybe the robber was trying to break the iPad. A double break-in, Jenn thought, sort of giddily from the stress. She took a deep breath and tried to calm down from the stress of knowing someone was in her house. The goal was probably not to break the iPad. Most likely it just fell on the ground—possibly twice—and technically it still worked, it was just cracked.

Jenn looked at her briefcase again to see if anything was missing. She had brought home various parts of three different cases, plus a folder in which she kept her time sheets.

She decided not to take her briefcase or iPad upstairs. She just left them in the kitchen. If someone was going to come back for them, she didn't want to be woken up. She thought about unlocking the deck door. Whoever it was that had broken in most likely wasn't interested in doing her any bodily harm. The person was interested in her work, or what she was reading about on the iPad. But on the other hand, there was a murderer loose in Mayfield. Why give them the opportunity to do her in so easily by just leaving her door open for a second time in one evening?

Jenn left the door locked and headed up to her bedroom. To be extra cautious, she also locked her bedroom door, which she had never done before. Jenn lay in bed and listened. Nothing but the sound of the crickets filled her ears. Her breathing slowed and she decided to risk falling asleep, comforted by the lock on her bedroom door and the cell phone next to her bed.

CHAPTER 30

J enn woke up again with Dr. Tilman's face in her mind. The dried blood on his right temple. The vacant eyes. When was this going to stop? Enough about the dead body. And, it was really not a pleasant waking thought. Jenn liked it when she woke up to much more pleasant dreams. She thought for a minute about the break-in the night before. Did that happen?

Downstairs she saw that yes, the iPad had been smashed, and her briefcase had been searched. As she poured her coffee, orange juice, milk, and water, she wondered whether she should do anything about it. While she sampled her morning drinks, she thought that maybe she should call Matt. He would brighten up her Sunday. But maybe it was better to let it go. They took nothing, and now, whomever it was who had broken in, knew she knew nothing. She didn't know who was murdering folks. She didn't know why there were salamander eggs near Dr. Tilman's body. She didn't know why the state archeologist would visit Riverfront Landing on a weekend. If the murderer thought she were on to him or her, they were sadly mistaken.

She was just as clueless as any other citizen of Mayfield. Maybe even more so, since her "head was in the trees," according to Claire. While she contemplated all of this, Jenn's iPhone rang.

"Jenn." It was Claire. "What are you doing today? Any chance you could take Sophia for us this morning?"

"Sure," said Jenn in her usual doormat manner. She hadn't even planned her day yet. It was free for the filling. Her days off from work were so infrequent, partially because she worked lots of Saturdays, that sometimes when she had no work, she didn't know how to occupy her time.

"Excellent."

"Hey, Claire, could you bring her up here? There's something I want to show you at my house. I could use Peter's and your opinions."

"What's up?"

"Just come up and I'll show you. What time are you thinking?"

"We'll be there around ten-thirty."

"Okay, see you then."

Jenn took her four drinks out to the patio and contemplated the day's weather. It looked like another good beach day. She might take Sophia to the beach, depending on how long they wanted a babysitter. After Jenn was fully hydrated, she decided to take on at least one house chore before the day got away from her. She looked around the yard and thought for a moment about the possibilities. Guess it was weeding time again. That was the trouble with weeding. You couldn't just do it once. It was a never-ending chore, like laundry.

Jenn went to the front of the house and got to work. The temperature was rising quickly. The deep brown wood chips along her front walk were interlaced with pale green weeds. She dug in and started working, but only a moment passed, and she heard a car in the driveway. She headed back outside to greet her brother and family, surprised to find her mom instead. She jumped out of her car, with the urn for Jenn's dad's ashes in her hand.

"Jenn, I'm sorry I was so upset yesterday. I'm better today," her mom said.

They were still standing in the garage hugging when Peter, Claire, and Sophia pulled into the driveway. Jenn and Linda stopped hugging and turned to watch the family exit the car. Sophia came running over. "Nana, Aunt Jenn," she called as she got closer, and gave them each a hug.

"Everybody come on in," said Jenn, and her family followed her in through the garage.

"Would anyone like a drink?" asked Jenn, smiling. Her family knew all about her love of multiple drinks at once, and often took her up on having a couple of beverages each while visiting her house.

"Coffee and tea, please," said Peter.

"Diet Coke and lemonade," said Claire.

"Apple juice and milk," chimed in Sophia with a huge smile.

Her mom said, "How about water, and I know it's early, but also a glass of white wine?"

Jenn got to work making all the beverages. She had her back to the kitchen table when she heard Peter exclaim, "Jenn, I know you complain about work sometimes, but really don't take it out on your iPad!"

"Oh, I didn't. Oh." Everyone turned to look at her. Uh oh, should she tell them the truth? They didn't like her all alone out in the woods in this house. It would only make them worry more. They thought she should be in a nice condominium with closer neighbors and less outside maintenance.

"Jenn," said her mom, reading her daughter's face. "What happened?"

"Someone broke in last night while I was sleeping. They must have dropped the iPad on the floor twice while they were shuffling through my papers. Look at my briefcase. I woke in the night, out of a strange dream, to what I think was the sound of the iPad hitting the floor."

"Someone broke in?" said Claire.

"Well, I don't remember locking the door, someone just kind of walked in. I guess it was really a walk-in," tried Jenn, hoping a little humor would lighten the mood.

"Jenn, you didn't call the police yet, did you? You need to call the police. You know you do," said Peter.

"I just don't want to trouble anyone," Jenn answered. "Really, it wasn't a big deal. It was just a little break-in. They didn't take anything and they didn't hurt anyone. It's probably a little bit my fault for forgetting to lock the door."

"Jenn, it is not your fault. You need to take this seriously," Linda said. "What if it was the murderer, in your house last night?" After she said this, she took a big swig of her wine, and glared at Jenn, her eyes bulging.

Peter pulled his phone out of his pocket and dialed 911. As the sound of the iPhone's beeps reached them, everyone turned to look at Peter.

"This has to be dealt with, Jenn. Your safety cannot be at risk. Whether it's connected to the murders or not, you have to be safe and protected."

Peter reported that it was not an emergency and proceeded to explain to the 911 operator that his sister's house had been broken into in the night, providing the address, and the particulars. When he finished, he said, "The police will have someone here within the hour."

Linda took another swig of wine. "Well," she said sitting down on the couch, still clutching the urn, "I guess I better finish this before the police arrive. It is a tad early for wine."

"Now, Mom," said Peter, "dare I ask why you are clutching Dad's urn? Didn't we just bury him for a second time yesterday? Do we need to do that again today? Claire and I were hoping for a little time alone today, Mom. Jenn said she would watch Sophia. But if we have to do that whole graveside ceremony and prayer stuff a third time, I guess we could. The Patriots aren't playing until four o'clock."

Jenn and Claire laughed at Peter's dry humor.

Linda laughed too, and replied, "No, I was just a little upset that I forgot to put any of Dad's ashes in Cockaponset. We had such a good time as a family hiking there. You guys used to bring back all those frogs and bugs, rocks, sticks, leaves—anything that you could, really. I just woke this morning and realized I had placed Dad's ashes everywhere around town that I wanted, but not the one place that he would have wanted, and now I'm out of ashes.

"I wanted Jenn to go with me to the cemetery to try and collect the ashes we left there yesterday on top of his grave, but she said no," Linda continued. "And I think she is right. Jenn said the cemetery is the woods, which means Dad's already in the forest. I guess he is at peace."

"You know, Jenn," said Peter, slumping into the chair next to Linda, "maybe I could use a small glass of wine, too."

Jenn walked over to where Peter was sitting, and pushing his shoulder up, said, "No, no, you guys get going. I'll deal with the police, I'll handle Mom, and I'll watch Sophia. You guys get your time together. Let me know what time you want Sophia back, maybe I could even run her down to you."

"Yes, let's go, Peter," said Claire, pointing to her wrist, even though there was no watch on it. "Now's the time."

"Alright," said Peter, getting up from the chair and heading toward Claire and the exit. "Let's go."

"Where are you two off to?" Linda piped up from the sofa.

"Oh, Mom," said Jenn, "they have plans." Jenn knew they were going home to work on conceiving a sibling for Sophia. Claire had shared that she had miscarried a couple of times since Sophia's birth, and that they wanted to expand their family, and that they were working on timing it properly with Claire's ovulation cycle. Because she knew all these facts, when Claire randomly asked for childcare on the weekends, Jenn just figured what they wanted was an empty house.

Claire and Peter said their goodbyes and left. After getting hugs from her parents, Sophia had grabbed one of the children's books Jenn kept on her bookshelf and carried it to her grandma, asking that she read it to her.

Since Sophia was occupied, Jenn decided to head back outside.

"Before you go, Jenn," called Linda, "could you top off my glass?" Jenn did, and as she reached in to pour more into her mom's glass, Jenn pulled her dad's urn out from under her mom's arm. She stuck the urn up on her fireplace mantel. Linda looked up at her from the couch, and Jenn said, "Just so the last particle of ash doesn't fall out on my sofa."

CHAPTER 31

◆

The sound of a car coming down her road drew Jenn's attention from her weeding. She looked up to see a Mayfield police car pulling into her driveway. Jenn rose and brushed off her hands, then headed toward the driveway. As she approached, she saw that it was Matt stepping out of the driver's side. He sure was an attractive man in a uniform, she thought.

"There's been a break-in?" asked the other officer. "Are you certain you're safe and the perpetrator is gone?"

His hand was on the top of his holstered gun, noticed Jenn.

"Yes. Yes. It's safe here," Jenn assured him. "The only danger is my mom. She's a seventy-year-old grieving widow, and has been acting like a crazy person lately. Yes, she's a danger and I guess my five-year-old niece is a little crazy, too."

"When was the break-in?" asked the older officer, still tense and at the ready, not smiling at Jenn's attempts at humor.

"Are you alright, Jenn?" Matt asked next.

"Hey, yes, there was a break-in, but relax, it was last night in the middle of the night. I'm fine. The thief wasn't interested in me. He searched through my briefcase, and possibly my iPad, which I think he dropped on the floor twice."

Jenn started to lead the officers through her garage to her kitchen. "Come on in," she said, beckoning them to follow her.

When she reached the kitchen, Jenn saw that her mom and Sophia had fallen asleep while reading picture books on the couch. They were each snoring at different decibels, with her mom's snore surprisingly loud.

"Oh, my mom and niece must have fallen asleep," Jenn noted. "There's my briefcase and the iPad. Unfortunately, I didn't think about fingerprints until I had substantially man-handled my iPad in the night."

"Jenn, okay if we sit down and you start from the beginning?" asked Matt, beckoning Jenn toward one of the kitchen chairs.

"Yes," she mumbled, and remembering her manners, asked, "Would you like a drink?"

Matt's eyes roamed into the family room to Jenn's sleeping mom. It was only 11:30 a.m., and Jenn saw Matt noticing the wine glass. Sticking with the less said the better, she offered, "Coffee, tea, water, or lemonade?"

The older officer said, "I'll take you up on the coffee if you don't mind. It feels like a long Sunday already."

"I'm all set," responded Matt.

Jenn made a mug of coffee for the older officer and brought it over to him. The officers were still standing, so Jenn sat down herself, and beckoned them to sit as well. The elder officer, who introduced himself as Steve Cornell, pulled out a small note-book and a pen. Jenn recounted the story as best she could, leaving out her strange dream, of course. When she had finished, Steve asked her a couple of follow-up questions.

Matt went out to his police car and returned with gloves, a camera, and an evidence bag, and then proceeded to inspect, photograph, and bag her iPad.

"Jenn, what are these papers in the briefcase? Could we bag the whole briefcase as evidence as well?" asked Matt.

"Oh my gosh, no," said Jenn. "I need all of that for Monday morning. You can't take it. Well, you can take the empty briefcase, if you think there could be a fingerprint on the leather, but I need all the papers. They're for various clients, and I doubt any kind of fingerprint would show up on paper, anyway."

"You're right. It's doubtful anything would show up on the paper. I'll go ahead and empty it out, since I've got the gloves," said Matt. He started to pull papers carefully from the briefcase. "I take it your papers were not so messed up before the break-in?" he asked.

"Yes. That's how I could tell they had been rifled through," Jenn answered. "They had been placed in the briefcase in an orderly manner, and now they're a wreck."

"Do you have any documents in here relating to Riverfront Landing?" asked Matt, stopping to glance at the top piece of paper he was holding.

"I don't, and I don't think you should be reading those," she said. "Some of those are confidential documents."

"Jenn is an attorney, and her firm represents the developer of the Riverfront Landing project," Matt informed Steve. "Jenn found Doctor Tilman's body behind P.T. Jane's."

"I didn't realize that there could be a connection to the murders. It seemed strange to me that nothing was stolen, not even the iPad, which would be an easy grab for a robber looking for something to pawn," said Steve. "With two unsolved murders, and a murderer on the loose in Mayfield, it's significant that your stuff has been rifled through but not stolen."

"I'm guessing someone was looking for a document in connection with Riverfront Landing," he said. "Do you access work emails from your iPad? Could the thief have accessed your work emails as well?"

"I do, but the iPad is password protected." As Matt and Steve started examining her bag, Jenn took a deep breath and realized how scary it was that someone had broken into her home. She had always felt safe there, even without the dog her family wanted her to get. Now she felt scared and suddenly angry that someone would just come on in to her house and mess with her stuff.

The officers went outside to check for any signs of the break-in. Jenn followed them out and waited in the driveway. Steve yelled out that he found some broken branches. Matt and Jenn headed toward Steve, and Steve pointed out two small broken white pine branches in the row of pines between Jenn's house and her neighbor's.

Matt turned to look at Jenn and gave her an "I told you so" look. Jenn spoke up and said her neighbor sometimes cut through the pines to visit her house, so they might have broken then, rather than last night.

"Well, they do appear to be fresh breaks and I'm not sure they would have happened if someone were just walking between the pines, rather than rushing," said Steve.

Jenn explained that her neighbor had visited just last night and had a drink on the deck.

For some reason, she blushed as she spoke these words, and felt Matt's eyes on her. She shook off her embarrassment. She had no relationship with Matt. After all his flirting, she had invited him to eat with her last Saturday, but he had run away at the invitation. Matt had inferred that the neighbor she'd known for many years was a stalker. Mark had been nothing but neighborly, and now Matt had her afraid of him. Why should she trust Matt, though? She didn't know him very well, and at least she had known Mark for a while.

Jenn really didn't know where the truth lay. Maybe Mark had broken into her home in the night. Maybe he was more involved in the murders or the mystery of Riverfront Landing than Jenn would want to believe. Or maybe Debbie had. But it was hard to picture Debbie doing anything in a quiet or sneaky manner. Although the burglar wasn't actually quiet, as they had managed to make two loud crashes.

"Let's get photos of those branches." said Matt. "Just in case."

"Matt, let's go back inside of the house and see if anything is out of order? Jenn, would that be okay with you? We just want to make sure there's nothing you missed," said Steve.

"Sure, that's fine," replied Jenn.

As they re-entered the house, Linda stirred, and opened her eyes. But with Sophia still sound asleep snuggled against her, she didn't sit up. "Jenn," she called, catching sight of the policemen in uniform, "is everything okay?"

"Yes, mom, no worries. The officers are just following up on the break-in, and they're almost done here, I think."

"Hey, Jenn," called Steve from the front of her house. "What about this desk? It looks like it's been rifled through as well."

Jenn followed Steve's voice to her home office. It contained a wooden desk and chair, and a small sofa. Papers were strewn all about the desk in a totally disorganized manner. Stacks of paper were on the floor and some of them had fallen over.

"Was this all messed up by the burglar, too?" asked Steve.

"No," said Jenn shrugging sheepishly. "That mess is just mine."

"Okay," said Steve, looking relieved. "Let's get going, Matt."

"Lock your doors from now on," admonished Matt. He had a stern look on his face. "You're more vulnerable out here than I'm comfortable with."

"I told her not to buy this house out in the woods," Linda jumped in. "And I know it's taking you officers forever to get out to the latest set of break-ins on this north side of town."

Steve took Linda's reference to the local criticism of the Mayfield police force head on. He even took a couple of steps away from the kitchen table and into the family room, so he could address her directly.

"I know our slow response time has been in the paper lately," Steve said. "I can assure you, ma'am, it's something we're working on overcoming. We've made a few changes and seen improvements already."

Linda slid to the side out from under Sophia while he spoke, rolled off the couch and got to her feet.

"Thank you, officer," she said. "Your assurances will help me sleep tonight. Although I'd feel better, Jenn, if you just come stay at my house, right near the center of town."

"Mom, I'm fine," Jenn replied.

"Just try to remember to lock your doors," Linda replied. "Write a note to yourself if you need to. You know, honey, a nighttime checklist."

Jenn just bit her tongue, unsure of how to handle her mom in that moment.

"Well, Jenn," said Steve, breaking the moment, walking over to shake Jenn's hand. "We're all set. We'll let you know if we discover anything from our examination of the iPad and the briefcase."

As Steve headed for the door, Matt stayed still and let them get ahead a few steps, out into the garage.

"Jenn," said Matt quietly, looking her right in the eye. He paused.

Jenn took a few steps toward Matt to hear him better, stopping just a couple of feet from him.

"I'm sorry we never got to have dinner last Saturday," he said softly. "I couldn't stay. How about next weekend we go out to dinner? Saturday night?"

Jenn was totally surprised. She couldn't figure this guy out. Hot, and then cold, and now hot again.

"Okay," she whispered back.

"I'll call you," Matt said and turned and walked out the door, closing it behind him.

Jenn turned back toward Linda, who had moved into the kitchen from the family room. "Jenn, what was he saying at the end there?" she asked.

"Oh, really nothing, Mom," responded Jenn.

"Well, I was wondering about the brother–sister connection between Doctor Tilman and P.T. Jane. Do you think the policemen have even figured that out? Should we tell them? Oh, and Jenn, that little conversation between the two of you, just now, sure didn't look like nothing to me."

CHAPTER 32

J enn was just pulling into the parking garage for work when she saw that Claire was calling.

"Hey, Claire."

"Did you sleep okay last night? Peter and I were worried about you. Any noises or trouble?"

"Nothing. I slept like a baby, or should I say like my mom does after she has morning wine."

Claire, Peter, and Jenn had laughed pretty hard the previous afternoon when Peter and Claire had returned to collect Sophia. They had chuckled over their mother's snoring while the police checked around her house.

"That's good," replied Claire. "Did you end up seeing Mark or Debbie at all yesterday?"

"You know, it's weird," said Jenn, pulling into a parking spot and turning off the ignition. The call switched from her hands-free car speaker back to the phone itself. Jenn grabbed her phone and put it up to her ear.

"Claire, are you there?"

"Yes, still here. Kiddies due any minute though. What did you say?"

"I was just realizing its weird Mark didn't come over and see why the police were at my house," Jenn said. "The last time a police car was at my house, he came over to see what was going on. Yesterday, there was no sign of Mark."

"Here they come, Jenn, my little Van Goghs."

Claire hung up and Jenn gathered her bundle of papers. She had tried to quickly find her old briefcase that morning on the way out the door, but no such luck. She finally grabbed a green recyclable grocery bag and stuffed the papers in it.

Jenn dug right into work, deep in thought, until her assistant Diana's knock on the office doorframe startled her.

"Hi Jenn, something new for all the lawyers," said Diana. In her hands was a box containing an Apple watch.

"What?" said Jenn. "An Apple watch?"

"Yes," said Diana. "All the lawyers are getting them. It's supposed to be all set up for you. Ready to wear. Here."

"Thank you," said Jenn, surprised by the unexpected gift. Diana turned and left Jenn's office. Jenn put on the watch. It wasn't as heavy a feel as it looked on peoples' wrists. She started to play with it a little. It was very clever and so easy to use. She would never have to dig in her purse for her phone again. *But wait*, thought Jenn. My iPhone that already felt like handcuffs, and I thought of it as a handcuff, and now, it is one. It's cuffed around my wrist literally. *Great*, thought Jenn.

She turned her attention back to her work, and did not stir until one of her fellow attorneys came by looking to see if she was ready to head up for the bragging lunch.

"Time for that show already?" asked Jenn.

"Yep. Another Monday in paradise," replied her friend.

At the meeting, Jenn's eyes glazed over and drifted toward the window and out to the cloudless, pale blue sky. She decided that the weekly luncheon was full of Grumpies today, no Happy, Bashful, or Sneezy, to be found. Not having much new business made them grumpy.

Although the same cast of characters sat around the table as last week, there was a downbeat atmosphere today. There was about as much discussion of vacation schedules and destinations as actual client-related work, but the tone still wasn't happy. It was more a resigned discussion of where things stood at the moment. The dwarfs were certainly not singing merrily on their way into the mine today.

Because she worked for both Jenn and a partner, Diana had access to a confidential distribution list, which showed how much each partner was projected to make in a given year. Diana would sometimes show the list to Jenn, and in recent years, David was slipping down the list. He used to be the top grossing land use attorney, but now he was behind four other partners. Jenn didn't think much of it in the moment Diana shared the memo. But now, seeing David's uneasy manner at the luncheon, while one of the other partners spoke of a new land use matter, Jenn could see it must have rattled him.

David said, "The Riverfront Landing project is forging ahead, despite the terrible murders that have occurred down in Mayfield." Jenn pulled her full attention to David. He continued, "With the passage of time, it appears the murders may be unrelated to the project and may be more reflective of an extramarital affair between the two murder victims. I believe Doctor Tilman's spouse is the prime suspect."

This statement shocked Jenn, for she had heard nothing of it from anyone in Mayfield and there was no indication of anything to this effect in any of the online articles or elsewhere.

David continued, "For those of you who don't know, Jenn lives in Mayfield, and her house was broken into over the weekend and her papers searched. There's been a string of break-ins in the north Mayfield area, and it may be unrelated to the Landing project as well."

Oh no, thought Jenn. She tried not to make a face. Why did that need to come up? She'd had to report the break-in to Ethan, the leader of the environmental practice group. Although David was the effective leader of both land use and environmental, and in a sense a step above Ethan, Jenn did not have it in her to call him. She started with Ethan because the three cases of papers being shuffled through were Ethan's clients. Ethan had in turn called the managing partner because someone unknown apparently viewed confidential legal documents.

Jenn had called Ethan yesterday after her mom had left, and based upon the limited exposure of documents, and the nature of the documents themselves, Ethan told Jenn that the plan was to call the three clients individually and explain the unusual event. The managing partner and Ethan were going to make the calls together and they would call her down for them if they needed her. Since she hadn't heard anything that morning, Jenn figured they were making the calls without her.

In the meeting, though, all eyes turned to her, and the questions started.

"You were robbed?" asked one associate. "Are you okay?"

"What did they take?" asked another associate.

"Nothing," Jenn responded. "They rifled my papers and broke my iPad. It's fine. I think it was someone interested in the Riverfront Landing project and thought I might have known more than I know, or thought I might have paperwork related to it.

"You need to get a dog," said Eric. "Dogs are great deterrents and you live alone in the woods."

Jenn didn't say anything. She certainly was not going to mention her pet trees. Or the dragonflies that kept her company and put on shows in the evenings.

Before Jenn could come up with what sounded like a normal response, she heard Stuart say, "An affair between the two victims. That's unusual. What's the scoop?"

Jenn breathed a sigh of relief that her personal choice to live alone in the woods was not going to remain the topic of conversation. Stuart probably had some interest in the murders, but it was nice that he generally stuck up for Jenn and picked up on the fact that she didn't like being the center of attention.

David said, "You know, I don't know all the details, but apparently Doctor Tilman and Dot Hutchinson had been having some kind of relationship and Doctor Tilman's wife did not like it. Doctor Tilman's wife is a geologist, and there is now some thought, since the victims were hit on their heads, that the weapon was a pickax, which, as you all know, is a common geologist's tool."

Jenn found her voice. "What? Where did you get that information?"

"I have some contacts in the Mayfield police department and they have been pretty open with me about the scope of their investigation because of the large nature of the Riverfront Landing project," replied David. "I'm not worried about the murders. I don't think they will stop our project, and it looks like the police are on their way to solving them fast."

"I haven't heard anything about this," said Jenn.

"Jenn, let's not waste the whole group's time on this," David answered. "Although you have some strong interest in what happened because of your ties to Mayfield, I doubt most of the group would like to hear about the police department's dissection of an extramarital affair."

Condescending ass, thought Jenn.

"I would," said Stuart. He must have had the same thought. Or else he was really interested in hearing about affairs. Stuart looked at David and held his gaze.

Silence.

Jenn opened her mouth to offer niceties and make the awkwardness go away, but then she stopped herself. Let's see what David does with this, she realized.

David raised his voice to its full boom and said, "Well Stuart and Jenn, we all can meet afterwards, if you want to hear all the nitty-gritty gossip about someone's affair."

As soon as Jenn heard the full breadth of David's voice, she knew a nerve had been struck. Something was afoot. *He raises his voice often when he is in the wrong*, thought Jenn. That's how he bullied or bossed those around him.

Jenn spent the remainder of the meeting trying to force her mind to remain on the meeting. She found it wandering to the murderers and wondering why both Dr. Tilman and Dot Hutchinson would end up dead. Jenn's mind was in the middle of wondering why salamander eggs were stuck in an ice cooler, if the whole thing was just about cheating spouses, when she tuned in enough to hear David say, "Meeting adjourned."

CHAPTER 33

S tuart caught Jenn's eye at the close of the meeting and signaled for her to wait so the rest of the room could clear out. David started to head out the door as well, but Stuart called him back. Stuart caught Ethan's eye, and Ethan, the alpha male of the environmental partners, stayed back as well.

Stuart sometimes rambled in his speech, as he had in his call to Jenn when she found the dead body, but today, as soon as the room was cleared, he went right to the heart of the matter.

"Spill, David. What's going on? No way those murders could be about an affair. And who do you know down there in the Mayfield police?"

David cleared his throat and his bellowing voice filled the conference room. "I'm quite close with Police Chief Scalini, and the state medical examiner has determined from the injuries that a pickax was used in both murders. Ingrid is a geology professor at New York University and leads geological expeditions with her students. Both of the Tilmans' residences have been searched, and more than one pickax was discovered at their summer residence in Mayfield. Although it's not clear who swung the pickax, it is clear that it was a pickax that did the damage."

Ethan and Stuart both looked surprised.

"Well, what about the salamander eggs Jenn found in the ice cooler?" asked Ethan. "What role do they have if the murder was about an affair?"

David replied, "Chief Scalini says they could have been placed there by anyone, and Jenn messed with the chain of evidence collection when she removed them from the scene and took them back to her house. Their presence near Doctor Tilman's body does not definitively mean that his murder was related to Riverfront Landing. Doctor Tilman himself could have put the eggs in the cooler for his own personal reasons, and could have been struck on the head while he was doing it."

"Wait, haven't the police determined that the murder took place somewhere else and Doctor Tilman's body was moved?" said Stuart.

Ethan and Stuart had obviously been following the murders pretty closely as well.

"I didn't see any blood around the cooler," added Jenn, "You'd think somebody would bleed a lot if struck with the pointy end of a pickax to the brain."

"Guys, guys, come on. I don't have all the answers. I have a conference call in five minutes," said David, looking at his watch. "I was just updating everyone on the investigation. I have to get back to my office."

David walked out the conference room door.

Ethan made a face.

"I know, Ethan, I'm thinking the same thing. Seems kind of fishy," said Stuart.

Jenn wasn't sure what they meant, so she decided to ask.

"You guys don't believe him?"

"Jenn," said Ethan, "we've known David a long time and David always gets his way. He is crafty and manipulative, and he lies, and I'm sorry, Jenn, but sometimes he cheats. We've seen some things over the years that we were not okay with and are not ethical in our minds, or how we want to practice law. There's a part of David that doesn't seem human, that doesn't seem to think of others or respect other people. I'm not implying or saying anything. I just don't feel like all the facts are adding up. But Jenn, you need to stay away from this whole thing from now on. Be careful."

"Jenn, get a dog, will you?" added Stuart. "Or better yet, borrow one for a while. We're just not sure what's going on down there, but something's afoot, and I'm not sure it's over."

CHAPTER 34

J enn stepped out of the elevator looking forward to the fresh air outside. It was already 8:30 p.m., as she had worked right through dinner, trying to make headway on a brief. Jenn was reflecting on Stuart's advice as she passed through the lobby toward the outside world. If she had a dog, given the hour, he probably would have peed somewhere inside the house by now.

There was still a bit of light in the sky. Late July brought a late sunset, and Jenn's eyes were drawn to the sky to see how much daylight was left. As she looked upwards at some pinkish clouds melting into a darkening sky, she heard, "Hey, Jenn. Have a minute?" It was David.

Shoot. Wish I had that dog. It would have been a good excuse to avoid this conversation. Perhaps, *My dog cannot make it past 9:00, I've got to go, can't have him wasting the couch.* No such luck.

"Sure," said Jenn.

"You know, Jenn, I felt today that the other partners believe I'm meddling in the murder investigation. I'm not. I'm just staying on top of the issue," David said. "I always stay on top of issues. I always take care of things." He stepped closer to her, and she resisted the temptation to back away. His voice lowered and slowed down, and he looked pained. "My whole life, Jenn,

I have had to stay on task, in charge, making sure that all goes as planned and as it's supposed to. I'm not sure anyone ever told you this, but my brother died when I was young. It's changed my whole life. He was two and I was seven. We were in the bath together." Jenn felt suddenly sad to hear of such a tragedy.

David continued in a whisper, like a confession, "I don't know what happened. I just know…I must not have been paying attention because he drowned. My mom told me a thousand times it wasn't my fault. She always says she shouldn't have left the room and put a seven-year-old in charge of a two-year-old. But inside myself, Jenn, I let him down. I let my brother die because I wasn't on top of it. So, yes, I've developed a relationship with Chief Scalini and I'm doing all I can to stay on top of this project." He finished with, "That's all, Jenn, that's why." David paused and looked Jenn in the eye.

How sad, thought Jenn. What a tough thing to live with. Jenn believed him. She saw pain, anguish, and even fear, fear of failing, in his eyes. Failing like he felt he failed his brother.

She responded from the heart. "I'm sorry, David. I never knew. That must have been so tough on you as a kid." She paused. "Look, I've tried to keep my ear to the ground down there in Mayfield, David. I heard you when you asked for help last week," said Jenn. "I just don't hear much because I spend all my time at the office. The one tidbit I've heard about is this crowdfunding site. Shelby Williams started a campaign to raise funds to preserve Riverfront Landing as open space. Apparently it's getting funded like crazy, and everyone in Mayfield is donating. You know how popular it is to be green and support the environment. I imagine the remaining leaders of Save Riverfront Landing, Robbie Hayden and Nat Harkins, are in on it, too. It is just that the funding site has Shelby's name on it."

"What's the name of the website?" asked David.

Oh, boy. He had not heard yet, and she had known since Friday. She must really want the project to fall through. She could have mentioned this on Friday, and now it was the end of Monday.

"Kickstarter," Jenn said. "I haven't checked it in a while, but last week, donations were apparently flying in."

"Thanks, Jenn," said David. "We'll check it out."

"Okay, have a good night," replied Jenn. She took about three steps toward the parking garage. Oh, the state archeologist. She hadn't mentioned the state archeologist to David. She could have told David that she now knew Christopher Collins had been on the site on a Sunday, and that he had been out to lunch the week of Dr. Tilman's murder with Nat Harkins, the leader of the opposition group.

Jenn thought about turning around and catching David, but she decided to stay her course. It could wait. She didn't even know what it meant anyway, and maybe David already knew. Jenn wondered if there were cairns at the site and if the state archeologist had been out to inspect them. Maybe Matt would know something about the state archeologist. Of course, to extract any information from him might be difficult, and might require her to get closer.

CHAPTER 35

◆

As Jenn drove through the parking lot adjacent to the baseball field, she saw that her family's cars were already there. It was one of those perfect summer evenings with both a low humidity and a slight breeze. Old maple trees lined the edge of the parking lot and shaded some of the cars. Jenn grabbed one of the remaining shady parking spots, and walked over to the spectator area to join her family. The game had already started. Her family was standing along the fence, just about in line with first base.

Sophia will be happy, thought Jenn. Her team, which was all in yellow T-shirts, was playing against the green team. As Jenn approached the field, she saw that Sophia's team was in the field, and the green team was at bat. She tried to distinguish Sophia from the other yellow players, and saw that all the players on the field had an adult standing a few feet from them. Sophia was a short stop. Peter was out there standing next to her, demonstrating a baseball stance, and encouraging Sophia to stop looking upwards, into the tops of the tall maple trees, which lined the parking lot.

"Hi, Jenn," said Claire, "Look, Sophia is taking after you. Her head's in the trees."

"Thanks. Hello to you, too, Claire," responded Jenn. "Hi, Mom."

Linda was standing along the baseball fence to the right of Claire. She turned and greeted Jenn.

"You know, I saw an article in the *New York Times* about how your generation is full of helicopter parents, constantly hovering over their children's every little homework project or interaction," Linda said. "When these kids get to college they can't function because their parents have taken care of every little thing for them. But this," she said, pointing her thumb toward the field, "gives the term 'helicopter parent' new meaning. They're literally hovering over their kids. For Pete's sake, can't they just let the kids be?"

"Too true," said Claire. "The culture we grew up in is totally different than the culture today. For example, at field day at my elementary school, there are no individual events. Each child is part of a team, and every team wins. I have a whole bunch of ribbons from my elementary years, which actually say, 'First Place,' and 'Second Place.' Guess that's not allowed anymore, all the kids have to feel good about themselves all the time, and ranking them would prevent the losers from feeling good."

"Ouch," said Jenn. "Since when are there losers in elementary school?"

"See," said Claire, "You've been brainwashed by politically-correct culture. If there is a race, some kids win and some kids lose. They are losers in that race. When we were kids that was okay. You would work harder, or practice more, and get 'them' the next time. Now everybody is a winner all the time. It undermines the concept of the work ethic."

"Speaking of work," said Linda, "How is it going, Jenn? Are you remembering to take care of yourself?"

Linda worried her daughter would fall into the same work-aholic trap as her father.

"Yes, Mom" said Jenn. "So, who is winning the game? Did I miss Sophia batting?"

"Jenn, did you not just hear my lecture?" Claire answered. "There is no winner in T-ball. Every game is a tie. And yes, you missed Sophia's first at bat, because every batter bats every inning."

"Did she get a hit?"

"Jenn!" said Claire. "Every player gets a hit. You stand up there and swing at that tee until you make contact and then every player stays on first, even if they get out. I find it to be the strangest thing!"

"Well, they look awfully cute out there," said Jenn, looking for the upside.

Jenn scanned the spectators and saw a few folks she knew from high school, including Dot Hutchinson's younger daughter Peg.

"Does Peg have a son or daughter playing?" asked Jenn.

"Yes. I don't recall her daughter's name, but she looks just like her mom," Claire said. "I'll point her out when she's at bat."

"Is that Sophia's first love at bat? Is that Freddy?" asked Jenn.

"Yes, it is," said Claire, acknowledging the crush.

Freddy was in his green T-ball shirt frantically swinging at the ball. On about the fourth swing, he made contact and the ball rolled out toward the pitcher.

"Run!" yelled Robbie, Freddy's father.

Freddy began the run to first base. He started out following the white baseline, but at some point he must have veered off it, because next thing Jenn knew he was standing in front of her on the other side of the fence surrounding the field.

"Hi," said Freddy, looking up at Jenn and Claire. "You're Sophia's aunt. Thanks for that special drink the other day. Could I come back to your house again someday?" he asked, staring directly into Jenn's eyes.

"FREDDY! RUN TO FIRST BASE!!!!" yelled Robbie "FREDDY, RUN!"

"Sure, sweetie," said Jenn, "but I think you better hop along over to first base before you get in trouble with your dad."

Robbie was storming toward Freddy with that crazed, intense look in his eye. "We're playing baseball here. It is not a social event!"

He glared at Jenn as though she had committed a mortal sin and intentionally pulled Freddy from the baseline.

"Did you call him over to you?" he demanded of Jenn. "WE are playing baseball here! He needs to get on first base!"

Freddy turned and ran to the base.

"Hey, stop glaring at Jenn as though she did anything wrong," Claire said. "This is not the World Series."

Robbie had already stormed off. He heard Claire because he turned and gave her an angry glare.

Linda said, "My, my, my, temper, temper. That was almost like the kind of temper tantrum your brother used to have, Jenn."

Jenn smiled at Linda's attempt to lighten the situation.

"Mom, it's okay. You don't have to smooth it over. That guy hates me, just because I work for Shipward & Waters."

"That guy would get a lot more done in his life, if he just channeled all that temper into something productive," replied Linda. "Hopefully, he'll figure it out one day."

"Oh, here's Peg's daughter at bat," said Claire. The next batter was a small blonde girl. Jenn could hear from the other team's cheers that her name was Charlie.

The rest of the game passed uneventfully. As they were wrapping up and congratulating Sophia on her game, Peg appeared alone with an expectant look on her face.

"Claire," she began, "I was hoping I could talk to you and Jenn for a few minutes."

"Sure, sure. Goodnight, Linda," began Claire, giving her mother-in-law a hug. "Peter, could you take Sophia to the car?"

"What's up?"

"I heard around town that you found a bucket of salamander eggs behind P.T. Jane's and it's connected with Doctor Tilman's murder," said Peg. "I'm afraid to go to the police, but there is some strange stuff at my mom's house. I want to show you, but I don't want her name smeared in the newspapers as a murderer."

Peg looked very upset and her face was turning red as she spoke.

"Peg, it's okay. We won't tell anyone. You can tell us what you're worried about," Jenn assured her.

"You may recall that my mom was always into gardening and the gardening club in town and stuff," said Peg. "Well, she usually stuck to roses and perennials, but she had all these weird fern plants and some sedges growing in pots outside her gardening shed. I didn't think much of them, except that maybe it was a new gardening style to grow swamp type plants. But then, in her little gardening shed, there were a couple of aquariums partially filled with water, and when I looked closer, salamanders.

"I cannot understand why my mom would have pet salamanders in her gardening shed," Peg said. "It bothers me because she never told me about it, and because now I hear that Doctor Tilman may have had some salamanders with him when he died, or found near to where his body was found."

"You haven't told the police?" asked Claire.

"Well, I don't know for sure why she had them, and I really don't want folks to think she had anything to do with Doctor Tilman's murder. I have some pictures of what she has," Peg responded. "I had been thinking about calling Jenn out of the blue and asking her about it because she had found Doctor Tilman's body. But it felt kind of weird to call you, Jenn, since we don't see each other regularly. I also know that it's your law firm involved in the whole thing. So when I saw you here tonight, I decided it was a sign that I should tell you." Peg looked down to her phone and quickly pulled up the photos. She handed the phone to Jenn.

The first photo showed what appeared to be five glass fish tanks lined up on a shelf, with some water and vegetation in each of them. The tanks were different sizes, and Jenn started to zoom in on the tanks individually. Toward the bottom of the photos were fifteen to twenty orange clay pots with various plants of different sizes. Jenn looked carefully over the different pots for plant species she could recognize.

"There is a second photo too," said Peg.

Jenn flicked to the left to view the second photo. It was taken from farther away, showing basically the same five tanks lined up on a shelf, with the plants lined up below them.

"Look at the last photo. It's some notes that were at the end of the shelf in the greenhouse," explained Peg.

Jenn flicked to the third photo. In cursive writing it was entitled, Operation Mincemeat. Below the title was a vertical list of maybe nine plants: Sword fern, cinnamon fern, creeping spikerush, iris-leaved rush, ovate spikerush, coyote thistle, common downingia, annual hair grass, mannagrass. She looked up to see Peg looking at her expectantly.

"I'm glad you told us. It might be significant," said Jenn. "Those plants you mentioned grow in and around vernal pools, as well as in and around swamps. I cannot imagine why your mom would keep salamanders in her gardening shed. Are they still alive? Did you look up what type they are?"

Peter walked back over to the three women and said, "I'm going to take Sophia home. She's hungry and so am I. Jenn, will you drive Claire home?"

"Of course," replied Jenn.

Peter turned and headed back toward his car.

"Well, here is the funny thing, you guys," continued Peg. "I didn't look it up, but I heard the ones found by Doctor Tilman were blue spotted salamanders, and some of these have blue spots. But other ones that are in the water have yellow splotches, and some have no spots at all but are around the same size. I thought they were just tanks of leaves and water, but after I heard what you had found, Jenn, I started digging around in the tanks and there are salamanders in there. At least there were last week when I looked.

"Oh boy, I bet I should have fed them," Peg realized. "They might not even be alive now. I'm sorry. With everything with my mom's passing, and my horses and Charlie, I didn't even think of it."

"Jenn, Jenn, what do you think?" said Claire.

Jenn was staring at the ground, apparently thinking, but possibly entering into some kind of trance.

"Jenn," tried Claire again. "I can see the wheels are churning in that brain of yours. What should we do?"

"Oh boy, the issues are so complex. Let's start with the legal analysis that I can't offer you attorney client privilege on," Jenn replied. "Because of my firm, I have a conflict of interest. Peg, you need to go to the police. You need to report what you found to them. Claire and I could have our friend in the Mayfield force meet us all at your mom's house now.

"Second, I think even the yellow splotchy ones are blue spotted salamanders as well," Jenn continued. "I read that larvae might have yellow splotches that eventually turn blue when they reach land. Eggs take about a month to hatch, so maybe they were eggs that hatched. Blue spotted salamanders are one of the weirdest organisms on earth. It's like they're an all-female species or something, and they borrow the sperm from other species to reproduce. So, I think—"

"Jenn, we don't need a history of the species here," snapped Claire. "Should we call Officer Matt?"

"Sure, sure, let's do that now. Maybe he could meet you or us at your mom's gardening shed. All I was going to say is that your mom may have needed the non-spotted ones to breed the blue spotted ones. But yes, the *real* question is why did your mom have salamanders at all?"

"Unlock your phone and give it to me," demanded Claire. Jenn complied, still somewhat dumbstruck that Dot Hutchinson must have planted an endangered species at Riverfront Landing. Why else would she have blue spotted salamanders? She certainly didn't seem like the criminal or zealous type, but wasn't planting endangered species taking the whole zealot preservation pursuit to a new level?

"Hey, Officer Matt. It's Claire, Jenn's sister-in-law. I have Dot Hutchinson's daughter here with me and she has something to report about her mother's gardening shed. Her name is Peg."

Claire handed Peg the cell phone. As Jenn listened to Claire's side of the conversation, she saw that Robbie, Freddy's dad, was holding a rake and was standing near them on the baseball field. He must be raking the infield dirt on the baseball diamond to clean up after the game. Robbie had been looking at them, Jenn realized, and he put his head down and turned slightly, as she looked up.

Jenn couldn't see his eyes as they were masked by his green coaching baseball cap. She had been so surprised by Peg's news that she didn't even notice Robbie's presence. She wondered how close he had been and how much he had heard? If Dot Hutchinson had been planting salamanders at Riverfront Landing, wouldn't Robbie be in on it, too? Or was she acting alone? Hard to picture a sophisticated, luncheon lady out planting salamanders in what was basically a pond.

"Do you want us to go with you?" asked Claire, as Peg ended the call.

"The officer said he knew my mom and where she lived, and that he had liked her a lot. I can go meet him alone," said Peg. "I'm just worried about my sister, Allison. What if she is mad? I didn't have a chance to talk to her about this yet, and she worries so about appearances."

"You know, Peg," said Jenn in a soft voice. "We really don't know anything yet, and even if your mom committed some kind of crime if she planted salamander eggs at the vernal pool at Riverfront Landing, half the folks in town are such tree huggers and in support of preserving the property as open space that they probably won't judge her harshly."

Jenn wasn't sure if this was true or not, but she wanted Peg to report her findings. To hide the salamanders from the police would be wrong. Of that, Jenn was sure.

CHAPTER 36

◆

Date night. Tonight was Jenn's long awaited date with Matt. She'd planned to go get some work done at the office, and then then get back in time for a fun evening. So far, Matt had not cancelled their plans for a Saturday night outing, but had actually texted to confirm. He was going to pick her up at six p.m.

After helping Peg last night, Jenn had driven Claire home. They made one spontaneous stop on the way. Claire had talked Jenn into eating dinner at Dunville's. Not surprisingly, Claire's friend was bartending again, and Claire's wine was on the house. They did not stay late this time, nor did they make any stops around town to unearth salamander eggs like last time.

Claire had joked that maybe the murderer was a zealot who didn't think salamanders should be taken out of the wild. After all, both Dr. Tilman and Dot Hutchinson had salamanders out of their natural state. Claire teased that the murderer was Mother Earth herself, or some other kind of earthly spirit and natural protector of the vernal pool species.

Jenn was having trouble joking about the murders after their interaction with Dot's daughter, Peg, and the reality of someone's life being abruptly ended with things left unsaid and tasks left undone. Jenn was thinking about that, about what that might be like for Peg to live with, and about what that was like for Jenn to live with after Alex's death, or her father's death. After dropping Claire at home, Jenn had started seriously pondering the likely suspects, wanting to make things right by solving the mystery of Dot's death.

On her drive to work, Jenn continued to ponder the murders. Surely her brain should be focused on her law cases, but it seemed like the Mayfield police were not making much ground in arresting the murderer. There were no new articles in the press or online about the murders. Were the police, was Detective Moffitt, even trying? Or were they too busy dealing with summer parking and food truck issues?

She wondered if the police had searched Dot's home after her body was found behind Starbucks. Wouldn't that be standard? Wouldn't the search have included the gardening shed? She tried to think back a couple of weeks to the timing of events. The search of Dot's house was before she had presented them with the painter's bucket of salamander eggs. But after they got the bucket, shouldn't the police have gone back and looked at the tanks in her gardening shed more closely? But then again, maybe they hadn't even gone in the shed, or didn't remember the tanks.

Supposedly, Ingrid, Dr. Tilman's wife, was the prime suspect because of an affair between Dr. Tilman and Dot. So maybe the salamander eggs and the salamanders were just something they had worked on together, but were not directly related to their murders. If they were lovers and shared a common goal of not having the property developed, then it made sense for them to work together to plant salamanders at the Landing. Peg didn't say anything about an affair, or about a close relationship between her mom and Dr. Tilman. And Jenn sure wasn't going to mention it. It certainly didn't seem like it was her place to tell Peg that the police suspected her mother of an extramarital affair.

It was hard to picture some kind of coldhearted killer living in bucolic Mayfield. And the thought of Ingrid brandishing a pickax was hard to accept. Jenn didn't know the woman at all, but didn't believe she was the murderer. Geology professors, like the stereotypical professor, were usually calm souls. Jenn couldn't recall having met a professor that was the highly strung, tightly wound type that could snap and start murdering folks.

Jenn's other suspects, in her mind, were the three other leaders of the citizens group: Nat Harkins, Robbie Hayden, and Shelby Williams. They all had motive to stop the development, and Robbie Hayden certainly had a crazed look in his eye. If it wasn't a murder for love and jealousy, Robbie sure seemed like the one most likely to snap. Anger management issues, if extreme, certainly could lead to murder. She didn't know Nat at all, except from his photo in the paper, and the middle school science teacher, Shelby, was probably sane and not capable of such a vicious act.

But then again, the idea that the murder motive was love, or really jealousy, made the most logical sense. Anyone who was murdering folks over the development would probably not need to kill both Dr. Tilman and Dot Hutchinson. If the murderer was for the development, he or she could have just murdered Dot, and if the murderer was against the development, he or she could have just murdered Dr. Tilman. The only person who would maybe want them both dead was Ingrid, the police's primary suspect. So, yes, letting the police do their work, and sticking to lawyering was probably the best bet.

Once in the office, Jenn plowed into her work. If she had to spend the day stuck inside, she might as well get as much done as possible. She felt someone's presence in her small office as she was reading. She looked up, expecting to see one of the partners, but it was Charlie Martins looking down at her. He was in his late fifties, tall and broad shouldered, with a receding hairline and a stern expression. Jenn had never met him, but recognized him. She had seen him at the firm before for meetings, and she had seen his photo in the local paper in connection with articles about Riverfront Landing. He must have a meeting with David today, which was unusual for a Saturday but not unheard of. But why was he standing in her office sternly looking at her?

"So, you're the Shipward & Waters attorney who lives in Mayfield? Jenn Bowdoin?" he asked, reaching forward and extending his hand. "I'm Charlie Martins. Riverfront Landing is my bailiwick. We almost have it into the construction phase. David mentioned you have been a help to him with your knowledge of the town and its people. I understand you grew up there. My kids might be about your age."

Jenn stood and shook hands with Martins, and told him her graduation year from high school. She was more than four years ahead of his kids in high school and did not know them.

"You know I've been made out to be some sort of bad guy in town, because I want to build houses. I'm not a bad guy," Martins said. "Folks would be better served to examine the motives of Nat Harkins, the leader of that supposed citizen's group. He may be charismatic and handsome, but not as good-natured as folks think. For him, it's not even about the land. Sounds crazy, but it's about me personally. Nat has all these folks believing he's a tree hugger and he's not. Tree huggers don't come as investment managers. You ever met one who was? When the market tanked back in 2008, Nat had a lot of money in one of my real estate investment companies and it plummeted. He hasn't forgiven me and he did lose money. But I didn't break any laws or do anything wrong. It was just a bad turn of events, and now he is seeking revenge and interfering in this endeavor of mine and acting like the pied piper against development."

Jenn wasn't sure how to respond or what to say. It was unusual for a client to track down an attorney in his or her office. She waited. It seemed like there was more to the story.

"I'm meeting with David today. He believes in my project. You have to go with your gut in life, Jenn, and my gut is that Riverfront Landing is going to make me a fortune," Martins said. "I'm like the Jimmy Buffet song, and it's no secret in town, I've made a fortune and lost it all. Now, I'm making it again, only this time, it will be larger and better, and I'll keep it for my grandchildren."

Martins had an odd smile on his face, like he was trying to charm her into believing him, or convince himself. But then the smile slowly faded and the sternness returned, and with it came anger. Intense anger. Directed at Jenn. She unconsciously took a step back to create space between them.

"You're against Riverfront Landing," he declared. "You don't want the homes built. I can see it on your face."

While she was busy reading his face, she must have forgotten to mask her own. Yikes. She was against the development in her gut. How did she get here, and how could she get out of this one?

"Oh no. I don't have a position. I'm not against it. I'm just helping David keep a pulse on the community," replied Jenn. This was weird. She was suddenly the recipient of his rage and she really hadn't done anything.

"I don't believe you." Martins seethed. "What good are you if you don't believe in the project?"

"It's not about whether I believe in the project." Jenn backed fully behind her desk, creating at least four feet of space between them. She raised her voice, trying to sound authoritative and lawyerly. "Look, I appreciate you sharing your thoughts on Nat Harkins. I've noticed myself that he doesn't fit the typical mold for a leader of a citizen's group against a development. I had no idea about the history between you two, but it is interesting. He certainly has a following of folks, but that doesn't mean he's leading them in the right direction." She hoped criticizing Nat would get the focus of the anger off of herself.

It worked. "Yes, I guess he's a good money manager in a small town and knows most of the folks in it," Martins said. "I'm sure he managed all or some of Dot's money, and maybe manages Robbie and Shelby's money as well. Although I doubt they have much, or at least not the kind of wealth the Hutchinsons have."

Jenn hadn't thought about this possible tie among the leaders of the citizen's group or about their financial resources.

"There you are," came David's loud voice from the hallway. "I'd thought I'd lost my favorite client. Come on, Charlie; let's go finish our meeting. Hello, Jenn."

"Well, Jenn, I'm glad to speak with you some," Martins said. "Thank you for anything you have done to help the Riverfront Landing project. I am still excited about it and I wish it had not been so sullied by Nat Harkins. If he weren't so personally vindictive, I doubt folks would have gotten worked up about preserving the property at all. He really knows how to push people's buttons."

"It was nice to meet you as well," said Jenn, sitting back down in her desk chair. *Wow*, thought Jenn, *suspect number four.* Her Nancy Drew list of suspects had just grown. One more person who appeared rational, but who could probably slip over the edge into zealotry.

So, if it wasn't murder for love, and Ingrid didn't do it, she now had one zealot in favor of the development, Charlie Martins, and three zealots against the project, Robbie, Shelby, and Nat. And then there were her neighbors, she couldn't forget them. Debbie and Mark, who definitely fell at least into the odd category, but probably not really the suspect category. And someone had broken into her house. Who on her growing suspect list had done that?

Jenn realized that if she were actually any good at the mystery solving, her suspect list would be shrinking rather than growing. Instead, now she had so many suspects she couldn't keep track of them all. It made her head spin. Plus, some of her theories were so tenuous, the murderer could have just as likely been the barista at Starbucks. The one who served Dot her last latte, or cappuccino, or whatever ridiculous drink Dot drank. Maybe Dot was as picky about her latte as Claire. With at least six suspects and no rational theories, Jenn decided she should just stick with the law.

CHAPTER 37

———◆———

L arge maps. Sometimes Jenn needed to analyze and review them to make sure she understood the nuances of a project. She picked up the rolled plans and headed to a conference room, so she could unroll the plans on the conference table. The room held a table surrounded by six chairs, and a side table that still had a few rolled up maps from someone else's project lingering on it.

The corner of the room housed a fake green ficus tree, which Jenn glanced at quickly. She didn't get the whole plastic plant thing, but guessed it was big business to make fake green plants that looked real and required no care. It was just that real plants didn't require much care, anyway, and actually improved air quality and grew and changed. In the many years she had sat in this conference room, the fake ficus plant in the corner remained the same. She and the others who entered the room had changed and aged, learned and loved, and grown, but the fake plant was exactly the same as it had been the day Jenn had her interview with the firm in this room. In fact, she realized the fake ficus might be sitting in this room long after she was six feet under. It would probably decompose long after she had.

Focus, thought Jenn. *I am really not stuck in this small room to ponder my own short existence.* She pulled out the plans to examine them. She liked examining plans. Green or sustainable buildings were the new trend in construction projects—new buildings designed and constructed in a manner that was environmentally responsible and resource-efficient. Plans would contain large notations about construction practices or techniques that would reduce the impact of a new building on the environment and human health.

The drawings in front of Jenn were for a small shopping center with one big box store and a few smaller supporting stores. As Jenn started to look at some of the wetland issues, she realized she hadn't brought any scrap paper with her and turned to the sideboard to grab some paper from its drawers.

Jenn saw that the keystone on the plan lying on the sideboard said "Mayfield." She unrolled the plans to see them from the right side up and saw that the full title of the plans, which were about twenty pages total, was "Riverfront Landing–Phase II." *Phase II,* thought Jenn. Phase II. What is Phase II?

She unrolled the plans, and although they were wider than the sideboard, she propped them up with her thighs and started looking. Phase II was a marina, with about 350 slots and all the accompanying buildings, including a pool and clubhouse. What did this mean for the overall development and Charlie Martins, who had just tracked her down in her office? The Hammonasset River at Riverfront Landing was uncharacteristically wide and there was even an existing bay-like area into which the marina would fit.

This is crazy, she thought. It was a clever piecemeal approach to take an already profitable development and turn it into a fortune. For the permitting, especially for the coastal permitting required by the state environmental agency, it was very clever to stagger the original housing request from this marina request. Although the developer would have to go back for a second coastal permit, now that the area was no longer pristine, it just seemed like a logical incremental step.

Jenn let her mind wander for a moment to a fact her father had mentioned to her years ago. The town of Mayfield had no natural harbor, as most of the wealthier Connecticut shoreline towns did. Although there were some smaller marinas up the river of the proposed marina location, the marinas were on the opposite side of the river, and were therefore located in the next town, rather than Mayfield. This would be the only marina in Mayfield, and really was set in a natural harbor created by the Hammonasset River curving to the east, right before the river flowed into Long Island Sound.

Jenn leafed through the twenty pages, which broke the project down into its components with a specific plan or two for each outbuilding, such as off season boat storage buildings, a ship's shop, shower, and bathroom facilities for the boaters, as well as a restaurant, parking areas, a pool and club house, and the actual marina slips themselves, including post locations for the docks.

Taking in the level of plan details, Jenn realized the engineering was already completed. Charlie Martins was probably just waiting for the final local permitting approval of Phase I before submitting these Phase II plans to the state to start its permitting. It looked like there was even space for some small commercial spots that could be rented. Jenn was examining these small commercial spots, wondering what they were for— possibly some small shops the boaters could patronize while at the marina—when she heard her name.

"Jenn." It was David. He was standing in the doorway.

"Hey," she answered. She backed away from the sideboard, and let the plans roll themselves closed.

"You found the plans I left in here?" asked David.

"Uh, yeah. I was just checking them out," she said. No use trying to lie. She had clearly been caught in the act. He could have been standing there watching her for a while; she was so absorbed in taking in Phase II.

"A marina in Mayfield will be fabulous, don't you think?" David said.

"Ye-a," replied Jenn. It was not the question she expected. "A marina," was all she could get out.

"It's the one thing the town is really missing," David said excitedly, "and even those in charge recognize that it would bring value to the community."

"What's the latest on the murders? Have they arrested Ingrid Tilman?" asked Jenn. If she asked him some questions, maybe he wouldn't fish for information from her.

David didn't answer. He had crossed the room and grabbed the Phase II plans. He moved the plans off the sideboard to the conference table and unrolled them. He didn't seem to have heard her.

"Did they arrest Ingrid Tilman?" Jenn asked again.

"Jenn, did you see how the river so naturally widens, and the coastal wetlands form a natural harbor or protective cove of the spot for the marina?" David unrolled the plans, stuck his phone on the left corner of the plans to keep them from unrolling.

"Here hold this," David said, motioning for Jenn to hold down the top right and bottom right corners of the plans. He held the left lower corner down with his left hand.

"Even the state agency would be hard pressed to suggest we're hurting coastal resources," he continued. "The natural cove is perfect and no dredging will be needed. We just need to sink some pilings, which really is a minimal natural disturbance. I was elated when I saw how well a marina fit the natural river's topography here. We had a bathymetry test done and even the water heights are perfect for landing boats here and creating a hub for recreational boat owners."

David motioned to the top page of the plans, which contained a drawing of the entire Phase II project.

"Here, look at the marina part in detail," he said, flipping the pages of the plans over to a more detailed view of just the boat slips.

Jenn readjusted her hands to help hold the right page of the plans open. She did as David instructed and examined the layout of the boating slips.

"I couldn't believe it had sat as an airfield for so many decades and no one ever thought to put a marina here. It was actually Charlie's idea. He envisioned it years ago and it was one of his motivators in purchasing this property. This layout is a conservative 350 slots, and as you can see," said David motioning with his hands, "there really is even room for more in this area. Imagine if Mayfield could catch the summer boating crowd that Block Island or even Martha's Vineyard has. It would be great for the town."

Jenn could see he was really excited, but she wanted to call him out a little. How was it acceptable to pull a bait and switch on all the citizens of Mayfield? First they were expected to accept the proposed 127 residential units. But now folks, that's not all, we are going to create a marina, with all the accompanying buildings, maybe even some commercial units for shopping for the boat owners and their families.

David hadn't stopped talking. "You know, Jenn, the coastal approval by the state agency even has some good language in it, which will support this Phase II. I couldn't believe it when I saw the openings in the first approval."

Jenn looked up from the plans. David's face was serious, although the tone of his voice was happy. She let go of the plans and backed away a few feet to create more personal space. They had been pretty close, leaning over the plans together.

David was talking about what exact land use approval was needed. How there was no category in the Mayfield town zoning ordinance for a marina, but that they would propose a new regulation and corresponding use. He was rambling on, and Jenn tried to listen. But when she stepped back, she started to think again about the murders. During the car ride to work, she had thought of David as one of her possible suspects. But how could she have thought that? He appeared to be such a reasoned attorney, navigating his way through the ins and outs of the land use requirements needed to meet his client's objective.

David stopped talking and was looking at Jenn like she was supposed to say something. She had no idea what, though, because she had tuned him out.

"Wow," she said. She thought that might fit the bill.

"Yes, isn't it great?" David was smiling, so Jenn smiled back.

"Yes, thank you for showing me the plans," she said.

David started rolling the plans back up. "You know it's too bad those murders had any association with the project at all, but they're behind us now. I'm very excited about this Phase II, and really, I can't wait to start working on the approvals we'll need for it. We just have to get those last few out of local wetlands and zoning. They should come soon, though."

David held the rolled up plans in his right hand now, and secured them with two rubber bands he pulled from his trouser pocket. "Hey, I did check out that crowdfunding site, but the chances that they will raise the $15 million needed to purchase the property is very unlikely," he said, "and even at that price, I'm not sure Charlie would be willing to sell it."

David headed toward the door, and as he passed Jenn, he affectionately tapped her on the shoulder with the plans. "Basically, I think opposition is dying down. Ouch, bad pun there," he called as he headed out the door. "But you know what I mean."

Jenn began to sit down, but remembered she still had no scrap paper, and wandered back over to the sideboard to get some.

CHAPTER 38

O n the commute home, Jenn returned a call that had come in earlier from Claire.

"Hey, Jenn," answered Claire. "I called because I heard about a new dating app that is perfect for you. It's called 'The Grade' and it checks the grammar in the texts from whoever you're dating. Of course, you have to actually put yourself out there and have someone texting you for it to check their grammar. Thought you could check Officer Matt's texts. You guys must be texting by now."

"Why do I need to check a date's grammar?" asked Jenn.

"Come on, Jenn, I know you lawyer types. You're all about nitpicking, site checking, and editing your writing. Isn't that whole law review thing about who can have the best writing with the least typos?"

"Well, no, it's about who has the best legal analysis, but it does need to be polished writing."

"Whatever, anyway," said Claire. "You have to download the app and see what kind of grade Officer Matt gets. Apparently, folks are turned off or turned on by good grammar."

"Claire, don't you have anything to worry about besides my dating life?" asked Jenn, somewhat annoyed by Claire's antics.

"Isn't it time to start worrying about Sophia's instead? Isn't she old enough? I mean, for God's sake, she could have a crush on a murderer's son."

"Oh, Freddy is a sweet boy," Claire answered. "And really, Jenn, a five-year-old dating? What are you, a supporter of pageant moms and their kin, pimping out a young girl's sexuality? I'll worry about Sophia's dating when its time, but right now, tell me what kind of texts does Officer Matt send?"

"You know I can't text and tell," replied Jenn. "You really need something to occupy your time better."

Sometimes Jenn was jealous of Claire's carefree lifestyle. Jenn had tons of responsibilities and stressors that came with practicing law. She carried her client's needs on her shoulders, whereas Claire didn't stress out over a child learning the difference between primary and secondary colors.

"Well, okay, but Jenn," said Claire, "can you wear a skirt tonight and not those old ratty jeans? You really have great legs, and it would be good to show them off."

"Thanks, Mom," replied Jenn. "Do you have any suggestions about what I should order?"

"As a matter of fact—" started Claire.

"Listen, can you just let me be?" asked Jenn.

"Fine, but heels, Jenn. Wear heels. And no talking about the trees," replied Claire, hanging up.

Jenn realized as she continued her drive home that she didn't want to fess up to Claire about the dearth of texts so far from Officer Matt. Claire seemed to think this was going to be a modern relationship with every thought, feeling, and experience of the day shared by text. Matt didn't seem to be in on Claire's texting plan, because Jenn barely heard a thing from him.

CHAPTER 39

C afé Chambord had the most unusual florae in it. Jenn tried not to stare at it too much. She could only identify one of the six plants potted together in a massive display at the center of the room. There was some philodendron, but she was unfamiliar with the other plants.

The restaurant was small with about twenty candlelit tables in one dim room with unusual small, silver pendent lights hanging from the ceiling. Scattered at intervals around the room were also three large pots containing the largest dahlias Jenn had ever seen. Each pot contained three dahlias and their large decorative orange blooms were each about eleven to twelve inches across. The blooms were so large and appeared to weigh so much that staking the stems was required.

Jenn extended her neck a tad and leaned right to get a better view of the plastic support, which surrounded each stalk and was barely visible from her vantage point at their table. As she stretched her neck a little farther, noticing that the plastic support surrounding the stems was green, not the clear plastic supports more typically used in florist shops, she realized Matt was calling her name.

"Jenn, Jenn, are you okay? Is there something you're looking at?" Matt turned his head to follow her gaze to its focal point. "The flowers?"

Oh no, realized Jenn. *I'm not supposed to talk about trees. Does that include the flowers?*

She shifted her gaze to Matt and saw that he was looking right at her now. She looked back at him and fessed up. "The flowers. I was just admiring those really large and beautiful dahlias in this lovely restaurant."

"I noticed them too. Unusually large, and so heavy. I saw that the stems needed to be supported. But really, the loveliest part of what's in this restaurant is you." He smiled at her sheepishly.

Jenn smiled back, but then felt her cheeks starting to burn with the somewhat cheesy compliment, so she looked down and tried to change the subject.

"So, how are you?" she asked. "Last week at my house you seemed upset about something when you left. I hope I didn't upset you."

"No, no. Just the opposite, in fact. I felt like I talked about myself too much. What have you been up to lately? Anything fun?"

Oh boy, there was not a ton of fun in her life. It's what she needed more of. Work, lots of work. Jenn ran through possible topics in her head. Her garden? Probably off limits. Her pet trees? Definitely not a topic Claire would approve of. Her trip to Dunville's on Friday night with Claire? Kind of uneventful. She thought again about talking about her work, but frankly it made her own eyes glaze over.

"I guess the most fun thing I've done lately is watch my niece's T-ball game," she answered. "The kids were adorable and most of them at age five had absolutely no idea what was going on. The parents tried to get them to pay attention to the game."

"Did you play T-ball when you were little?" Matt asked. They exchanged innocuous stories from their childhood throughout dinner. Matt was very charming and quick-witted, but there was also a kind of darkness to him Jenn couldn't figure out.

As the waiter was asking if they wanted dessert, Jenn noticed Robbie enter the restaurant with a woman, who must have been his wife. Robbie did not seem to notice Jenn, but a second couple followed him in, and Jenn recognized Shelby Williams as well, with a man, who was probably her husband.

"Those are some of the folks opposing Riverfront Landing, right?" asked Matt. As Jenn turned to look back at him, she saw Matt was gesturing by tilting his head toward Robbie's table.

"Yes. I recognize Robbie Hayden and Shelby Williams. I'm guessing those are their spouses," Jenn said.

The restaurant was busy now. Since they had arrived, dinner guests had trickled in, and the volume of noise had increased substantially. As Jenn glanced around the crowd, she realized it looked like the restaurant was catching the New York summer tourist crowd. There were many New Yorkers who had summer homes in Mayfield and came out just for weekends or parts of the summer. Jenn realized there were an awful lot of folks she didn't recognize.

Jenn cleared her throat and raised her voice so Matt could hear her. "What kind of tasks are you working on lately at work?" she asked him.

"The typical summer stuff, I guess. Parking issues, ticketing New Yorkers for speeding or driving too aggressively, a couple of fender bender accidents," Matt said. "I'll be honest though, I'm personally mostly still focused on solving those murders, but that's not to be repeated. It's not my job, or my role to work on them. I'm just having trouble with the whole situation. I think it's because I knew and liked Mrs. Hutchinson."

Wait a second, thought Jenn. *Previously Matt had been so tight lipped, but now he is willing to have a conversation about the murders?* Jenn just smiled at him expectantly, hoping he would continue.

"Have you heard the latest theory? The love triangle?" Matt asked. "The idea that Doctor Tilman's wife, a mild-mannered geology professor, would murder first her own husband, and then his lover?"

Jenn nodded but didn't speak, hoping he would continue.

"If you were an angry wife, why would you murder your husband first, and then wait a few days and murder his lover?" Matt inquired. "It's the order of the murders, and the timing that has me troubled. Double murders in love triangles happen in the heat of the moment and start with the lover being killed first. They don't start with the spouse turning up dead. I don't think there are statistics on this or anything, but it deviates from common sense."

He stopped. Jenn waited again just in case there was more.

"I'm really not in a position to talk about the Mayfield police force. You know how new I am to this job, and you can't change jobs too frequently as a police officer, particularly when you've been somewhere less than a year. But, and I guess all I can say at this point, is that I do have some concerns, and the concerns extend into whether the murder investigation has been properly handled."

Jenn waited. Matt didn't speak. The waiter had brought their desserts and Matt pushed his berry tart around his plate.

"Jenn, here is what I want to say to you in a very upfront manner and it's why I didn't stay with you the other evening.

I've been separated from my wife for over a year, but technically I'm still married," Matt confessed. "I'm getting divorced. We were married for three years, when we decided to separate. We have no children. We just grew apart. It's why I moved up here from Westport, to start over. It was both my partner in the Westport police force, and my partner at home that I needed a change from. But now that I'm here, I am finding it hard to fit in with this police force. There are dynamics within it that I don't understand and I'm not sure I'm going to be able to stay at this job. Once I'm a year in, I may move on, but I don't know where that will be."

Matt paused and looked up from his tart. "What's worse, Jenn, I'm really attracted to you. You are gorgeous. I know it's crazy to say this to you so soon, but I can tell already how I feel. I really like you, Jenn. Everything about you."

Jenn was taken aback. No one had ever said anything like that to her. They had barely spent any time together. How could he know so soon?

"I don't want to start something with you I can't finish and I don't know if I'm able to handle a relationship with you right now," continued Matt. "I'm not sure I'm ready for something serious. I will be officially divorced soon, but I'm not yet. I don't know if I'm going to have to change jobs and move again, and I can tell already that you and I together…are a serious thing."

"Shelby! Shelby! That is not true!" It was Robbie Hayden at full volume. All twenty patrons of the restaurant turned their heads to see Robbie standing at his seat. Even in the dim light, his face was an angry red.

"That's not true! I never did that!" he shouted in a rage.

"Robbie. Robbie. Sit down. You're making a scene." It was apparently Robbie's wife, or Shelby. Jenn couldn't see their faces.

She saw Robbie sit back down and Jenn turned back to face Matt. He was still watching the other table. The restaurant had gone silent. The background hum of conversation went silent.

"Matt," said Jenn. He did not turn back toward her. "Matt?" He was still watching the other table. His body was tense and his face like a concrete mask.

Jenn turned back to look at the other table and saw Robbie stand up and say, "Let's go, Kathy! We don't need to stay here and listen to lies!" Robbie reached for his wife's shoulder and prodded her toward the door of the restaurant.

Jenn heard Matt sigh and watched him finally turn back to look at her and let his taut body relax.

She smiled at him. She heard individual conversations start back up at other tables and the general hum of conversations resume.

"Well, that was something," said Matt. "That kind of rage is really dangerous."

"His intensity scares me. It makes me think he is capable of murder," Jenn admitted. "And he hates me. I sometimes wonder if he's who broke into my house."

"Oh boy, he's my prime suspect. There is something going on with that citizen's group and I can't put my finger on it," said Matt. "I've seen Ingrid Tilman in the station. She looks like she's about as capable of murder as you are. Really, doesn't seem like she could hurt a fly. And she's really short, I noticed, like maybe just five feet without her shoes. So, I'm not sure about the angle of hitting someone in the back of the head with her pickax. Why do you think it was Robbie that broke into your house?"

"He's been to my neighborhood, to a party next door at Mark and Debbie's house," Jenn said. "You know she's involved in the Save Riverfront Landing group as well. While the party was going on, his son wandered over to my yard to see if my niece Sophia lived with me. I spent some time with his son Freddy, gave him a fancy lemonade, and Robbie came into my driveway looking for him. The guy hates me. He stares at me as if I'm the devil incarnate because I work at Shipward & Waters and my firm represents the developers. Guess it's not a big leap for me to think he would channel all that rage into an impulsive act of murder."

"Do you ever think maybe it was one impulsive act of murder and one copycat murder, made to look like the first one?" Matt asked.

"I did think of that once, but it's even harder to accept two crazy murderers in Mayfield, instead of just one," Jenn answered. "Seems like you and I both struggle with the fact that it doesn't make sense to murder suspects who are apparently on different sides of an issue. You know, one an expert for the developers, one a leader of the citizens opposing it. And although I hadn't thought of it, you're right about what you said earlier, that it doesn't fit the stereotype murder for passion. Why murder the husband first and then the lover a few days later? So, two different murderers does make some sense here."

Matt leaned in a little toward Jenn and stared deeply into her eyes. "Jenn, I hate to break it to you, but there are hundreds of crazy folks living in Mayfield. Not just two. People are crazy. Most folks are good, but the stresses of their lives can cause them to do crazy things. On a given day anyone can cross that line from reality to loony tunes. Usually it's not as dramatic a line as murder, but smaller lines. The lying, cheating, stealing lines get crossed by folks all the time."

Jenn stared back into Matt's eyes. He was really so handsome. Did he just tell her he was married? Was he saying he was crazy? Wait a second; did he just break up with her before they had ever really started going out?

Matt leaned in even farther. "You know, one of the reasons I'm worried about the Mayfield police force is that Chief Scalini has been really involved in the murder investigation," he said. "Detective Moffitt, who is in charge of it, admitted to me that Chief Scalini is adamant that Ingrid is the murderer. He's not sure why the chief is pressuring him to wrap up the murder, but he definitely is. You know there is a state police detective assigned to the case, as well, and he is the one with the overall authority. But the state police detective has done nothing, and is apparently accepting of the chief's determination that Ingrid Tilman is the murderer." Jenn's mind was spinning from this revelation. How could they really think Ingrid Tilman was the murderer?

Matt continued, "Detective Moffitt and I are speculating that the chief may be under political pressure from First Selectman Fritz Robinson. Folks want to believe their police force is competent and puts the bad guys behind bars. All those news articles lately make the Mayfield police seem like they're the bad guys. Fritz probably understands that folks don't want to live, or especially vacation, where there are murders. It doesn't help them escape from the realities of life the way a vacation town should."

Matt paused. "It's really hard to work within a police force where you're not sure who you can trust. I feel like I can trust you to keep my confidence on this. I'm just not sure about this police force. My gut on Chief Scalini is that he is a man on the take. I'm not sure who he's taking from, but the prostitution issue, the competency issues, I just don't think this is the force for me. But I have to bide my time, Jenn, and look for another force where I will fit in better."

Jenn tried to take it all in. It was hard to work somewhere if you did not respect the folks you worked with. This guy had a lot on his plate, which was about the only conclusion she could reach at the moment.

Jenn felt a presence at the side of the table and looked up to see Shelby Williams staring down at them.

"Hello, Matt. Hey, Jenn, I wish you could get your firm to just back off this project," Shelby said. "My Kickstarter request has taken off, and there will be no need to develop Riverfront Landing. I'll get to whatever amount I need. I'm not going to back off this. We're not going to back off this. We need to start somewhere, in terms of accepting responsibility for our environmental footprint on this planet, and there is no reason to take the last pristine spot of coastal land all the way between Boston and New York and turn it into another fancy subdivision."

Shelby took a breath and continued. "The coastline is not just for the rich, who can afford half-a-million-dollar- or million-dollar homes. The shoreline is for everyone to be able to access and enjoy, and preserving this as open space will only increase public access for all the people, not just the rich people."

Oh no, thought Jenn. *Folks are really worked up tonight.* She started to think about a response.

Before she got out any words, "Oh, hey, Mrs. Williams, is it?" said Matt.

He didn't wait for an answer. "I'm Officer Matt Banks with the Mayfield police force, and I might have to give you a citation for interrupting my romantic date with Ms. Bowdoin here. This restaurant isn't cheap and I'm really trying to convince her I'm worthy of her love. I know preserving land is important, but aren't affairs of the heart also worthy of some respect? The Riverfront Landing issue will be here Monday morning, but the moonlight, the candles, and those large orange dahlias which help set the mood, the nice buzz from our fine wine; it will all be gone. How about we call it a truce until then?"

Shelby seemed surprised. It was not the response she expected. She had been gearing up for a battle.

Jenn thought for a second and joined in.

"You know, Shelby, truth is, I haven't had a date with a man this handsome and well, dashing, really, in forever. How about a little sisterhood support here? Plus, Shelby, you look awfully fine this evening in that lovely sweater or poncho, I guess, is what it really is. How about letting all the business of Riverfront Landing wait until Monday, and we all just enjoy our Saturday night?"

Maybe not the best proposal, but Jenn hoped it would make Shelby realize that she was far too zealous.

"Oh, this sweater," said Shelby looking down at it. "Why, thank you." It was a dark brown poncho with a Western-like zigzag pattern on it. Shelby looked back up at them both and appeared to take in the fact that they were on a date, looking down at the almost empty bottle of wine and the candle on the table, and even turning to glance at the large orange dahlia. She looked back at Officer Matt's face and then at Jenn. She pulled her purse off her shoulder and started to unzip it. Then she stopped and looked up at Jenn again, apparently changing her mind about taking anything out of it.

"Jenn, I put a call in to Charlie Martins this afternoon. You know I've got almost nine million dollars raised," Shelby said. "I can't believe it. The funds just keep pouring in. Folks seem to get it nowadays. The beauty of this earth is for everyone to share, and the coastline is one of the most beautiful parts. It's time for Charlie and me to start talking numbers. I'm just really happy about it. I had no idea the people of Mayfield would put their money where their mouth is on this issue. It is remarkable that Riverfront Landing, with its picturesque Hammonasset River opening to the sound, is still as pristine as it was hundreds of years ago, and with enough funding it will remain open space forever."

Shelby realized how long she'd been talking. "I'll let you be tonight. I'm sorry to interrupt your date. I just never realized how much difference folks banding together could really make."

Shelby headed toward the door and Jenn looked back at Matt. "Boy, that was intense and odd all at the same time," Jenn opined. She didn't know how to get back to what they had been talking about. His marriage, his work situation, his earlier declaration of a connection between them.

While Shelby had been speaking, the waiter had left the bill in the standard black folder. Matt quickly picked it up, put some cash in it, and said, "Come on, let's go."

He dropped Jenn off at her house, begging off coming in. She kissed him lightly on the cheek. She wasn't sure what was going on in his head. She thought he was great. Maybe she should tell him that, but during the car ride home he had been quiet and distant. Shelby's interruption had broken the mood and it wasn't recoverable. Jenn didn't know what to make of it.

"You know life never goes as expected," was all she could think to say as she started to open the car door. "It isn't a bad thing. It's what makes it interesting. Thank you for a lovely dinner. I had a great time."

She smiled, and could see Matt's eyes as the car light turned on.

"I did too," he said, smiling back at her.

CHAPTER 40

s Jenn walked into her kitchen, she noticed the microwave clock only said 9:36 p.m. *Strange*, she thought. And there was still a touch of light in the sky with the sun setting so late in July. The day had been beautiful, but she felt like she missed it, between being stuck inside at work for the bulk of it, and spending the evening inside Café Chambord.

Jenn felt like she had been gone for hours, but it really wasn't that late. Matt had said something about getting all the Sunday shifts as a newbie on the force, so maybe he had work tomorrow morning. Maybe that's why he didn't want to come in. Or maybe she had food in her teeth that had scared him away. She swiped her tongue over her teeth. Who knew? Overall the date was great. But she couldn't tell what happened at the end there, why Matt would get so cold after Shelby came over to the table. Maybe he was the moody type. She would have to wait and see.

Jenn sat down in her family room and kicked off her shoes. She thought about getting some drinks, maybe a nightcap of red wine, some water, and she also had a craving for a nice cold glass of milk. She poured herself the three drinks and returned to the couch to ponder her day.

The discovered plans for Phase II of Riverfront Landing were a shocking development. David was awfully far along with the plans, and it was odd he had never once mentioned this Phase II concept at their weekly business luncheons. From a developer's perspective, the marina, and all its accoutrements, was a fantastic further use of the property. The plans had been interesting to Jenn because from Hammonasset Park, and from Larry's Bagels, you really couldn't see the river's curve that sheltered the proposed marina from the currents and waves of the Sound, and the predominantly western wind.

It truly was a great natural spot to harbor boats. Marinas along the shoreline of rivers didn't always have such protection from the elements. The aerial plans for the original development focused on the inland portions of the property and Jenn had never seen an aerial view of the river itself, and the way a natural harbor existed.

Where the end of the river curved east, its western coastline was part of Hammonasset Park, and any maps she had seen to date had ended at the property line, and didn't include that land, which was part of the Park and owned by the state. She had never seen a full aerial image before. The day she had walked to the river's edge from the beach at Hammonasset Park she became aware of the curve, but she hadn't gotten the full extent of the sheltered landing area.

Maybe what Shelby said had affected Matt's mood. She said that Riverfront Landing had remained untouched for hundreds of years. Hundreds of years. Suddenly Jenn got it.

Dear Lord. It was right before her eyes! Sometimes she was so dense. The property had been an airport, hence Riverfront Landing. She could still recall the airport sign she drove by in her childhood. The sign had a picture of a plane along with the name. But it wasn't called Riverfront Landing because of the planes. It was a landing area on the riverbank, like the Pilgrim's landing on Plymouth Rock.

The state archeologist had been at the site. He'd been there because the property was probably significant for American Indians or maybe even early settlers. Why hadn't she realized that? Why hadn't David mentioned the state archeologist at the weekly luncheon, or even today? Did David know he was examining the site? Jenn stood up. She went for the iPad. She typed in "landing."

"A landing is an instance of coming or bringing something to land, either from the air or from water."

Jenn couldn't believe that she, along with the whole town, had missed it. Maybe the other misnomer in town, the Surf Club, prevented folks from looking for what was right in front of them. The property's name had been in the shadow, and was now in the light.

There was some sort of organization Jenn recalled, which still honored or celebrated the American Indians that had lived at Hammonasset. She'd seen notices about it in the local paper, but had never thought about it, and had never been interested. Yes, the internet revealed that there was a Supporters of Hammonasset organization, which held a biannual festival to honor Native American culture and tradition.

And, of course Hammonasset was an obvious American Indian name. She learned that it meant, "Where we dig holes in the ground." *Funny name*, thought Jenn. But apparently it was a reference to the fact that the Hammonasset tribe of eastern woodland Indians had an agricultural way of life and grew corn, beans, and squash. The property had changed hands a number of times during the town's earlier years, but was set aside as public park land as early as 1918.

The state archeologist must have found something of significance at Riverfront Landing or why else would he have been there twice on a weekend? Plus, it must be something the citizen group knew about, specifically Nat Harkins, since he was having lunch with Dr. Tilman the day before he was murdered. David, the attorney for the project, and probably Charlie Martins, might have no idea about an archeological find.

Jenn thought back to the coastal permit that Charlie and David would have had to obtain from the state environmental agency. She knew from other applications that there was a question on the application about whether there was any archeological significance to the site. She guessed that Hammonasset Park held the significant sites used for farming. But a settlement along the river's edge at the landing would have been much more protected than any of the coastline in the park itself, which was directly on Long Island Sound.

Maybe there were archeologically significant findings over near where the marina would go, Jenn pondered. *But how would the state archeologist know about the marina plans, unless Nat Harkins knew about the marina plans as well?* Jenn's head was spinning. The only thing she knew for certain was that she had no answers.

CHAPTER 41

S he stared silently at her iPad for a moment. There was something else she had seen recently that she wanted to look up. Something she had seen on a piece of paper. What would it have been? She racked her brain for a second and then it came to her. It was the photo of Dot Hutchinson's paper. The title, she struggled to recall. It had made no sense. Finally it came to her: "Operation Mincemeat." Mincemeat was a type of pie her mom still made at Thanksgiving. It was called mincemeat but it was not really made of meat. It was made of fruit. Why would a list of plants be labeled, "Operation Mincemeat?" So strange. Jenn typed "operation mincemeat" into the iPad.

The results shocked her. They had nothing to do with Thanksgiving or mincemeat. The name referenced a deception used during World War II to get the enemy to move its troops, to make the invasion of Sicily go smoother. Jenn had never heard of it. A British dead man was dressed up to be a pretend British officer, and fictitious letters between two real British generals were planted in his pockets. The body was taken by submarine and released close to the shore of Spain. The letters stated that the allies would not invade Sicily, but rather would invade Greece and Sardinia. Troop reinforcements were made by the

Germans and Italians, but based upon the falsely planted information, no troop reinforcements at Sicily. Forensic examination later showed that the fake letters were read and relied upon by the Germans and Italians, and it was accepted that Sicily was liberated more quickly and fewer soldier losses occurred, probably as a result of this complex British deception.

Jenn's head spun. Why would Dot Hutchinson label the plants "Operation Mincemeat?" The logic was not linear and clear to Jenn. The plants were a deception. How? Why?

Suddenly, Jenn heard loud knocking at her back door. Was it Matt? It had seemed early to end a Saturday night date, and Jenn felt some kind of connection between them. She started across the family room, glancing at the clock on her way through the kitchen. 10:16. Well, he certainly waited a while to come back.

"Jenn?" came a voice from her back door. "Hey, Jenn, are you still up? I see your lights on and need some help." It was Mark, not Matt. Jenn was immediately disappointed. How strange. Mark never actually knocked at her door. He just seemed to linger in his garden and catch her when she was going outside.

"Everything okay?" called Jenn as she opened the door.

CHAPTER 42

◆

"**N**o," replied Mark. "Debbie isn't back yet. She went to meet someone, and although I'm not certain, I think she went to the Riverfront Landing."

"What? Why would she go down there on a Saturday night? What's going on?" Jenn asked him.

Mark looked stressed out. His face was contorted and he was agitated. At least he was fully dressed in casual clothing and not half in work clothing like he was the last time he seemed out of sorts. He came right into her kitchen and leaned on the counter, palms down. He hung his head as he spoke.

"Debbie went out three hours ago. She texted that she was meeting someone, but she didn't say where and she didn't tell me more. I know it had to do with Riverfront Landing. Her notes are on her pad on the coffee table from a conversation she had. It said '8 p.m. Riverfront Landing.'"

"I take it she's not answering her cell?" said Jenn.

"No, of course not. It was the first thing I tried. I texted her, too. Now I know there are spots down there at the park beach where the reception is iffy. We've been down there. But I wanted to ask you to come down with me. I could call the police, but I think they would think I'm overreacting. It's just with all these murders in town, I'm worried. It's not like her. I know she's a bear, but she means well. She was just born angry inside and takes it out on everyone around her. I was just pulling out and I know you know the property from your work. I thought maybe you could help me."

Mark needed help. *Of course*, thought Jenn, and she grabbed some sneakers, a lightweight jacket, and her phone. They headed out the door. Mark's car was in her driveway. She walked around to the passenger side of the vehicle and glanced up at Romeo and Juliet. Their outlines were visible against the starry night. In the darkness, the trees looked beautiful. You couldn't see the orange cankers or distinguish the branches, which held dead leaves. They still seemed strong and powerful, ready for anything. Jenn glanced around the full sky, looking for the moon, but didn't see it. Maybe it was still low on the horizon.

Mark paused at his open door and said, "Let's go, Jenn."

Jenn could see his troubled face in the glow of the car's inside light. She grabbed the passenger door, opened it, and climbed in. Mark backed out of her driveway and proceeded quickly toward the Landing.

Jenn glanced at Mark's profile. He gripped both sides of the steering wheel, in exactly the position driving students were told to put their hands. One at ten o'clock, as if the wheel were a clock's face, and one at two o'clock. She could see his right eye in the dashboard light and it looked strained on the road before them.

"What's really going on, Mark? What are you afraid of?" asked Jenn. "You are way too worried for your concern to be that she has a flat tire or her car broke down. What role does Debbie have in all of this? I take it Debbie really was at the property that early morning when Dot spotted her. And you know I saw her there, too. What was she doing that she didn't want to be spotted? Besides trespassing of course."

"I'm not certain. And what I think, I can't say," Mark replied. "It could get her in big trouble and even though I hate her, I love her, too."

What kind of answer was that? thought Jenn. She saw the moon out the window. It was a half-moon just about rising in the east. She was about to pester him with another question, when she realized a very specific question might help him share with her.

"What exactly was Debbie doing at Riverfront Landing when Dot spotted her?" Jenn asked.

"The iPad at our house has a history of websites viewed that are all about Indian artifacts and the Hammonasset tribe in particular," Mark said. "She must be connected with the state archeologist. I think she must have met him at the property a couple of times. I don't know if that's who she went to meet tonight or why they would need to meet on a Saturday night, but she is definitely mixed up in all of this. She's been so withdrawn. I can't even get her to get angry at me, even when I do stupid things around the house, which would normally set her off."

Oh boy, thought Jenn. Their dysfunctional relationship was certainly evident in that statement. Mark was upset because he couldn't even get his wife's anger as a form of attention.

"I've been thinking that she switched sides and wanted the properties developed for her realty business," said Mark. "That would make sense in that it would give us more money. She always wants what we can't afford. The house isn't nice enough. We need this or that new furniture. We don't go on exotic vacations. Why can't we have a boat? How will we pay for our only daughter's wedding, or graduate school? She goes on and on and on."

He took a breath.

"I know my career as a scientist is disappointing to her. I'm uncomfortable saying this out loud," admitted Mark, "but it doesn't seem like she would care about the greater good and whether all individuals, as opposed to just wealthy individuals, have access to the Riverfront Landing property. It never seemed to fit the Debbie I know."

Jenn's brain was churning. "Does she know the developer Charlie Martins?" she spewed out. "Maybe she made a deal with him to infiltrate the citizen's group? You're right that she doesn't fit with its other members, who seem to be more philanthropic. At least Dot certainly was, and so is Shelby Williams, being a middle school science teacher. I guess Robbie Hayden, the engineer, although crazy angry, is convincing as a father of three young boys, who would like more field space in town. Nat Harkins is the leader of the group, though I've never understood his motivation or amorphous statements against the project. But now I know he has it out for Charlie Martins. Charlie told me himself that he lost a bunch of Nat's money and Nat hates him for it."

Dear Lord. Why did she say that last part? Hadn't Charlie Martins told her that earlier today, thinking there was an attorney client privilege that existed between them? The day had been way too long already.

"Jenn, I don't know," said Mark. "Debbie is smart and savvy, duplicitous and deceitful, maybe. She certainly deceived me into marrying her. I thought she was a sweet, kind and patient woman. You know, she gets herself into trouble sometimes, and I have to bail her out. I don't know if it is a personality disorder or what, but sometimes her relationships with others break down and she needs help extricating herself from situations."

Jenn turned to look at Mark. She couldn't see his face very well in the car's darkness, but to the extent she could see, he looked really sad.

"Is she capable of murder, Mark?" asked Jenn.

"I just don't know anymore, Jenn. I just don't know."

They reached the turn for Riverfront Landing, and with the streetlights from Route 1, Jenn could see that the gate across the dirt road was open.

"Well, it looks like someone is here," was all Jenn could think to say. Mark turned the car onto the entrance road, and into the unknown.

CHAPTER 43

Jenn was hesitant. It was trespassing. Even if she was helping out a neighbor and friend, she wasn't sure she could talk her way out of this one if the police arrived. They already were a little suspicious of her, from her peripheral involvement in finding Dr. Tilman's corpse and the salamander eggs.

The dirt road led about a quarter mile into the property and ended in a dirt parking lot, which could hold about twenty cars. It held just one car tonight though, Debbie's Lexus.

"She's here," said Mark.

Immediately east of the parking lot was an old airport building. Actually, the first building was the office or management area, and then beyond the first smaller building were two large airplane hangars. Jenn had never been down here. She had driven by the "Riverfront Landing" airport sign thousands of times in her childhood, but her mother and father had never, ever turned down the lane to see what was there.

To the south of the parking lot was an open grassy area for about a quarter mile, which Jenn guessed was one of the old runways, and then beyond that was an oval shaped wooded area with old deciduous trees. The wooded area was dark, but Jenn had seen it in the distance and knew it was there from when she looked north to the property from Hammonasset Park. To the west of the parking lot was more grassy area, which was an older runway space, and further west of the property was a small modular home neighborhood.

Mark pulled his sedan up next to Debbie's car. He jumped out and walked around the front of his car to the driver side door of Debbie's car.

Simultaneously, Jenn opened the passenger door of Mark's car, climbed out, and walked toward the rear of Debbie's Lexus, to get out of Mark's way. Mark tried the door and it was unlocked.

He leaned in and reported, "Her purse is here, and her cell phone. Strange. Why would she go walking alone at night on the property?"

"Is her phone locked? Do you know her passcode?" asked Jenn. "We could see who called or texted her recently."

"I might," replied Mark. "Let's see." He was holding Debbie's phone and trying different possible passcodes. "Nothing." With the car door open, Jenn could see Mark's face and he looked frustrated. "I think she changed her passcode. I knew it a month ago or so," he said, adding, "It's weird that there's only one car here. Why would she be the only one here if her note said Riverfront Landing at eight o'clock?"

"Well, what would make sense?" asked Jenn.

"There must be someone else here. She wouldn't come down alone on a Saturday night. The other person must be parked somewhere else," said Mark.

"But who is the other person? The developer Charlie Martins, Nat Harkins, the head of the citizen's group, or maybe Christopher Collins, the state archeologist? She met him before." Jenn wondered out loud. "And why would they need to meet on a Saturday night? What's the rush?"

"I'm going to go looking for her," Mark said. "My bet is she's out there somewhere. Come on. Let's look around the old buildings."

Jenn hesitated and didn't move.

"Come on, Jenn. Let's go. I need help."

He needed her. Jenn turned and started walking across the dirt parking lot toward the buildings. She thought about using her phone as a flashlight, but she could see well enough in the moonlight. The sky was clear and the stars were visible. She didn't stop to look at them though, but tried instead to focus on the path in front of her. With her back to Mark, she suddenly thought, *what am I doing?* Why was she down here in the dark trespassing, just because Mark asked for her help? For all she knew Mark could be the murderer—Matt thought he might be obsessed with her, stalking her. It was strange how Mark seemed to watch her comings and goings. How he could easily have been the one to break, well, walk into her home and go through her work stuff and iPad. He'd just readily admitted he'd gone through Debbie's iPad.

Matt had made a couple of suspicious comments about Mark. Was Matt warding off another suitor, or was he joking? Mark seemed so harmless, like a puppy dog, really, always trotting back to Debbie, no matter how many times she kicked him.

Jenn glanced over her shoulder at Mark. He was about five steps behind. She could tell he was looking at her, but in the moonlight and at about a five-foot distance, she could not quite make out his eyes.

"I hope she's okay," he whispered quietly, almost to himself. Jenn turned back around to see where she was going and felt reassured. *Mark is like a puppy who just wants to find his owner,* she thought. *He's lost without someone to boss him around.*

About seventy-five feet from the edge of the parking lot, there was a worn path through the grass that led up to the first building. Jenn walked along the path, suddenly thinking she had reached tick heaven. The grasses had grown to almost three feet high on either side of the path. The property hadn't been open as an airport in three or maybe four years now, while Charlie Martins was trying to get it developed.

Jenn reached the cement stoop in front of the building. She paused for Mark to catch up. The lights were all off. She could see into the building through the large glass windows at its front, but she couldn't see into the whole interior because there were a couple of smaller doors at its rear. Yet it seemed pretty unlikely that Debbie was inside.

"Is it open?" asked Mark.

Jenn stepped up and tried the door. "Locked. I really don't think she is in there, Mark. Maybe just her car is here and she went somewhere with someone else in their car." Jenn leaned in and peered through the glass door. Toward the rear of the room she could see what looked like the kind of a counter that would be in a larger airport.

"But her purse and her phone, Jenn," Mark said nervously. "They're in her car. She must be on the property. She would take them with her if she went somewhere else. Let's look at the next two buildings."

Jenn stepped back down and waited for Mark to lead them, but he gestured for her to lead, so she started on the next grass path, which headed toward the second building. Now the path was narrower and less worn. Jenn paused and thought about the fact that she didn't want to be here trespassing, and she didn't want to check the other buildings, and she certainly didn't want to lead. She thought maybe it was time for her to stop letting other people take advantage of her and to think about what she wanted. She paused.

"Jenn?" said Mark.

"You lead, Mark, I don't want to." She turned to face him and moved to the side of the narrow path so he could pass. "I probably should just wait in the car. We're trespassing and I could get into all sorts of trouble for this."

"Okay," said Mark, and walked past her.

"It's complicated, Mark, because my firm represents Riverfront Landing. I don't know the possible repercussions of me being out here tonight," Jenn said to Mark's back, as he was continuing down the path. Jenn still followed though. She did not turn back to the parking lot.

They reached the second building, which was an old-fashioned airplane hangar. It would have housed about four or five small, two or four passenger planes. Jenn guessed it dated back to the 1940s or so. It had cinderblock walls, and the only windows were over ten feet above the ground. Jenn could see in the dim moonlight that some of the windows were broken. The large wooden doors the airplanes would have gone through were pulled closed. The path Mark and Jenn were on led to a smaller door to the left of the large doors. The large entry doors were on the shorter end of the rectangular-shaped hanger.

Mark stepped onto the stoop and tried the door. It had an old circular doorknob. Mark turned it gently. Locked.

"I guess we try the third building," said Jenn.

She paused and Mark took the lead again. The third building was a newer airplane hangar and larger than the second. Jenn had no idea how many airplanes would have fit inside, but it looked almost as large as a football field. It was also cinderblock and the path led up to its shorter side, to a normal-sized door. It was strange to Jenn that there was no pavement leading out of either hanger, and as she looked around, she could see that there was no pavement anywhere. You could tell that in the past the grass had all been kept short and simply driven over by the planes traveling back and forth to the runways. She knew from the map that two different runways crossed the property, and their use depended on wind direction. Jenn wondered what it must have been like as an airport.

A gunshot sounded from the far side of the third building. Mark whipped around, and yelled, "Debbie?" He started to run past Jenn. She grabbed his shirt with her left hand to settle him. Jenn put her right hand to her mouth to gesture quiet with her index finger. Mark brushed her hand off his shirt.

She whispered, "Mark, be rational. It's probably not the best idea to go running toward a gunshot in the night while we're trespassing, and there's a murderer in town."

"Okay, Jenn, I'll be careful." He continued down the path.

Jenn stood still for a moment and thought. This couldn't be good. She pulled out her phone. Calling the police would be an admission she was trespassing. But then again, no one was hunting at eleven p.m. on a Saturday night in the dark. At least not hunting animals.

She heard another gunshot and glanced away from her phone to see Mark fall to the ground about fifty feet in front of her. Oh God. Did he fall? No, no. He'd been shot.

Jenn dropped to the ground as well. She could detect movement. There was someone out there. She needed to get off the path. The hanger was probably locked. Into the grass was the only option. She slid her phone into the back pocket of her jeans and started crawling in the grass. But there was no cover; the grass wasn't tall enough. In the wooded area to the south, she could hide and have a moment to call the police. It was about 100 feet away through the tall grass.

She could hear someone coming up the path from Mark's direction. The low army crawl she was doing, was too slow. She had no choice; she stood and sprinted toward the wooded area. The tall grass was difficult to run through, but her adrenaline had her heart pounding and it felt as though she was moving like the wind.

Jenn heard another gun shot. She started slowing down to look, but then realized it was probably directed at her. The woods were getting closer. She sprinted even faster and broke through the bushes and undergrowth at the wooded glen's edges. She felt a sting Ouch. Thorns. Probably raspberry bushes.

As the thorns scratched her arms, Jenn leapt through the undergrowth and sprinted behind one of the larger deciduous trees. She paused for a second and looked around in the dark. It was harder to see in here where the tree canopy blocked some of the moonlight. The wooded grove was small. There were only about fifty taller trees. Jenn needed somewhere to hide. She thought whoever had fired those shots was chasing her now. She had no idea if Mark was dead or not. She started running through the trees, speeding up into a full sprint. It was difficult to see, but she put her arms in front of her and hoped for the best.

Jenn's heart was pounding and her breathing was ragged. She was about 100 feet into the woods, when her left sneaker landed in water. She could feel it seep into her left sock and her other foot slid out from under her. She fell, landing on her back. She reached down to try to catch herself and felt water and leaves. But the back of her head hit the ground and she blinked, looking straight up into the trees. She was lying in a pool of water about three inches deep. Her hands had slowed her down, but her head still hurt some and she felt disoriented.

What was she doing? This was crazy. She felt something sticky, smooth, and weird under her right hand. Plastic. She turned to her side and looked. Black plastic. Her fall had pushed away a covering of old leaves revealing black plastic. She rolled to her side and pushed more leaves and dirt away and saw that the plastic extended over a large area. She grabbed at a fold and lifted. It bucked, creating a hump, dispersing more leaves. The plastic was preventing the standing water from seeping into the ground, creating a pond. This was the vernal pool, she realized. It was fake. Man-made. A fake vernal pool. With fake plant species added to make it look real. In the dark, she could see ferns and sedges. The whole little ecosystem, the whole vernal pool, was fake. Crazy.

Jenn reached for her phone. It was wet. She ripped at the double layer waterproof case, hoping it worked. She typed in her passcode and then dialed 911.

"911. Please state your location." It was a woman's voice.

"I'm at Riverfront Landing. In the back of the property. In the tall trees. I think there's someone out here shooting people," she said in a steady voice. She stood as she spoke and started moving toward the south, away from the gunshots.

"Jenn!" someone yelled. It was a male voice. He didn't sound that far away. Jenn paused behind a larger tree. She had no way of knowing how far away he was. But she needed to hide. Was it Charlie Martins? It was his property and he seemed so strange at the office earlier that day. *He's going to be mad I'm on his property*, Jenn thought.

"Jenn!" Angrier this time. Wait, was it Robbie Hayden? It sounded angry like Robbie. Intensely angry. Or could it be Matt? Was the person here to help her or hurt her?

"Jenn." She heard her name again. "Jenn." In a loud whisper this time. Not angry. Hold on. It was David. She recognized his voice. "Are you okay? There's someone with a gun over by the hangers. Have you been shot?"

"Hello? Are you okay? State your name. Please stay on the line." Jenn could hear the 911 operator in her ear. She paused for a brief second and was about to answer David. David running around in the grasslands, and now the woods at night with a gun, shooting people? Or David out at the property, caught off guard by the commotion and coming to help? She wasn't sure.

Jenn turned away from David's voice and saw that there was nowhere to go. There were just a few small trees, some brush and bushes, and then the open beach between her and the Hammonasset River. She could see the river in the moonlight and realized there was nowhere to hide if she left the cover of the deciduous trees.

Jenn pulled her phone away from her ear, turned up the ringer volume and at the same time repeated herself. "Help. I'm at Riverfront Landing. There's a killer out here with a gun. Come quick. On the south end of the property."

Jenn turned up the volume on the side of her phone and stuck it on one of the branches of the tree at about shoulder level, and sprinted to the west. She ran as fast as she could. Twenty feet, fifty feet, seventy-five feet. She dodged the larger trees and tried to stay along the southern edge of the wooded area. She saw that there was nowhere to go west of the property, either. The two-foot-tall grasses spread out for hundreds of feet before the neighboring modular home community, and she didn't have enough of a lead to make it through before the murderer caught up with her. It was a small island of deciduous trees surrounded by grasslands. So, instead of running out in the open grassland, she eyed the trees.

There were two large enough for her to climb. She avoided the bigger, older tree, and went for the smaller one. The lowest branch was chest high, but by putting her arms around the branch and her feet on the trunk, she was able to pull herself onto the tree. She kept climbing. She could hear someone coming now.

She risked the light of her Apple watch. She dialed her iPhone number and hoped it would ring. She wasn't sure. Could you call an iPhone from an Apple watch? She had to try something. After a moment, she heard the iPhone ringing. Both quietly on her wrist and loudly from about 100 feet to the east, where she had left it on the tree. She could hear someone walking or running through the leaves and underbrush. She wasn't sure if they were coming toward her or heading back toward the phone. She thought the sounds of footsteps might be fading. Going back toward the phone. But ugh. She wasn't thinking clearly. Now she was stuck twenty feet up in a tree. She might have been able to make it through the grasslands if she had waited for the phone to distract him.

Jenn had no choice. She couldn't get down in time now to make it across the grassland. She climbed a little higher and tried to find the best spot in the tree to hide from someone looking up from the ground. She calmed herself and attempted to still her ragged breathing. She remembered reading about the Mayfield police department's slow response getting to robberies on the north end of town. How much time would she have to wait for them to come? She wasn't even sure they were coming. What if they hadn't heard her? What if she was stuck out here with a killer stalking her? What if the 911 operator hadn't even heard her location? She remembered the bad cell coverage the day she called Matt from the other side of the river.

Jenn took in a long deep breath. She needed to control her brain. It was out of control, churning out one fearful thought after another.

Think productively, Jenn told her mind. Her heart pounded. What could she do if he found her? A productive thought. She needed a rock to throw at him. She looked at the tree in front of her and saw that portions of the trunk were not uniform. There was something on the trunk. She reached her hand toward one of the irregular spots and realized it was lichen growing on the tree's northeast side. It was pale green and thick enough in some spots that it was separated away from the trunk, and she could peel it off with her fingernails.

Jenn pulled at the lichen and some upper layers of bark came off with it. Maybe she could crumble it and drop it down into his eyes. She filled her hand and stopped when she heard a voice approaching from the east.

She started to think about how, as children, she and her brother, Peter had hidden in trees. They had played hide and seek in their yard, sometimes just the two of them, and sometimes with other children from the neighborhood. There were three trees that she climbed in her yard as a kid. The secret was to keep perfectly still and stick your arms above your head so they didn't create a bump on the trunk when viewed from the ground.

Jenn thought about her pet trees. She wished she were hiding in one of them, so that whoever was chasing her wouldn't know about the bad branches; the ones weakened by the cankers that might break under the weight of a man. She remembered her dream, from a week ago, where she was hiding in her pet trees. Was that a premonition? How strange.

"Jenn." It was David. "Jenn. Help. There's some kind of killer out here. Where are you hiding? I need somewhere to hide. I'm scared. I can't run as fast as you. I think he's behind me."

Jenn didn't answer. She stayed perfectly still. She thought about how she had been so easily manipulated her whole life by people asking for help. She liked to be helpful and she wanted her mother, her brother, her sister-in-law, Claire, all to be happy. All they ever had to do was show some disapproval, anger, or frustration, and she would jump in to make it all okay. Then, she thought about David. It was in the break room when he first asked her for help. She recalled the locust leaf stuck to the top of his shoe when he cornered her. She looked at the tree she was standing in. Its leaves were locust leaves. She looked at the other trees around the grove and tried to make out their leaves. Some maple and oak, but mainly locust.

"Help! Jenn. He's coming!" David again. She could hear the false ring of his voice that time, though. He's the killer. He's lost his mind. He must be so desperate for this development to succeed. She would not be manipulated into helping him. She would stay her course. She would stay hidden.

She could tell that he was pretty close now. He was at the larger tree about twenty feet from her. She couldn't see him through the leaves, but she could see he had some kind of flashlight or maybe the light from his phone.

"Jenn, are you up there?"

She was as high as the branches could hold her and she was worried that if she shifted her weight, they would shake, or even worse, break. David fired the gun up into the other tree. It really was loaded. Shit. He was certifiable. He could have killed her if she were in that tree.

"Come on, Jenn," David yelled.

A moment before, Jenn had heard the Doppler effect of police sirens in the distance speeding closer. She didn't move. The sirens had stopped. They were at the property, but so far away. They were behind her to the north.

"Maybe you're in that tree," said David. He must have turned toward her tree. She could hear him walking over. She did not think the police would get here in time. She thought she was pretty well hidden from the ground, but she wasn't sure. She really wasn't that high up. She stayed still until she heard his footsteps stop. She was afraid to look down. He probably couldn't see her, but there was really only one side of the tree that wasn't visible from the ground. He would fire right into where she was standing. She had to act fast.

Jenn grabbed the lichen and stepped down to another branch out of the densest leaf coverage. She looked down and saw David looking up at where she had just stood. He held his phone as a flashlight, in between his thumb and index finger of his left hand, and the gun with both hands over his head. He fired right into the leaves next to her. Before he could shift his vision to where she now stood, she threw the lichen at his face. He let go of the flashlight and reached with his right hand for his eyes.

"Jesus, Jenn!" he yelled.

Jenn jumped down about what looked to be almost fifteen feet and hit him on the legs. He fell backward, landing on his back. Pain seared through her left ankle, but she frantically crawled up David's body, grabbing his right wrist, which still held the gun, with both her hands. She stuck her right knee into his big gut and kneed him repeatedly.

"Help!" she remembered to scream, as loud as she could. "Help. Over here."

David tried to pull Jenn off him, and he weighed more, but it was mostly fat. He got his right hand free for a second and started pulling her hair with his right hand.

At that moment, she knew it was either keep hurting him, or he would kill her. She whipped her head around, getting her hair out of reach, and kneed him again in the gut. She saw lights in the woods, and knew the police were close.

"Help! Help!" she cried again. David tried to move his right arm, but with both of her arms pinning him down, he couldn't get it free. Jenn kneed him again in the gut. And then she squirmed lower and kneed him in the privates. His resistance waned, but she kept kneeing him. It was all she could do.

"Drop it," she heard. It was the police. She turned and saw Matt and another officer with their guns and flashlights out, aimed at her and David.

David let the fingers of his right hand open and the gun was released.

Matt quickly stepped closer and kicked the gun a few feet away. Then he walked to where he had kicked it and picked it up.

Jenn was blinded by the police flashlights. She edged off David, moving toward his feet. David turned to his side to grab his stomach in pain.

"Don't move," said the other officer, gesturing with his gun.

Jenn paused for a second, but then realized he didn't mean her. She sat down with her back toward David and looked at her left ankle. She wasn't sure it would support her weight. She just sat, breathing.

Matt handcuffed David while he lay on the ground. David didn't say anything.

Jenn turned and looked at him. She could see that his eyes were wet with tears, and one tear rolled down toward the ground.

Suddenly, Jenn felt anger. Intense anger. She turned to David and said, "Have you lost your mind? Did you kill Mark and Debbie? What the hell are you doing? Running around killing!"

David didn't answer her. She couldn't believe him. She couldn't believe it. In the end it was all about ego and money, about David continuing his success as the best land use attorney in the state, about him continuing to make money. It wasn't about saving salamanders, or preserving an American Indian settlement or artifacts, it was just about money.

Two other officers arrived on the scene. After the officers conferred, one of them pulled David up off the ground and started walking him away. Jenn still wasn't sure if she could stand. Matt came and squatted next to her.

"Are you okay?" he asked, looking worried.

"Are Debbie and Mark dead? Did he really kill them, too? And Doctor Tilman? And Dot Hutchinson? Over having his development go through?"

"Jenn, I'm sorry. Debbie's dead. Mark may not make it. Maybe you could tell us what happened tonight. But let's get you over to the ambulance. Your ankle needs medical attention."

CHAPTER 44

M att acted as Jenn's crutch and she hobbled out of the woods, across the grass and over to an ambulance. They sat her on a gurney and the ambulance technicians treated her ankle and checked her vitals. Matt hadn't asked her a thing on the walk and she was too tired to speak, anyway. As the adrenaline left her body, she felt an incredible wave of exhaustion roll in. Once they had her lie back onto the gurney, she closed her eyes and let the ambulance technicians help her.

Jenn felt someone tapping her upper right arm, and when she opened her eyes, she saw Detective Moffitt looking down at her.

"Ah, Jenn Bowdoin. My favorite attorney and trouble-maker," he said. "You can't just sit at a desk and hang around the courtrooms like all the other lawyers. You have to go stomping around at night fighting killers."

"I was just helping my neighbor," she stated. "He was worried about his wife. I guess she had come down here to meet David. I'm not sure I understand why. I think David found out the state archeologist was getting involved. I'm guessing he lured her here to kill her because he didn't want another setback in the development of the property."

"Hey, Jenn, rest up. Don't worry. I'll figure it out," Detective Moffitt assured her. "Looks like the citizen's group was throwing up whatever they could to stop the development, and David needed the permitting to go through. Talk about a little man with a Napoleon ego. His head isn't screwed on right. Sooner or later, he would have snapped. I suppose we're lucky there aren't more causalities tonight, at what, I guess, was his Waterloo."

Jenn grimaced at Detective Moffitt's bad analogy. She said, "Hey, I figured out it was not just the salamanders that were faked. Look at the vernal pool out there," she said, pointing toward the grove of trees. "It's the whole vernal pool. It was created by black plastic. If you check out the plant species at Dot Hutchinson's house, you'll see they match the species growing around the pool. Operation Mincemeat she called it, creation of fake information, a fake vernal pool, named after an old WWII strategy."

Detective Moffitt looked surprised. "A fake vernal pool. They faked the whole pond? That's crazy. I'll check it out, Jenn, and I'll see you at the hospital. I'll come get your full statement," he replied. "Now go get your ankle checked out."

CHAPTER 45

◆

Jenn sat on her deck with a water, a beer, and a lemonade, and the tray she had used to carry out all the drinks, along with a plastic bag of crushed ice. She had her ankle propped up on another chair and the bag of crushed ice sitting on it. The dragonflies buzzed about the yard. Her ankle injury wasn't really that bad. It was a clean break that was healing nicely. No surgery required. And Mark, thankfully, had lived. He wasn't home yet. The bullet had hit him in the shoulder and although he had lost lots of blood, no organs were damaged, and he was recovering nicely.

At the hospital, Detective Moffitt had taken her statement. The hospital had taken X-rays and kept Jenn through the night. But they quickly determined she was fine and discharged her late Sunday evening. Her mom had come up and stayed with her a day or two. But now, four days since Saturday, Jenn could hobble around her house on one crutch when she needed to. She wasn't going to work until next Monday, so she could sit around and watch the dragonflies.

Matt appeared around the corner of her house. She had been expecting him. She started standing up to greet him as he walked toward the deck, but he stopped her, greeting her with a kiss on her cheek.

"Would you like a drink?" Jenn asked. "Is it okay if you help yourself?"

Matt went into the kitchen and came out with a water, a beer, and a lemonade. Jenn smiled at him. "Thirsty?" she asked.

"Yep," he replied, sitting in the chair next to her.

They sat for a moment in silence.

"So, from what Detective Moffitt has pieced together, it looks like Doctor Tilman found the salamander eggs at the site, but didn't realize that it was a fraud, or that the whole vernal pool and the eggs were planted by Dot Hutchinson," Matt launched into an explanation.

"So when Doctor Tilman told David about the eggs, David didn't want the eggs of an endangered species, or the fact that the species lived at the landing, to end up in Tilman's expert report," Matt went on. "David asked him to meet him in the parking lot behind O'Malley's. According to Mrs. Tilman, the two had met before on various cases over the years at the coffee shop. Maybe the coffee shop was already closed, but for some reason, at some point in the evening, Tilman must have climbed into David's car. The police had checked Tilman's car for evidence and found nothing, but David's car is full of it."

Matt continued, "Moffitt speculates that Tilman had brought a few salamander eggs to show David, and had stored them in the ice cooler. We don't know why he did this, except maybe for security in case the conversation didn't go well with David. Or alternatively, it was a very hot summer evening, and maybe Tilman was worried about the eggs getting too hot in a hot car. Tilman's younger sister owns P.T. Jane's, so he probably felt comfortable sticking something in the cooler for safekeeping. The owner said she keeps it on and sometimes uses it to keep catering food trays cold when they have popular authors in for a book signing.

"Anyway, David won't admit to any of this, but now we've gone back and David's car has remnants of blood on the passenger seat that were revealed by ultraviolet light," said Matt.

"So did David hit Tilman with the pickax in the car?" asked Jenn.

"Detective Moffitt is still working on figuring out that part. The best guess is that there must have been an old pickax somewhere in Tilman's car. David hit Tilman in the car, or as he was turning to get out of the car, and dragged his body behind the ice cooler at P.T. Jane's. Maybe Tilman had the pickax to use as a stick to look into the painter's bucket and move leaves to see the salamander eggs. Moffitt's alternative theory is that David bought and used a pickax on purpose to frame Mrs. Tilman, but that seems less likely."

"Why?"

"Well, you know, I mean it is a whole worse type of murder if it's planned and intentional, and if he bought a pickax ahead of time, as opposed to him acting on impulse," explained Matt.

"Detective Moffitt is working on figuring it all out. I guess David also must have driven Tilman's car back to their Mayfield cottage and then walked back for his car. It would have only been a mile walk. Mrs. Tilman has no idea whether a pickax was missing, and she had six pickaxes when we searched that summer cottage, all different sizes. She says they are for a variety of different uses while excavating a site."

"If Doctor Tilman had found the eggs, why did his report not mention them?" asked Jenn,

"David forged the final report from Doctor Tilman and eliminated any reference to the blue spotted salamander," Matt replied. "We were able to recover different versions of the report from both David's and Tilman's laptops.

"Hold on," said Jenn, and then after a long pause and a sip from each of her three drinks. "But why kill Dot Hutchinson?"

"Dot Hutchinson had already started talking publicly around town about the salamander eggs. She assumed they would be in Doctor Tilman's report and that his report would be submitted to the state agency or the Mayfield Wetlands Commission," Matt said. "All we can figure is that David found out that she knew about the salamander eggs. We think he caught her at Riverfront Landing. We now know she visited it in the early morning hours to check on the pool, and believe he followed her to her house, maybe even saw the salamander tanks in the gardening shed. Whatever he did and wherever he did it, we know he used the pickax on her and dumped her body behind Starbucks. We found evidence of her blood also in David's car, so we know he used that vehicle to at least move her body."

"So Tilman and Hutchinson weren't having any kind of affair? That was all rumor," Jenn asked.

"There is absolutely nothing to support it. But the other way David may have known about Dot, is that Dot did place one call to Doctor Tilman, and it may be that call David found out about if he looked at Tilman's phone after he killed him," reasoned Matt. "That call may be what put Dot Hutchinson on David's radar. It might have caused him to follow her to the site."

"Crazy stuff," said Jenn.

"Meanwhile," continued Matt, "while Dot was sabotaging the project by planting salamanders, the leader of the citizen opposition, Nat Harkins, was trying to establish that the site was a rare historical Native American settlement or contained artifacts. I'm not sure which. I just know that you and I saw the state archeologist at the site, and he has admitted that he was first contacted and told to check out the site by Nat Harkins."

"Well, what about Debbie? What was she doing?" asked Jenn.

Matt explained, "Mark says Debbie was working both sides. She acted like she was part of the citizen's group, but she might have reached some sort of agreement with Charlie Martins, or David, to handle the real estate sales once the development was built. In searching Debbie's laptop, we found drafts of marketing paperwork that supports that that was her approach."

Jenn's head was spinning from the tangled web of it all. She asked, "But why would David need to kill Debbie then? Sounds like she was on his side by the end."

"Detective Moffitt thinks her strong personality and David's controlling personality might have clashed, and with David's break from reality, maybe he lost his patience with her," said Matt. "Hard to get into the mind of crazy person. We think their argument the night she was killed was about her wanting compensation for filling him in on what she learned about the state archeologist's findings."

"What a crazy thing, for three people to end up murdered over a piece of property," was all Jenn could say.

"Police Chief Scalini resigned today," Matt informed Jenn. "Although it hasn't been one hundred percent verified, David's phone records indicate he met with Chief Scalini and there is a $9,900 bank withdrawal from one of David's accounts."

"David tried to bribe Chief Scalini?" Jenn was surprised.

"Well, not all the dots are connected yet, but yes," Matt said. "If you remember, Chief Scalini was pressuring Detective

Moffitt to substantiate the love triangle between Doctor Tilman, his wife, and Dot Hutchinson."

"Yikes!" exclaimed Jenn. "You know, I thought the whole time it was about preserving nature. About keeping the property in the public trust for the benefit of everyone. And then I kind of thought it was about saving the blue spotted salamander, protecting its habitat, keeping that rare ecosystem alive. A unique vernal pool located in a forested grove in the middle of a coastal plain. And on that very last night, I thought it was about preserving some sort of American Indian artifacts from when the Hammonasset tribe possibly lived and farmed at the Landing. But it wasn't really about creating public, green beaches, or any of those green, tree hugging, environmental issues," concluded Jenn.

"No?" replied Matt.

"No. It was really all about the money. Money, money, money. The dough, the greenbacks, " answered Jenn. "David needed to continue his success as an attorney for developers in a slower economic market, his distributions from the firm were falling, and he lost his mind trying to get his project passed. He took matters into his own hands, literally," said Jenn.

Matt smiled at her attempt at humor. "Well, there are two good things that will come out of all this horror," replied Matt.

"What are those?" Jenn was thinking about Mrs. Tilman, who had been accused of murder, and Dot Hutchinson's daughters. They each had to live with the loss of a loved one. She couldn't think of anything good coming out of all this craziness.

"Shelby William's crowdfunding site now has well over $14 million," Matt answered. "That's easily enough to purchase the acreage and preserve Riverfront Landing as open space for everyone to use and enjoy. Since David's arrest and the storyline making the national news, funding has flown in from all over the country."

"That's awesome!" replied Jenn. "I guess folks do understand the value of preserving land as open space for all to use."

Jenn knew most Americans weren't the perfect environmentalists and might not always recycle or leave no carbon or ecological footprint, but they sure seemed to understand that the only way future generations would see the beauty of this earth is to preserve what we have. Or cynically, at least enough folks want to be considered socially aware and green supporters to kick in to preserve the largest undeveloped piece of coastline from Boston to New York. Jenn preferred to believe the former of these two explanations. It was not social pressure that made folks make green choices, at least not always. It was that most folks naturally appreciate the beauty of nature and got respite from nature. It wasn't just her that enjoyed a beautiful sunset, or a quiet walk in the woods. It was the majority of people who recharged, refueled, or forest-bathed from time spent in nature. They ought to be called *greeners*, pondered Jenn, those who were refueled by time spent in nature.

Jenn had been staring at the ground while her mind wandered. Matt cleared his throat and Jenn's eyes moved back up to his face. He said, "I think people do understand." He paused. "Really, we are all tree huggers at heart. Hey, do you want to hear the other good thing that comes out of all this craziness?" He looked at her intensely with his dark brown eyes twinkling and a big smile.

"Not at all. Couldn't care less," said Jenn, smirking. She couldn't resist teasing him. Because she had an inkling of what it was.

Matt snorted, crinkled his nose and continued. "Well, tough. Here it is anyway. With Chief Scalini resigning, the whole atmosphere of the Mayfield police force seems to be changing, so I don't need to go running off looking for another police force to join."

"You don't?" asked Jenn.

"Nope, I'm not going anywhere," Matt said, with a big smile.

Jenn smiled back at him. Jenn thought his eyes looked like an even richer soil color tonight. Tomatoes. Tomatoes would grow so well in there.

"So, how about we go out for dinner?" asked Matt.

"Tonight, with my crutch and everything?" replied Jenn. She smiled and felt happy at the prospect of dinner, and at the prospect of a relationship. Wait, what had changed? She hated dating and relationships. Maybe climbing a tree in the middle of the night and fighting a psycho-killer had made her braver? Could that be it? Was she willing to maybe try? She had stayed guarded so long after her fiancé died so suddenly, and hadn't wanted to date anyone Claire had found for her. She had just gone through the motions. Now she was going to date a truly great guy, and not be scared. Life was about the living, and it was time for Jenn to start living.

"Yep," said Matt. "Your crutch doesn't scare me. Makes you more interesting. Let's go get some food and have some fun."

ACKNOWLEDGMENTS

In memory of my brother Noah and my Dad, both of whom had the gifts of humor and kindness.

It might sound a little odd, but I would like to thank the beech tree on my childhood street, and the woods at Lake Louise for always providing me a safe haven and solace from all the world's demands. Thank you to my mom, Adam, Scott, Thomas, Tyler, Michael, Ryan, and to my supportive friends. A special thank you to my Aunt Gailey, and to Permuted Press, Anthony Ziccardi, Heather King, Lisa Levinson, and Amy Barry.

ABOUT THE AUTHOR

Photo by Gailey Teller

Karen Perry is an attorney and math teacher in a small town in Connecticut. She has four children, three cats, two jobs, and one husband, which makes for a busy life! She tries to recycle but hates washing out the peanut butter jar.